All the Things that come Between Us

A Re-Kindle Romance Novel

by Sarah Ruth Hickner

Sarah Ruth Hickner

All the Things that come Between Us

"I Do" is only the beginning of the love story...

Author: Sarah Hickner

Title: All the Things That Come Between Us

Paperback ISBN: 978-1-967990-00-9

Subjects: Love story, romantic comedy, religious/Christian, marriage, relationships, animals/horses

Initial publication date May 6, 2025

Contents

To Joey – my favorite person.

1

Rolling Out

"Who put their half-eaten sucker in here?" I slammed the silverware drawer shut and looked up to see three cherub faces with eyebrows raised.

The youngest was off the hook, since she could barely stand, much less reach that high. I haven't fed her the crack we call sugar yet, but it may be overly hopeful to think her brothers hadn't.

I looked at the other two. Both had their lips sealed shut, eyes wide. Syrup dripped from Tucker's chin.

"Who did it?" I asked again.

They stared into each other's eyes. One nodded while the other shook his head. If anyone doubted twin telepathy, they needed to spend a day in my house.

It was time to pull a King Solomon. Yanking the drawer back open, I grabbed the sucker to brandish it and threaten its demise. Would this work like those two moms in the Bible arguing over the baby? Would the true owner melt in sorrow while the other shrugged in nonchalance?

The white paper stick looked like it had spent a lot of time in a slobbery toddler's mouth. Half of it was worn away and more red than white. I grabbed the sucker and thrust it into the air, "It's going in the trash!"

Two forks clung to the lollipop, and the stick sagged sideways under the weight. My jaw clenched involuntarily. The plan was quickly going south. I couldn't trash this candy with forks attached to it. Sure, we didn't pay for them, but wedding guests spent a cool $30 each, for which I will forever be grateful.

Three sets of eyes stared. Gravity was apparently stronger than sugar, because one of the forks fell free, clanging to the sink. Anger swelled in my chest as I tried to breathe deep and stay calm. No matter how hard I try to keep the house clean and raise these kids right...

"That's Tate. Tate sucky," Tucker piped up, interrupting my thoughts. I turned to see Tate's eyes doubled in size and his head shaking.

"No, Mommy!" his eyes filled with tears. Tucker's were dry.

Krista screamed and chucked her leak-proof sippy cup. It landed on the table, missing my favorite salt and pepper shakers by two inches. "Krista!" I scolded.

I need Scott. I closed my eyes and took a deep breath, rubbing my temples. *Once the kids are at school, after book club, I can get out to the barn.* Remembering I'd have a few minutes with my horse gave me the energy to keep moving forward.

"Mommy, OK?" Tate asked. His words were a balm. *The sweet one*, I thought, and then mentally slapped myself. They're all sweet. They're all wonderful. *But Tate is definitely sweeter than the other two*, my inner voice retorted. I looked at his big blue eyes. It was true.

I strode to the table and retrieved Krista's cup. There was a small puddle of watered-down apple juice under it. *Of course. I wish Scott was down here helping*, I said to myself again before moving on with life. Because wishing and wanting didn't fix things. I wiped the puddle and handed the cup back to its owner.

I'm a capable woman. If I can push two babies out in one night, I can certainly keep a house clean and raise three kids while Scott is only in the house long enough to sleep, occasionally eat, and pack bags for his next trip. I've always been capable and I still am capable. I'm practically a Proverbs 31 woman.

Except I'm not up before the sun unless a kid forces me to be. And neither my kids nor my husband have ever called me blessed. And I seem completely incapable of losing this baby weight that clings to my body with the determination of an angry toddler.

The sound of dry cereal clattering to the ground grabbed my attention, followed by the click-clack of Baxter's claws on the hardwood floor. Who knew my favorite thing about our family dog would be his assistance with kid messes? While Bax hoovered the cheerios scattered across the floor, I decided to wrap up this debacle.

"Y'all," I took a second to look into each innocent face, "We don't put candy in drawers."

"But you haf candy there," Tucker said matter-of-factly.

My face heated, and I clenched my teeth. "Well, that's... It's..." How did he know about that? This isn't about me, I reminded myself. I took a risk and targeted the most likely culprit. "Tucker, did you put the sucker in the drawer?"

Panic passed over his little face before a look of calm took over. "Tate put booga on wall!"

"You said you woodint!" Tate melted into a wail.

"I didint tell abowt de udder," Tucker put his fists on his hips.

"Boys! What other?"

Tate's lips were drawn into a tight line, but his eyes were filled with moisture. Tucker pursed his mouth and crossed his arms. They glared at each other, Tate lurching with hiccups.

"Breakfast is over. Go to your room," I said, shaking my head.

"But Kwista thwows food and scweams!" Tucker's defiant voice filled the kitchen.

"Krista is eleven months old and not capable of putting a sucker in a drawer. Go to your room now."

The boys climbed down from their chairs, disappearing up the stairs. Krista's bottle hit the floor and she let loose a yell that would have made Tarzan proud, while I threw the fork tethered by candy into the sink to deal with later.

The day was already long and it had just started.

"Hey, Abs." Scott rushed into the kitchen, a carry-on suitcase rolling behind him. He paused next to Krista and tickled under her chin. "Hey, my precious girl!" his voice was a bit higher when he talked to the baby. Her responsive giggle was spitty, but she looked at him like he hung the moon. He leaned down and picked up her cup, setting it on her tray before striding my way.

Tension radiated up the side of my face. My dentist is either going to love me for all the money he makes from my ground-down teeth, or hate me for all the work he'll have to do. I think he's sending his kids to private school, so my bet is on loving me.

"Hey, Scott!" I moved towards him, aiming for a quick kiss. He plowed across the kitchen, not even noticing my approach and nearly taking me out with the roller bag.

"What's with the bag?" my heart rate kicked up a notch. "I thought you didn't have to leave until tomorrow. We've got a family night tonight. Remember?" Blood ran towards my face and my neck started itching. I knew red splotches were appearing.

"Dave called and said they needed me a day early in Pennsylvania. New potential client. Tragic car accident." His thumb scrolled on the screen of his phone while he talked and chugged a protein shake, and I wondered just how bad I looked if he preferred the light-up rectangle over his own wife.

"Sorry Abs, I know your hands are full with the kids. I promise I'll keep 'em for a night over the weekend so you can have a girls' night with Lacy Lee. And we can do pizza and games next week."

My breath was coming in short and rapid spurts as I tried to act normal.

When I didn't answer right away, he glanced up. "That would be good, right?"

"Yeah." I finally pushed out. "Great." He had no idea how devastated the boys would be, and he's leaving me to deal with it. I wanted to love this man and have warm parting words, but anger was boiling inside of me.

Scott stood by the door, ready to go. His shoulders were wide and his waist narrow. That body still made my heart race, even if I was filled with a ridiculous amount of shame when I stood next to him. Why couldn't men carry the babies or at least gain baby weight? He walked over and pecked my cheek. "Love you, Abs."

Krista screamed, followed by a long coo. Scott glanced over at our bundle of chaos. "Where are the boys?"

"I sent them to their rooms, they—"

His phone buzzed, snagging his attention. "Sorry Abs. Gotta go." He leaned forward to give me another quick parting kiss that didn't reach my face. "Give the boys a hug for me!"

His suitcase bumped over the threshold behind him, the Virginia luggage tag mocking me as the door slammed. I thought the tag would remind him to come home more, but apparently he felt like he was taking us with him when he had the shape of our state dangling from his bag. The house was silent for an empty moment before Krista's little pounding fists filled it back up.

First, a stop at the drawer. I dug in the back, past the sticky forks, behind the silverware tray, until my fingers landed on the heart-shaped foil-covered piece of goodness. My racing pulse settled for a second as I peeled the wrapper off, closed my eyes, and took a bite. The milk chocolate melted over my tongue, and I paused to savor it. Ignoring Krista's demands, I pulled out my phone to check in with social media. Sometimes, this was my only way to interact with adults.

My thumb paused its scroll on a photo of a picture-perfect family—two parents and two kids, all with white shirts and khaki pants posing on the beach. The two-year-old wasn't eating sand and the older kid who appeared to be four or so was holding onto his sibling like he loved her more than life itself. My stomach turned. Why did my kids never behave like this?

A text came through as I was envisioning the outfits I'd have my family wear for a beach shoot. The name Bri was at the front of the message. The only Bri I could think of was the sister of my ex-fiancé, and I hadn't heard from her in years. Why would she be texting me? I clicked on the notification, and her words were all in caps:

Bri:

> **HAVE YOU SEEN?**

There was a screenshot of an Instagram post. The chocolate nearly dropped from my mouth. My ex-fiancé's face smiled at me. A gorgeous blonde with even lighter highlights clung to his arm. She wore a lace wedding dress that reminded me of a Hollywood fairytale. I had to make the picture bigger to read the tiny words under the photo. "God bless the broken road that led me straight to you."

It took every effort not to throw my phone and scream. Instead, my fingers were flying as I shot out a response.

Abby:

> **FOR REAL?!**

Bri:

> **YES.**

> And the caption. He's got some nerve, considering the "broken road" was all his fault.

Bri may be his sister by blood, but when I found out he'd been cheating on me in the middle of planning our wedding, she was always on my team.

My chest burned at seeing their happiness. I hoped for the blushing bride's sake that he'd changed his ways, but it was hard to believe.

The memory sent a cold chill through my body. The happy text I'd sent him about wedding venues—*should we do a church or a farm?* And the text he'd sent back—*Hey babe! Last night was amazing.* My mind stumbled through the events of the previous evening—ramen noodles on the couch with Lacy Lee followed by studying until I couldn't keep my eyes open for a huge accounting test.

Oh yeah. Incredible. Lol, I typed back, but before I hit send, his next text came through.

Next time let's try it in the back of my truck ;)

Standing in my kitchen, with chocolate melting in my mouth, my fingers started to tingle. It was the same panic re-action from that night when my entire perfect world I had meticulously built crumbled around me. I squeezed my phone, determined not to spiral into that pit of darkness again.

I tucked my phone into my pocket. *I am happily married*, I told myself. That was in the past. Good for them and their new smooth road.

"I dodged that bullet!" I said to Krista as I unbuckled her from the highchair to go up and check on the boys. But even as I said it, the events from the morning played through my mind: Scott leaving a day early. Scott's kiss not even reaching my face. Scott staring at his phone instead of me, his wife, the mother of his kids. A part of me knew it was just a ghost from my past coming back to haunt me, but I couldn't help but wonder why

Scott was really leaving a day early and who was on the other end of his glowing screen.

2

Bible Study

"**C**ome *on!*" I whisper-yelled at the carpool moms ahead of me. I was trying to set a decent example for the kids but also, *how long does it take for your kid to get out of the car?* School had been back in session for two weeks. These kids should know how to get out of a car by now. I needed to get to Bible study and this slow line was going to make me late. Being late was bad, but being late on the first meetup since summer break was inexcusable.

Bam! Something smacked against the glass in the back of the car. "What was that?" I demanded from the boys.

"Kwista thwew sumfin'," they said in unison before a happy squeal erupted from the rear-facing car seat. Looks like she'll be a better softball player than I ever was.

My knuckles turned white as I gripped the steering wheel, willing these dawdling kids in front of us to hurry up already. Didn't they want to get away from their parents and go do whatever preschoolers did in class? Don't we call them three-nagers for a reason? What's Scott doing right now? Why am I worrying about this?

"Boys, when it's your turn I want you to be ready. Are you ready?"

"Yeah!" they exclaimed.

"Like a pit crew in a car race? Can you be faster than any other kids?"

"Yeah!" they cheered again.

"And do you have your lunchboxes and backpacks ready to go?"

"Yeah!" Tate yelled before Tucker's wail cut through the joy.

"I fugot my wunch!"

Oh. My. Breathe. I cannot be late for Bible study. Or book club. Whatever it is, my church group of women who get together to study Christian books.

"It's ok! Tate, will you share with your brother?" I tried to soothe little Tucker.

"No!" Tucker cried. "No no no no no!"

Krista's voice piped up as she hummed along, trying to copy her brother. Sure. Copy the negative.

"Tucker, Mommy doesn't have time to turn around. You'll be late and miss the welcome circle."

"I share, Mommy!" My heart warmed at Tate's kindness, as Tucker answered with another, "Noooo!"

A click sounded from the side of the van and the door slid open. Sunlight streamed in and one of the teachers smiled so big rays of sunshine reflected off her perfect white teeth. "Ok boys, are you ready for school?" she asked.

"No no no!" Tucker shrieked.

Tate was climbing down from his seat and I threw up a quick prayer of gratitude that my kids could finally unbuckle themselves.

"Tucker, I'll bring your lunch later. You've got to go." I felt every ounce of anger from the moms behind me now that my vehicle was the weakest link.

"You pwomise?" he asked. I calculated in my brain. If I left Bible study book club as soon as it ended and brought a muffin from the coffee shop for his lunch, I'd still have time for a quick barn trip.

"Yes, bud. You go with your brother and have a great day. I'll bring you food before lunch bunch starts."

"Ok, Mom! Wuv you." And he was out the door. My foot hit the accelerator before the van door clicked closed and I swear Krista squealed with glee. That one would be a handful when she figured out how to walk, and even worse, ride anything that had speed. God help us.

Krista and I pulled into the Java Lava parking lot at 9:16. One minute late already, and I hadn't even ordered my coffee. I threw the van into park and leaped from the vehicle, scanning the parking lot for Lacy Lee's car. Not here. Am I really surprised? No.

She'll probably show up at the pearly gates and God will be checking His watch, I laughed to myself. And then she'll smile and say "What? I got distracted!" Or "I had to help Abby with the kids!" or something. God would smile because no one can be mad at Lacy Lee. Plus, isn't that the whole thing? God loves us and will be thrilled when we get there?

I stuck my book, *The 5 Love Languages: The Secret to Love That Lasts*, into the bag slung across my shoulder, and reached in to lift the car seat out of its holder. The way a 13-pound baby and a 2-pound car seat defied physics to become a 40-pound lump of dead weight was beyond me. And to make it even worse, my arms were as flabby as ever.

Shouldn't moms of babies have bulging arm muscles from all the lifting and toting? It was as unfair as my husband's drool-worthy body while mine had rolls and dimples and strange translucent marks in places he used to run his hands over. I shivered at the memory of his fingers grazing up my thighs and around my formerly toned abs.

Then I remembered how he left early today with the lamest explanation ever. I imagined him lounging in a hotel room with his tie loosened and a suit jacket thrown over the chair. An action movie with explosions, good vs evil, and a damsel in distress playing on his TV instead of the cartoons I'd seen every episode of seven times. He wakes up from an accidental nap as the credits are rolling and heads down to happy hour at the hotel bar, sitting with work buddies or a client. And then my mind conjured a beautiful blonde with glowing skin, leaning into him and giggling, reaching out and touching his arm.

I could see his gentle smile and his cheeks turning pink at the attention. He has a bourbon and she has a drink with a piece of fruit on the edge. She knocks back the last sip, stands, and grabs his hand to pull him away from a public setting. They step into the elevator alone, and as the doors close a hundred elevator scenes from Grey's Anatomy compete for attention.

"Stop it," I told myself under my breath. I had to stop the spiral. Just because that one jerkface from college proposed and then cheated on me did not mean I attracted cheaters. Scott would never cheat on me.

Krista looked up from her carrier and blew the loudest, wettest raspberry. The mist of her slobber landed on my bare arms, and I had to resist the urge to drop her and grab the hand sanitizer. But when I glanced down at her to scold, she smiled. It was kind of hard to be mad, even if my arms felt like I'd been through a spit sprinkler.

"Abs!" the unmistakable loud and cheerful voice of my best friend called from behind me. "Hey Abby, wait! I'll get the door for you!"

She nearly crashed into us, crushing me and the car seat with her embrace. "Oh my gosh I can't believe we got here at the same time!" she said with a wicked grin. "Rough morning, I guess?"

"You have no idea," I mumbled. Lacy grabbed the door handle and tugged. The door didn't budge, and we shared a mutual eye roll at the notoriously sticky door. Lacy yanked and when it came unstuck it nearly smashed her in the face. She yelped as she jumped to the side, and a laugh spilled out of me.

I lugged Krista and the diaper bag across the threshold onto the cappuccino colored tile floor of Java Lava. It was the perfect color for a coffee shop that didn't value cleanliness as much as it valued charging top dollar for locally roasted beans and the fanciest espresso machine in town.

"Hi, Abby! Hi, Lacy Lee! Oh, look how big baby Krista has gotten!"

"Hi Steph!" I managed a smile to my favorite barista. "I thought you were leaving this place to start college in the fall!" The eleven that formed between her eyebrows confirmed it wasn't exactly a happy topic, but in the way of our favorite barista, she kept a smile pasted on her face.

"I decided to wait until winter semester to go back. I couldn't miss my favorite Tuesday morning group, could I?"

"Oh well, don't hold back your future for us." I smiled.

"But if I left, I wouldn't get to see baby Krista grow up!" Her voice slowly morphed into baby talk. Krista let out a string of sounds that sounded like she was speaking in another language. "Do y'all want the usual?" Steph started typing into the iPad before I even confirmed.

"Sure. And add a cranberry muffin to-go. Tucker forgot his lunch today." I glanced at Lacy Lee. It was more an explanation for her than Steph since Steph didn't know my preschool kids. "Oh, and I'll cover Lacy Lee's today. She got mine last time."

"That was weeks ago!" Lacy objected.

"I don't care. It's my turn!" I handed Steph my card.

"Is that baby Krista?" The singsong voice of Gabriella, a high school girl whose mom was in the group, broke in. "Krista, you got so big!"

I smiled at the homeschooled teenager who was my saving grace for these meetups. "Oh, good, I'm so glad you're here. She has a bottle in the bag and lots of snacks. The girl loves to eat. And there's spare..."

"Diapers in the side pocket and an outfit in the car. I've got it, Mrs. Abby! Don't you worry! Is it ok if I take her for a walk outside if she gets fussy?"

Gabriella took Krista and the bag from me and a million pounds were lifted from my shoulders. "Yes of course. Here's my keys. The stroller is in the back of my van." I smiled, giddy with this moment of freedom.

I turned to finish paying for the coffee. The machine pre-calculated the tip offering 3 options, and I nearly sighed in disappointment. I miss doing the calculation in my head. I clicked the 25% button, grabbed my coffee, and headed for the mass of Bible study ladies in the corner.

We were an odd crew, but I'd grown to love these ladies. Names were always a struggle, even with people I'd known forever, so I made alliterations to help me remember.

Commanding Cathy started us off. Ok, I didn't say they were positive. Control can be good though, like when you're leading a group of women who tend to talk off topic. "Welcome back everyone!"

We all smiled and nodded. Lacy Lee raised her latte in the air, "Cheers! So good to see y'all."

"Cheers!" We said, turning and tapping our cups. Coffee sloshed left and right and women grabbed for their books to keep them clean. Only a few splashes hit the floor, but it matched the tile so it was ok. Ish.

I ran to grab some napkins while Cathy reeled us back in. "For today's icebreaker, instead of sharing what we did over the summer, let's talk about our favorite meal we had."

Dodged a bullet with that one. Our vacation was four days at the beach, and Scott spent every one of them on his laptop. I took two toddlers and a baby to the ocean by myself. The boys weren't allowed in past their knees because I couldn't leave Krista, and still, little Tate got walloped by a wave. I had to abandon Krista—who knows how much sand she ate—to scoop up Tate all while Tucker yelled, "SUPERFROG!" and jumped every tiny wave, splashing Tate and me in the face.

Even when they were safely and happily making sand castles, I kept working on a game plan for saving them if a sand sinkhole suddenly swallowed my babies. I never came up with anything, but thankfully it was a nonissue. Vacation was stressful.

Please, let's talk about food.

"Lacy Lee, why don't you get us started?"

Lacy beamed. She loved to try new things. The complete opposite of me.

"Well, I flew to Vegas with the hubby and we had the most incredible food! At the Guy Fieri restaurant there were bucket nachos. Like literally, they serve it in a bucket, and when they lift the bucket up from the table the cheese spillllsssss!"

My stomach started hurting from listening to Lacy talk. I clung to my simple latte.

"Oh, and there was a burger topped with mac and cheese!"

I marveled at Lacy's slim figure. If I even looked at something like that, I'd gain five pounds.

"Wow, Lacy Lee, that sounds amazing! Ok, thank you, who wants to go next?" Cathy tried to lead the group, but once Lacy Lee got going, she was a runaway freight train.

"Oh my gosh, *and* there was a *cake vending machine*!" she gushed, and I was all ears.

"No way! Was it fresh or like Little Debbie cakes?" Gassy Gabby piped in. She's not actually gassy, but the first time we met, the toddler on her lap let one loose. I was convinced it was Gabby until the kid excused himself.

"Did they have a bunch of flavors?" Peppy Priya asked, her cheeks glowing. This girl was always in a good mood, and her skin always looked like she'd been slathered in oil, laid in the sun for a few hours, and then spritzed her face with dew. It reminded me of the models from those free underwear pamphlets that come in the mail.

Sara sat there smiling in her own little world. That's how she became Silent Sara.

"I've seen those before. Steve went crazy and we got one of each flavor." That was Winning Wendy. She always had to win. Whether it's the hardest day, the best muffins, the fastest to read the chapter, it's like she's turned everything into a competition and I'm pretty sure she doesn't even realize it.

Lacy Lee smiled, took a sip of her latte, and spent five minutes describing how the vending machine was full of fresh baked cakes. She got red velvet and her husband got chocolate, and all I could do was dream of a perfectly baked white cake with vanilla frosting. Not the fondant crap, but that soft, fresh whipped frosting that's so light I could eat it with a spoon, or put a dollop in my coffee. Not that I'd ever actually do either but a girl can dream.

"Ok, who's next?" Cathy tried to get us back on track. The rest of us were boring compared to Lacy. I talked about the ice cream I had at the beach with the kids. Somehow, ice cream tasted better at a hole-in-the-wall local joint where you can hear the crashing waves. Plus, the boys were in swimsuits so we rinsed the sticky off in the ocean.

Ready to get to the heart of our meeting, I made a show of grabbing my book from the bag on my chair and placing it on the table. Then I set my notebook and pens next to it all lined up.

"Are those color-coded sticky notes?" Gabby asked. My face flushed over the pleasure of being noticed.

"Yeah! I like to take notes when I read."

"Wow, I barely got my chapters read before I came in the coffee shop," she admitted.

"Same!" said Priya.

"I read the whole thing over the summer and now I'm going back and reading a chapter at a time." Winning Wendy wins again.

Sara smiled and pulled out a slightly worn book with a couple of sticky notes peeking from the pages and a bookmark with a pink owl dangling from it.

Lacy Lee grinned at me, and then she plopped her book on the table. It looked brand spanking new. I'm not sure she even opened it yet. I almost snorted. It was so hard to hold back my laughter. Sara smiled too, joining our inside joke.

Cathy took a deep breath, preparing to corral us before she lost control again. "Ok, ladies! I have a leader's guide for the book, but I came up with some of my own questions. Plus, I'd love to hear what y'all think of our book so far. You should have read the first two chapters of *The 5 Love Languages*."

I glanced around the table. Lacy Lee was taking a swig of her drink and Sara waited with what looked like a smirk on her face. What on earth is that about? Gassy Gabby was smiling, but was that sweat on her hairline? Winning Wendy looked a bit angry. As my eyes landed on Priya, she started to talk.

"Oh my gosh, I'm totally intrigued! I mean, I always wondered how some people could be married three times like that guy he talked about in the book." She made a face that looked like the teeth showing emoji. "I mean, way to go for believing love might happen again, but…"

"For real! People need to learn to stick it out. That's the problem with the world. No one knows how to do hard things anymore." Winning Wendy cut Priya off. She always seemed so judgy. I mean, on the one hand I agree, but what if it's really bad? What if the spouse is abusive or cheating? Really, I always swore I'd never marry a cheater, and if somehow, I did, I'm out.

At this observation, my heart picked up. What would I do if Scott was cheating? It seems absolutely ridiculous for work to call him out a day early on such short notice. What if there's more to it? My face was getting hot when something slammed into my leg. My head jerked up to see Lacy Lee staring at me with wide eyes, pointing to her phone.

Mine was next to me, screen down so I wouldn't be distract-ed. Flipping it over, there were two text notifications.

Scott:

> Sorry again to cut out early. Why don't you order takeout for dinner? Love, S

Was that a text from a husband who feels guilty leaving his wife with three small kids again, or a husband who feels guilty because he'll spend the evening with another woman?

My phone buzzed and a text notification from Lacy appeared at the top of the screen. I clicked over to see what she was saying.

Lacy Lee:

> Why is your face turning red?

> Are you ok?

> ???

Pinpricks in my eyes told me if I didn't do something quickly, I'd be the center of a lot of unwanted attention. I wasn't ready to talk about any of this. It probably wasn't even real. It's probably my mind going crazy.

"Hey ladies," the warm voice of Gabby interrupted my mini meltdown, "I'm so sorry, but my coffee went straight through me. I've got to run to the bathroom." She smiled sheepishly and as she turned in her seat to go, her elbow grazed the cup of water she had sitting there. It tilted for a second as if deciding whether or not to cause a ruckus, before making a decision and toppling onto its side. Water spread across the table, soaking into everything in its path.

Cathy snagged her book a moment before the water reached it. Gabby's appeared to be targeted as if the liquid had some vendetta against *The 5 Love Languages*. The book was instantly sitting in a puddle, absorbing at least half of the spill. Gabby lifted it and water dripped from the pages like it had taken a dip in the ocean.

"Oh gosh!" she squeaked in horror. "It's ruined! I'm so sorry! Did I mess up y'all's books, too?"

Lacy Lee grabbed Gabby's book and all but shoved her to the bathroom. "Don't worry! It's fine! Accidents happen! Go take care of business and we'll get it cleaned up!"

"Are you sure?"

It looked like pee might come out of her eyeballs if she didn't hurry.

"Go!" Commanding Cathy demanded.

Gabby rushed off, just as my favorite barista, Stephanie, showed up with a brilliant smile and a stack of paper towels. Hands reached in from all directions, grabbing the towels and helping to mop up the mess. It was unfortunate more water didn't land on the floor. I struggled to trust the cleanliness of a beige floor in a coffee shop.

"Ok, ladies! Now that the spill is cleaned up, let's get back on track," Cathy said.

Gabby returned, trying to pull the chair away from the table without making noise, but it screeched, drawing the attention of the entire coffee shop.

"Welcome back, Gabby!" Cathy nodded towards her and then kept going. "Ok, I wanted to see what y'all's answers are to the question at the end of chapter one. It said, *fill in the blank: There would be fewer divorces if only people would...*"

I prepared for a pregnant pause when Lacy Lee slammed her cup onto the table and declared, "Date night! Everyone needs to do regular dates. I don't care if it's morning or afternoon or night or at 2 am," her eyes snagged on mine, and I looked away.

Gabby piped up, "Yes, I agree with Lacy Lee. Although, I will say it's hard when your kids are young. Gabriella is old enough to babysit now, but for many years a date for us looked like ice cream on the porch and hoping none of the kids got out of bed."

That's a really good point. Scott and I could at least do that when he was home.

Gabby kept talking, "There would be fewer divorces if the husband and wife, even the kids, share the work. It takes a lot to maintain a home, and it definitely shouldn't fall on one person. Although if it needs to, maybe you just have a messy house. No one died from a slightly messy house."

"I knew this girl who said mice chewed her foot when she was a baby because her house was so messy. She has scars!" Priya looked horrified as she spoke.

Lacy lurched forward like she was dry-heaving and I rolled my eyes, while all the other women said a combination of "aw" and "ew"!

"You know what I mean." Gabby's tone was almost like she was scolding a kid.

"What else would make for fewer divorces?" Cathy asked.

It was smiling Sara's serene voice that came next, "People need to realize when they get married that this is a covenant before God."

"Yes! Hear hear!" Lacy Lee slung her coffee forward like she was doing a cheers. Only Sara tapped her cup with her. "So many people think it's basically a contract and they can break it when they're tired of dealing with it. But we stand before God and make this commitment to each other and to Him."

"It's the three C's," Wendy piped up, and I marveled that it took her so long to share her opinion. "Commit, communicate, and cherish. If everyone did this, there would be zero divorces. People just need to suck it up and commit."

Stephanie was wiping tables nearby and I wondered if she was listening in on our conversation.

"But what if there's abuse?" Sara prodded. "If there's abuse, it needs to end."

Wendy sat up straighter. "Yeah, but if they both cherish each other, there won't be abuse."

"Have you seen those Hannibal Lecter movies? I'm pretty sure he eats the people he cherishes."

I had to shake my head to keep from laughing at Lacy Lee's response.

"Separate bank accounts is the key," Priya interjected. "So many couples disagree about money, so if the wife has a separate bank account, she can do what she wants without Big Brother watching over her shoulder."

"But then you're not communicating well." Wendy was starting to sound angry. "That leads to secrets."

"Yeah, well, my husband doesn't need to know every tiny detail about my life. We trust each other. I don't need to know if he ate out for breakfast and how much it cost. Honestly, it probably saves so many fights. I swear, he loves shoes more than I do. If I knew how much he spent on that newest pair of Italian leather dress shoes, I'm sure I would have lost my mind on him. But it was his money. He does what he wants with it. Same with my purses. I have expensive taste!" She held up her bag. The leather was buttery soft and I fought the urge to reach out and touch it.

"But what about stay-at-home moms with no income?" I asked. I liked this idea, but what would go in my bank account? Not that Scott ever complained about me spending money, but there's always the niggling of guilt.

"Some husbands give their wives an allowance," Cathy said.

"Why does the idea of a husband giving me an allowance annoy me so much?" Lacy Lee asked. "I mean, it should be like, 'Yay, free money'! But I guess it feels like the wife is demoted to kid status or something."

"It's the wording. You've got to think of it differently," Sara offered.

"I'd just like to find a way to make my own money," I said, my mind already spinning with how on earth I could work while taking care of three kids. It's not that I wanted to slave away in an office or be apart from the kids five days a week, but a little more adult time would be nice. "I just... sometimes it seems like I'm constantly taking from the family. Every time I spend money, it's like I'm taking instead of contributing."

Cathy leveled me with her stare. "Abby, you stay home with three kids under four years old. If you were a daycare provider, you'd be making about $5k a month."

"Scotty boy better pony up!" Lacy Lee nearly shouted and sporadic laughs erupted around the table. Gabby, who had several kids and homeschooled most of them, just smiled and shook her head.

"People just don't get that sometimes you have to agree to disagree. What do you think, Abby?" Cathy put me on the spot.

I pulled my hair behind my ear and opened and closed my book, searching for answers. If I had the answer, my marriage would be happy. Scott wouldn't rush off all the time, and when he was with us, he'd actually be with us. I'd want to go on date nights with him so we could hang out. The truth is, while I'd love help around the house and with the kids, a date night sounded like torture—the two of us alone together? What would we even talk about? Which maybe was my problem and solution.

"Communication." I nearly stuttered as I said it. My cheeks were hot with shame. Scott and I barely talked these days.

Heads around the table nodded in agreement and I happened to catch Stephanie's eye as she stood up from wiping down a table. She gave me a weak smile and headed to help a customer.

3

A Moment with Henry

"I'm dropping off food for Tucker in Ms. Smith's class. He forgot his lunch." I handed a brown bag to the lady at the front desk. She looked like the preschool's grandma, but she could get scary. Miss a payment or pull around stopped cars during carline, was a one-way ticket to the death glare.

"I'll get it to him!" She grabbed the bag containing the cranberry muffin and headed towards the preschool rooms.

"Ok, thanks. See y'all at one," I said and rushed out the door. Car line for lunch bunch started at one. That gave me one hour and fifteen minutes to drive the twenty-five minutes to the barn, hang out with Henry, and drive twenty-five minutes back. Three loads of laundry and the breakfast dishes were waiting at home, but I needed this. Time with my horse calmed me.

My my hand itched to stretch out and grab my phone, but I resolved not to touch it while I drive. Then a call came in. Lacy

Lee's name appeared on the radio screen and I pressed the green button.

"Hey, Bae!" her cheery voice blasted through the car speakers.

"Hey, Bae." Mine was a little less than enthusiastic.

"Are you on your way to see our buddy, Henry?"

"Yes. I need some barn time." I didn't have to explain it to Lacy Lee. She'd known me for over a decade. She'd been one of three non-equestrians who actually came to the collegiate horse shows and cheered.

"So, what happened at Bible Study?" Lacy Lee jumped right to the point.

"What do you mean? Are you talking about Gabby spilling the water?"

"Come on, Abs. Something was happening right before the fateful water spill. If I believed in magic, I'd say you made the cup tip over to cause a distraction. You were about to have your own flood over there."

"Ugh," I groaned. "I don't know, Lacy. It's probably all in my head, and I don't want to make something out of nothing. My brain has been spiraling worst-case scenarios ever since Scott left for his trip this morning."

"He left already?" Her tone was defensive. "I thought he wasn't supposed to leave until tomorrow. What about family night?"

"Same. Yeah. But he rolled through the kitchen with his little suitcase. That thing's been on more trips in its short life than I ever will." I imagined his hands on the suitcase and how often he zipped and unzipped it. It has felt more of my husband's hands than I have. It's his constant companion.

I dropped my voice an octave to mimic him. "We'll do family night next week. Man, Lacy, I wanted to punch him!" I hit the steering wheel. "Just sock him in the nose. Is that bad? Anyway, they asked him to go a day early for his work trip."

"Um, you probably shouldn't punch your husband in the nose, but I'd have wanted to in that situation."

"I mean, he's the main guy on this account and without him, the company never would have nailed it. But to ask someone with three kids to up and leave a day early with no warning? It makes me wonder."

She waited a second before speaking. "You think he's leaving to see another woman?"

"Well," I sighed, "I totally believed him when he said it was a work thing. And then I opened up my phone and saw that Thad," I basically spit his name out, "just got married."

"What? Who did he marry?" Lacy's shriek had me covering my ear.

"Some gorgeous blonde. You wouldn't believe the caption. Are you ready for this?"

"Yes! Tell me."

Krista babbled, matching the shrill pitch of Lacy's voice.

"It said, 'God bless the broken road that led me straight to you'."

"No."

"Yeah, I'm for real."

"The road of broken hearts! What a toad."

"Lacy Lee, did you just call Thad a toad?" Now I couldn't help but laugh a little, even if I was fuming and spinning with the emotions.

"Yeah! I mean, he's all hot on the outside but lumpy and fat on the inside. You know it's true."

"Doesn't the toad become a prince or something? He is not a prince."

"The frog becomes a prince. The toad is a toad and will always be a toad, and if he pees on you, you get warts. Good riddance, and I feel sorry for that girl."

"Ok, but you went off track, Lacy. I saw his post and it made me so angry. Like I was part of that broken road. Except the only reason I was broken was because he broke me."

"You're not broken, Abs. He is. But keep going."

"And then my mind just started spinning with all these crazy ideas that Scott left a day early to see some other woman. No matter how hard I try, I can't get this idea out of my head. I mean, he's always looking at his phone, and maybe it's not work. Maybe it's, I don't know, some hot coworker he hooks up with on work trips. Someone whose body isn't so..." I didn't have words for what my body was; not words I wanted to admit at least.

"A body that didn't carry three babies in nearly three years, two of them being twins?"

Hot tears streaked down my cheeks. "Yeah. I get that I'm supposed to be grateful for what this body did for my family and those babies. But I can't even look at myself in the mirror. It's no surprise he doesn't look either. I wouldn't blame him for finding someone hotter. Someone with abs you can see." I wiped a tear off my face and Krista chatted away in the backseat, as if she understood and was telling me her feelings on the matter.

"Don't you dare talk to my best friend like that," Lacy Lee scolded. It was her non-joking joke whenever I talked down to myself.

"You're right. Anyway, that's what's wrong. But I think it's in my head. I mean, just because Scott and I haven't been exactly swoony over each other the last couple of years, doesn't mean he'd actually cheat on me. He's a good man, right?"

"I'd never let you marry him if I thought he would mistreat you."

I took a deep breath. "Thanks, Bae."

"But he is human."

"I'm pulling up to the barn." I cut her off. "I've got thirty minutes here before I need to head back to the preschool."

"Ok, Abs. Give Henry a nose boop and a kiss for me. And tell the best barn dog in the world to take care of baby Krista."

"I will. If it turns out Scott is cheating on me, and something happens to Luke, can we get our own farm? We could be like the equestrian edition of Golden Girls. It'd be early years, of course."

I could hear her smile, "Only if I can have a pet chicken that lives in the house."

A snort escaped me as I put the car in park. "Gross. There will be absolutely no chickens inside the house. Have you ever stepped in chicken poop? Henry's looking at me through the stall window. I'm hanging up. Bye, Bae!"

"Bye!"

Jack, the muscled up Rottweiler, came bounding to me, tongue lolling to the side. If I didn't know him, I would have dived back into my car.

I grabbed one of the dog treats from the console that I kept for him and Baxter. "Hi, Jack!" He sat, furrowing his little tan eyebrows in anticipation, his tail nub practically digging a hole in the bluestone parking lot. I tossed it to him and he snatched it from the air before swallowing it whole. He nudged at the back door. "Ok! I'm getting her, I'm getting her!"

Baby Krista started talking again, and I wondered if it was a secret language that only she and Jack understood. She was in love with the barn and animals. I unsnapped the chest and leg buckles and pulled her out, pressing her warm body against me and inhaling the baby smell that still barely clung to her. Jack's wet nose pressed into my leg and a laugh escaped. "I'm hurrying, Jack!"

With Krista in one arm, the pack-and-play in another, and Jack at my heels, we paraded into the center aisle barn. A nicker sounded from somewhere in the middle, and I would bet it was Henry. His beautiful copper-colored head, with a tiny dot between his eyes we called a star, was stretched over the stall door, like he was begging me to hurry.

"Hey, Abby!" Tracy's voice came from the office to my left. She was the head trainer and owner of the barn. In our younger days, we competed together, moving up the ranks in the equitation world as juniors. When we graduated from junior competition at eighteen, she made the move over to jumpers, and I occasionally would compete against her. But I preferred the hunters. There was something so comforting about a perfect, rhythmic hunter course. Thanks to Henry jumping with his knees square and up to his eyeballs, we had a *lot* of champion rosettes at home.

When I got pregnant, Tracy had a client who was the perfect person to lease Henry, so he moved into her barn. At the time, the girl was thirteen and a fantastic rider. She'd been leasing him for nearly four years now. Next year was college, and I wasn't sure what would happen. For now, he was being excellently cared for. I didn't get to ride often, but I could come out and dote on him while she was at school.

Henry nuzzled Krista's toes and then her belly, sending her into a fit of giggles. She stretched her chubby arms out and grabbed either side of his nostrils, and he blew a big, hay-smelling breath at her. She squealed and I swear Henry's eyes lit up. These two. As soon as Krista was old enough to ride, I'm pretty sure Henry's allegiances would change, and I'd need a new mount.

"Ok you two," I smiled.

"Here, I'll help!" Tracy grabbed one end of the pack-and-play, and we set it up in the barn aisle in front of Henry's stall. I set Krista in it, and Jack pushed his nose against the mesh from the outside and made a strange growling noise. Krista reached for his nose, and as her fingers touched him through the mesh, he darted to the side. This was their favorite game that would continue the entire time we were here unless Jack got his toys to share with Krista. That was something I discouraged. It was adorable, but also—ew, gross.

I opened the box with Henry's things, and everything sat aligned. My heart swelled that I'd found a teenager who liked order as much as I did. The massage brush was the best way to start a grooming session. There were twenty-five minutes left of barn time, and I was going to soak up every single one.

4

Noodles in the Air

I shot the text to Scott. The kids were eating dinner, and I finally had a second to grab my phone.

> Yeah, well, kids love it. It cheered them up. And it's easy. I'm tired. What are you eating?

> Ruth's Chris :) :)

Anger swelled in my chest. Oh, what I wouldn't give for a good steak. At least he took the time to respond to me on work trips.

"Mom! Mom!"

I looked up to see my boys. One had a speck of red sauce on his cheek and red covered the lower half of the other's face. It was the latter who beckoned.

"Yes, Tucker?"

"Look at how long this noodle is! And watch me eat it!" He put the end of a noodle in his mouth and started slurping. My insides cringed at the sound, but I tried to smile through it. In a couple of seconds, the noodle completely disappeared.

"Wow, Tucker! Impressive!"

"No, No! I mess up. Watch again." Before I could object, he had another noodle in his mouth.

A pterodactyl scream filled the air before a rubber-coated spoon clattered across the table. A reddish-brown blob landed next to it. Something wet hit my cheek. I reached up to touch it, pulling a tiny noodle off my face. Tucker and Tate both stared wide-eyed at me, a long noodle still trailing from Tucker's mouth.

"Krista! No, ma'am!" I scolded, moving towards the table. The kitchen island was determined to stand in my way.

She squealed in glee and submerged her hand into the bowl.

"No, Krista! *No!*" I turned on my junior high basketball skills and shuffled sideways around the corner of the island. Once the path was clear, I lunged at her, and the world moved in slow motion. Her hand came out of the bowl, a human ladle holding a mound of spaghetti. I didn't think I'd given her more than a couple of bites.

She cocked her arm back like the hammer of a gun, and I reached forward. My left foot hit something slick, and instead of propelling me forward, it slipped out from under me. The shining white, sauce-speckled floor approached my face as her arm released, slinging forward and flinging spaghetti. I followed the trajectory of a tiny noodle sailing through the air. It landed on the wall and my knee slammed into the tile floor.

Pain ripped through me. I wanted to curl into a ball and cry. The bowl clattered next to my head and spaghetti splattered onto my arms and face. Krista screamed, morphing from a silly joy to anger. It took all of my restraint not to scream back at her. *I'm the one who should be angry.*

"Mom!"

"Mumma!"

Tucker and Tate stood over me.

"Mumma, you ok?"

My knee throbbed, and tears streamed down my cheeks when I looked up to see two concerned round faces.

I croaked out a simple reply. "Yeah."

"Mom! You cry!" Tucker spread his arms and crashed into my chest. "It ok, Mom." He held me tight, pressing his spaghetti sauce face into my white shirt.

"Mumma, I call Dad." Tate held my phone in his chubby little fingers and I wondered how on earth he even reached the thing.

"No sweetie, it's ok." Good thing three-year-olds can't work phones. Scott did not need to witness this. He was on his way to Ruth's Chris in fancy clothes with beautiful women and fine wine and good steaks. I'm supposed to be capable of holding down the fort. He'd never pick me over them if he knew how the fort was falling.

"Here, hand me the phone." I stretched my hand out, and the Facetime ringtone filled the air. A wave of panic seized me and the kitchen spun for a moment. "Tate, how did you...?"

He grinned, and I wondered how I ever questioned the capabilities of the kid who opened child-proof door knobs and cabinet catches easier than any adult.

"Hello?" Scott's voice came through the phone, sounding a little annoyed. "Abs?"

I pressed the palm of my hand over the phone camera, smearing spaghetti sauce.

"Oh, hey, Scott." I swallowed down a sob.

"What's going on? Why is it so dark? Is that Krista crying? Everything ok there?"

I glanced at the screen to see his handsome face. The front of his hair was gelled into a wave that swept across his forehead and he wore a skinny tie. Everything about him was pristine and my insides went from wilted to dried to a crisp before crumbling to the floor.

"Yeah, we're fine." LIE LIE LIE. "Tate apparently knows how to use my phone! Who knew? Lol!" Did I just say lol? Scott's eyebrows furrowed together. "Krista's just being a baby," I kept rambling. An ugly cry was fast approaching. My lungs were constricting.

His eyes shifted to the side, like someone else was talking to him. "Ok, well, I've got to go."

"Ok, have a good dinner."

"Bye, Abs." The phone reverted to the home screen.

"You lie!" Tate accused.

"God says lie is bad. Now you have to kill animals." Tucker piped in.

"Don't kill Baxter!" Tate ran to the dog and wrapped his arms around the golden-orange torso. Bax paid him no attention as he stayed on task cleaning up spaghetti.

"What? Tucker, I think you're confused." The pain in my knee had reduced to a dull ache, and I made my way back onto my feet. It looked like my evening would be spent cleaning the kitchen once the kids were in bed. Marinara sauce dripped from counters, and noodles I had carefully cut into tiny baby-safe pieces clung to the walls and lay in small clumps on the floor. The kids and I were all covered in food. Well, except for Tate, who still had a single red dot on his cheek.

"It's bath time," I stated, and hobbled over to Krista to unstrap her from the high chair.

"But in Sunday Skoo, dey say people kill animals when dey mess up," Tucker persisted.

"Yeah, Tucker, that's in what we call the Old Testament." I glanced over to smile at him and nearly had a stroke. "Um, kids, new plan. We're all stopping right here and taking all our clothes off, even our socks! That way, we don't get sauce anywhere else in the house."

Tucker gave a whoop and started ripping clothes off. "Don't throw your clothes, Tucker," I demanded, halting the throwing motion he was in the middle of. "On the floor, right here." I slipped off my shirt, having to peel it away from my chest, and dropped it onto the floor, demonstrating for the kids.

Tate leveled me with his eyes. "Even our underwear?"

Through the ache of my knee and the horror of the moment, I almost laughed. "No, Tate. We can leave our undies on until we get to the bath. But please remove your socks and then watch where you step. Absolutely no stepping on sauce and tracking it all over the house!"

"Maybe Bax will cwean it up while we baf!"

"A mom can dream."

"Hey, Sweetie!" Scott came through the door Friday afternoon. The bags under my eyes must have told him the story of my week. He looked refreshed, like he'd spent four days eating meals on a corporate credit card and sleeping in a hotel room all by himself. Hopefully by himself.

"How was your trip?" I asked. For a moment I fantasized about things going wrong—a flat tire, a client getting mad, overcooked steak—something so I didn't feel so alone in this.

"It was great! They've referred us to another rehab facility opening soon in the tri-state area that will specialize in prosthetics. It looks like we'll be signing on another big account."

"Wow, that's amazing," I said through gritted teeth, imagining his travel schedule getting even worse with a new account. Scott gave me a side hug as Tucker and Tate barreled through the door.

"DAD!"

Scott turned away from me, and I imagined he was glad for an escape. He scooped the boys up—one in each arm. I stood on a tiny island, cold and alone, yet overjoyed for the boys and their moment of pure bliss with their daddy.

Krista squealed, and it sounded suspiciously like "Da!" She abandoned the coffee table she'd circled for the last several minutes, collapsed onto all fours, and crawled like a speed racer to Scott's feet. My husband took turns blowing raspberries on the twins' bellies. Snorts of laughter filled the house, while Krista screamed, "Da!" and pulled up on his pant legs. It was hard not to smile.

Scott tiptoed away from the baby, making a beeline for the living room, where he dumped the writhing bodies of the boys onto our overstuffed couch. "Again! Again!" they demanded.

"Daaaaa!" Krista was catching up with the boys.

I turned to the kitchen sink. This was my chance to wash dishes without the kids needing something. I donned my rubber gloves, turned the water to scalding, and got to work. At least here I was useful. I may not be great at a lot of things, but dang if I wasn't magic with a kitchen.

Spaghetti sauce was burned into the pan and I attacked it with the fervor of a dog going after the treat in a Kong toy. This would sparkle like new. I worked the bristle pad in aggressive circles, the suds turning rust-colored.

Something brushed my side, and I turned to see which twin was interrupting my therapy session at the sink. A large hand gripped my hip as I looked up into my husband's eyes. His cologne momentarily overtook my senses, and I stared up at him. My mind cataloged the feeling of his warm hand grasping my other hip and tugging me toward him. But I was lost to the scent of man.

"Hey," he said with the barest hint of a grin, breaking the spell I was under. "I missed you."

"Uh. Hi!" Heat rushed from my abdomen to my face.

The oxygen disappeared from the room, and I stood there like a fish out of water. Was he being for real? Did he miss me? Or is he trying to cover up what he was really doing on the trip? Maybe this is a guilt moment.

He stared at my mouth, and my mind drifted to the chocolate I'd snuck from the drawer while they were playing on the couch. Did I smudge it on my face?

"Ew! Daddy's gunna smooch Mommy!" Tucker's voice yelled over the running water and blood rushing through my ears.

"Scott." I tried to get his attention, but he was in some kind of trance. "Scott! The kids! Plus, the water's running."

My husband's tiny smile slipped into the indifference I was used to, and a buzzing sound filled the air. He pulled his phone from his pocket and glanced down. "Oh, sorry. I've got to get this. It's someone from work." He stepped away, taking his warmth with him. I swayed for a moment before refocusing.

"But you just got home from a work trip," I bit out, not even trying to hide the annoyance. "It's Friday after 5 pm. They can wait until Monday." The steaming water was making sweat drip down the back of my neck.

"Sorry, Abs. I'll be quick." And he rushed off, gone again.

5

Motion Sickness

"Tucker, what's on your shirt?" I tried to maintain a calm, kind voice, but I was on the verge of losing it. We needed to leave in six minutes if we were going to be on time for church. Tate was waiting, dressed to perfection by the door. Did he fix his hair by himself? Impossible. He's only three years old.

Krista wore a diaper and sat trapped in the pack-and-play. Her outfit, socks, and shoes were waiting upstairs, and I was still in a slip. My grand plan of getting everyone fed and clothed before getting myself dressed was going downhill. It seemed like a good idea—waiting so I don't ruin my dress with spills and stains. But we were running out of time and Tucker needed a fresh shirt or a solid wipe-down.

"I drop my jelwy toes," he said. That baby accent took the edge off everything except my nerves. The oven clock changed. Five minutes.

Scott walked into the kitchen and I fought the urge to fan myself. He wore olive green pants that hugged the muscles of his thighs. My cheeks heated when I realized everything I had was on display in this slip. It was so tight across my hips that the seams were ready to pop. The ladies were threatening to jump out every time I bent over. The only redeeming feature was the loose fabric at my waist, hiding my fat rolls.

A burst of frustration clouded my vision. We go through nine months of stretching, growing, reflux, Braxton Hicks, swollen feet, greasy skin, and so much more. Then we're left with glistening stretch marks and extra fat rolls.

"Something wrong?" Scott asked with furrowed brows. I stared at the perma-scruff on his face. It may be uncomfortable to kiss, but it sure was easy on the eyes. My hand itched to reach up and touch his chin, to have his arm wrap around my waist. But then I remembered how thin my slip was, and how he'd feel every lump and bulge. I imagined that same hand wrapped around another woman's thin waist, caressing her skin. Squeezing my mouth shut, I shook my head.

"Ok," he responded. "You ready?"

"Yeah. I mean no. No dress. Jelly on Tucker's shirt. And..."

"Eeeeeeeee!" Baby Krista's scream cut me off.

"And Krista's still in a diaper."

"Tucker! Why did you get jelly on your Sunday clothes?" he reprimanded.

"I dwopped my toes." he lifted his hands in an overdramatic shrug. I shook my head.

"If you can handle the baby and yourself, I can take Tucker," Scott said and scooped the messy twin up, holding him at arm's length and disappearing up the stairs.

Krista lifted her arms, eyes squinting as she said, "Dadadada-da."

"No, Krista. I'm 'Momma.' You can do it. Say 'Momma'." I tucked my hands around her torso, underneath her armpits, and lifted. A shot of pain exploded across my lower back. I yelped in shock, dropping Krista into the pack-and-play and melting onto the floor.

Krista howled as the cold tiles cradled me. I closed my eyes and took a deep breath. It was love at first sight when I saw these tiles on a home renovation show. I had imagined how they'd look with my kitchen table and counters. I'd envisioned wiping spills off them. But I had never thought about how they'd feel against my spasming back. *It's fine. I'm fine. Everything's fine,* I told myself.

One of my muscles must have tried to detach from my body and leave the premises, but found itself trapped and in a knotty ball. I closed my eyes, focused on the cold floor, took a deep breath, and held it. Ten, nine, eight—if I can make it to one—seven, six. "Uuuuuuugh," I groaned, releasing my held breath, but the muscle relaxed its grip a fraction.

"Mumma? Mumma you k?" Tate had left his perch by the door to peer down at me.

"I'm fine, baby," the pain muffled my voice.

"Daddeee! Mumma hurt!" Tate yelled.

Please, no. I took a few deep breaths. It's fine. I'm fine. Everything's fine. The hard knot of muscle relaxed enough that I rolled onto my hands and knees. Using the edge of the pack-and-play, I pulled myself upward.

"Daddeeee!" Tate screamed.

"What?" Scott yelled back as he exploded through the door with a cleaned-up Tucker in his arms. "What's wrong?"

"Mumma!" Tate exclaimed.

"I'm fine," I scolded, though anyone with a lick of sense could see my white knuckles gripping the edge of the pack-and-play. "It's fine. I just... I don't know. My back flared for a second. Like a muscle cramp or something. But it's going away now."

"Abs? Are you ok? Should we stay home?"

"No!" I closed my eyes and pressed my fingers into my temple. God, is it too much to ask that we go to church like a normal, happy family? "We have three minutes or we're going to be late. Can you help with Krista? My back flared when I tried to pick her up."

"Yeah. But Abs, why don't we stay home? We can watch church online while the kids play with their toys."

"I said no! I want to go to church! Just help me with Krista and we can still be on time." Two minutes. We had two minutes to get to the car if we wanted to walk in before the music started. Scott disappeared with Krista and I dragged my uncooperative body up the stairs, grasping the banister for support.

There was a lingering twinge of pain, like a guard dog on the edge of a property line threatening to attack if I moved too fast. But I had less than two minutes to get ready and out the door.

I did my best imitation of a marching band performer, like my suite mate, a proud member of the University of Alabama's Million Dollar band, showed me. Walk like you're stepping on a tube of toothpaste so you don't jostle your instrument while you're playing, or in my case, my back. A royal blue dress hung in the doorway of my closet, already pressed. I flung it over my slip, threw some hoop earrings on, traded the three-inch heels I'd planned to wear for some basic black flats, and scooted down the stairs as smoothly as possible.

"Dadadadada!" Krista blubbered behind me and I turned to see her in leopard print pants and a yellow polka dot shirt.

"That doesn't..." I started to scold and thought better of it. If we wanted to be on time for church, she'd have to look like a circus clown.

"What?" Scott asked.

"Nothing." I smiled with tight lips. "I had laid a dress out for her. But it's fine. Thanks for helping."

"You ok?"

I marveled at how he seemed to care. Where was this side of him when he was on work trips 4 out of 7 days? "I'm fine." I wanted to shout, *We get along fine without you!* But here we were nearly running late for church. We'd never be even close to on time if he hadn't helped. Ugh. I used to keep a high-end competition barn of twenty-seven horses spotless and organized, ready to go to a show at the drop of a hat. Now I can't even get myself anywhere on time.

"To the van!" Scott yelled. He threw Krista over his shoulder like a sack of flour, sending her into a giggle fit, and marched forward. The boys followed like little soldiers, climbing into their car seats in the minivan.

I was the caboose and felt every bit of that title. I helped the boys buckle, careful not to move fast or bend over much, while Scott got Krista situated. When I turned to the passenger door, my husband was waiting next to it. "Let me help you, Abs," he offered, and supported me as I climbed into the van.

"Time to see Jesus," Tate's voice piped in from the back seat when we were all settled.

Scott and I laughed. "Yeah, bud! Let's go learn about Jesus!" But let's not see him for a while.

I pushed the radio button for number three in the favorites list and the local Christian radio piped in from the speakers. My insides cringed. It's like the Christian radio stations all conspire and time hop three decades for the Sunday morning commute. Praise is praise, I tried to tell myself.

Scott reached down and changed it to classic rock.

"Scott! We're on our way to church."

"What? Do we have to pregame church?" He pushed another button and 90s country filled the van. "Compromise. God's music."

His victory smirk was so adorable I almost laughed.

"What's pwegame?" Tate asked.

"I'm remembering Mommy's college days," Scott said.

"Scott! You know I never did anything like that! I either studied or went to the barn, except for when Lacy Lee dragged me out."

"Well, explain how we met out dancing, then! And that dress you had on." He had the faraway look of someone slipping into a memory.

"That is not how we met. We shared a class." I cringed remembering the night Lacy Lee convinced me to wear that scrap of fabric, and it led to a terrifying, nearly life-altering event in the dark hallway of a bar. Although, I guess it did change my life because that cute boy from one of my classes swooped in and saved me.

"Was it a pitty jess?" Tate's curiosity made my heart warm and cheeks redden.

"It was quite the dress buddy, and your mom looked—"

My face was on fire. This was not an appropriate topic for our kids.

"It was a beautiful dress with long flowing skirts that fanned out when I twirled," I said.

Scott narrowed his eyes at me, and I heard the unspoken words. *I thought you never wanted us to lie to the kids.*

I changed the station back to Christian radio, hoping the move would work double duty and change the subject. Another warbly song nearly as old as I was filled the car. Can't they play something from the last decade? With a heavy sigh, I switched back to the country station.

"My tummy hut," Tucker whined. Turning over my shoulder, we made eye contact. His skin had a greenish hue.

"You ok, buddy? We're almost there."

"Uuuuu," he moaned.

"It's probably car sickness from your dad's crazy driving." The joke fell flat as everyone sat tense, waiting to see what would happen. Even Krista was quiet.

"Just a couple more lights and we'll be at church," Scott said.

"Mumma!" Tate exclaimed as Tucker lurched like an invisible creature had punched him in the gut and made him double over.

Baby Krista squealed, piercing our eardrums, just as jelly toast made a grand reappearance, floating in orange juice.

"Oh no." I closed my eyes and brought my hand to my mouth, looking out the window. I needed a moment. Otherwise, my sympathetic vomit response would kick in.

The odor filled my nostrils and my stomach roiled.

"Mumma!" Tate exclaimed, like I could save him from this. Like I could fix anything.

"Scott." I groaned and pressed my quickly warming head against the cold glass.

"On it." He whipped into a parking lot and threw the mini-van into park. I grasped for the door handle and stumbled out, gasping for fresh vomit-free air and grabbing my back, begging it not to seize up.

Scott was like the Dad version of a NASCAR pit crew. He unclipped the booster and lifted Tucker out of the van, out of my line of sight. There was a heaving sound, followed by splattering. The other kids were quiet as I closed my eyes and called, "You ok, Tucker?"

There was a brief silence before my baby responded, "Uh huh."

Scott stripped Tucker to his superhero undies and gave him a butt wipe bath while Krista chanted, "Dadadada!" from the backseat, and little Tate sat in silence.

"Thank you Lord for Tate," I whispered, "the easy one."

Scott led an underwear-clad, sedate little boy to my side. "You think you can handle him now? Without, you know..."

A glance and sniff confirmed he was vomit-free. "Yeah, I've got him." I crouched to my knees and grabbed his hands. "You ok, bud?" Tucker nodded and wrapped his little arms around my neck. A slight odor survived the wipe-down, but I held him anyway. While Tucker and I clung to one another, my husband did a complete car detail job with a single pack of wet wipes. That man was a miracle worker. At least I gave good hugs.

A mound of desecrated disposable towels was the only evidence of the fiasco. Scott grabbed a garbage bag from a roll he kept hidden in the side pocket. "Preparedness is next to godliness," he quipped, and I rolled my eyes. His dad always said that quote from the Boy Scout Promise...or at least that's what I think it's from.

Either way, I couldn't disagree. That roll of trash bags in the van had always seemed excessive, until now.

We strapped Tucker in and climbed back to our seats. Scott rolled all the windows down, and I leaned my head out, relishing the clean air. "To church?" Scott asked with humor in his voice. How was this funny? I wanted to scream.

I chewed on my thumbnail for a second, imagining walking into church mid-sermon and the sideways glances we'd get. If Tucker got sick there, I'd have a lot of apologizing to do. "I guess we can go home and watch online. Get takeout for lunch. Hopefully, it was from your crazy driving, but I'd hate to subject his Sunday School class to a stomach bug."

Scott pulled out of the parking lot towards home as I finished my thought, "Plus he's, you know, in his undies."

My husband turned to me with his brows furrowed and offered a half smile. His hand stretched across the center console and gripped mine, giving it a quick squeeze before returning to the gear shift. A drop of water in the desert.

"I'm sorry, Abs. I know you wanted—" Scott stopped talking when his phone buzzed. He glanced at it and put it back down to focus on the road.

"What was that?"

"Oh, nothing. Just work stuff."

6

Family Dinner

"Mummy, can I hep?" Tate looked up at me with round, hopeful eyes.

"No, baby, Mommy's got it." I grabbed five paper napkins and a handful of utensils to set the table for dinner. The oven beeped, reminding me I needed to get the lasagna out, grab bowls for the salad, and prepare the bread.

"Pweeze!" he begged.

I let out a resigned sigh. "Ok, bud. You can help set the table. Let Mommy show you, first."

"I know how."

"Well, let me finish here, and then I'll come show you in case you forgot."

I set my silicone trivets on the counter. The manufacturer said the quartzite was heat resistant, but we'd spent so much money on it I never could just set a hot platter directly down.

"Hey, Babe." Scott walked into the kitchen. Sweat dripped from his hairline and darkened his shirt in places, most notably in the small of his back just above his shorts. He grabbed a cup and pressed it against the water dispenser button on the fridge. "Can I help with anything?"

The oven door slammed closed as I stood up with a platter of lasagna gripped between two mitt-clad hands. "Mom!" Tate called, reminding me he was waiting. I took a step towards the counter, and the front of my leg slammed into a furry warm body. A hand grabbed me at the waist as Baxter's claws clattered away and liquid sloshed out of the platter, splattering onto the floor. I muttered a string of toddler-appropriate not-curses under my breath.

"You ok?" Scott asked, making sure I was steady before releasing me. I set the platter of lasagna down and turned to my husband.

"Mom!"

"In a minute, Tate," my husband and I said in unison.

I clenched my jaw.

"How about I get Baxter out from under your feet?" Scott offered and turned to leave before I responded. "Bax, come on," he called over his shoulder.

Gathering the garlic butter and loaf of French bread, I set to work cutting it into pieces and slathering each one with the spread. My mouth watered, and I regretted I wouldn't be partaking in my favorite part of the meal. According to everyone I'd ever heard who lost weight, if I just cut carbs, the pounds would fall off. Once the bread was wrapped in foil, I tossed it in the still-warm oven.

I grabbed a stack of bowls from the cabinet and headed to the table. "Ok, are you ready, Tate?"

"All done!" He stood next to the table and held his hands like a model from The Price is Right. His grin was so big that his eyes nearly disappeared. I surveyed the table. Napkins were opened up and set out like placemats, and knives and forks rested on either side. There was no consistency to it. Some seats had the knife on the right, the others had a fork on the right.

Food from his play kitchen was placed in the center of the table. A sixth spot had one of Krista's dirty burp cloths instead of a napkin with toy utensils. The space in front of the high chair had an actual metal knife and fork. I could envision her throwing the fork and stabbing an unsuspecting victim in the eyeball. I rubbed my eyes and walked over to push the utensils far out of reach.

"Wow, Tate! Why didn't you wait for me to show you how? I could've—"

"Tate, you did such a good job!" Scott barreled into the room, followed by the dog. "Who's the extra spot for?"

"Batter!"

"Dogs don't eat at the table, silly boy!" Scott reached down and tousled Tate's hair. The intro music for Bluey came on, and Tate yelled, "See ya!" before running to join his brother and sister in front of the TV. I stared at the place settings, an inner battle being waged over whether to move everything to its proper place or leave it.

"Leave it," Scott mumbled low enough that the kids wouldn't hear.

"But it's—"

"Leave it, Abs. He helped, and he's proud of it. Just get out more napkins in case people need them."

I took a deep breath and counted to five. "Fine."

"What's that sm—"

"The garlic bread!" I cut Scott off and dove for the oven, pulling it open. The thick smell of char filled the room, and a bit of smoke wafted out. Scott grabbed the bread. "Your hands, Scott!"

He yanked the loaf out and threw it on the stove in a quick, fluid motion. "It's fine. Let's just crack some windows and turn on the fan." He reached up and flipped the switch, filling the air with a whirring sound, and I dashed to the two closest windows, cracking them just enough that a baby couldn't escape but the odor would.

"Dinner looks great, Abs. The bread's just a little crispy on top. We can cut that part off if the kids don't like it. But it won't bother me." He paused for a second, pulling his phone out of his pocket and glancing down. "Hey, I've got a phone call coming in, I'll be right back."

He made his escape, leaving me inside with three kids and dinner ready to eat. "Hey boys, it's time to wash up for dinner!" I called. "Help Krista put away her toys."

"Otay!" Tate said and grabbed the fabric bin for Krista's stacking toys. He carefully set each one inside while Krista grabbed them back out of the bin and threw them on the floor.

"Tucker, help, please. Grab that box."

"Jusa secon," he declared, his eyes never leaving the screen.

"Tucker, help your siblings."

He was lost in the show, and didn't respond. I was losing my patience. I reached for the remote and clicked off the TV. Tucker lurched sideways, flopping onto the floor like a fish yanked out of a pond to die on the bank. "Noooo!" He screamed the word for so long that his face resembled an apple. When he ran out of air, tears sprung from his eyes. The dying fish charade kept going, complete with flopping and screaming, "Nooooo!"

Krista reared back and threw a block, nailing him in the shoulder. He grabbed at himself and descended into sobs. "My so!" he said between hiccups and tears.

Scott rushed inside. "What's going on? Is everything ok? What's wrong with Tucker?"

"It's fine, Scott."

"My so," Tucker wailed and did a little flop.

"What happened to his show?"

"I turned it off when he wouldn't listen."

"Tucker, it's ok. Maybe we can watch it after dinner," the father of the child, who was rarely there to parent, bargained.

I wanted to scream and throw the remote into the TV, ending this whole mess for good. The TV rotted their brains anyway, but I needed those short bursts of alone time it gave me, so I kept my temper in check. "Tucker didn't listen when I asked him to help clean up numerous times, so I turned it off. He's done with TV for the day. He can help pick up and wash his hands, and then it's dinner time."

The kid kept moaning and crying, but I moved on, leaving Tucker and Scott to deal with each other.

"Come on Krista!" I scooped up the baby and took her to the sink. "Hands!" She held her hands out flat and I squirted a fluffy ball of foaming soap into one. "Now ruuuub them together!" She giggled and clapped, sending tiny bubbles soaring into the air. "Rub, Krista," I clarified and reached down with my free hand to massage the soap between her fingers and all around her hands.

I turned on the water, and she stuck her hands under the stream. "Good girl, Krista! Clean hands!"

"Aaaaah," her jabber mixed with giggles when I made a game of grabbing her fingers with the towel to dry them. I toted Krista over to the table and lowered her into the high chair.

"Kween hans!" Tate declared, sticking his hands in my face while I buckled Krista in.

"I see! Good job!"

"This one's all cleaned up and ready for dinner," Scott declared as Tucker came to the table and climbed up into his chair.

"I'll fix our salads," I offered.

As I walked to grab the big bowl, Scott's hand reached out and grazed my hip, sending shivers across my skin. I made a point not to look at him—to pretend nothing had happened because nothing would happen with the kids right here. What was he thinking, touching me in front of them?

"Here, I'll help," Scott said and grabbed a stack of salad bowls.

I glanced at him before I responded. "Ok, could you fix Krista's?"

"Sure thing," he smiled and dumped a handful of salad into a bowl. "Krista, what kind of dressing do you like? Ranch?" He laughed at his own lame joke.

"I usually put a little honey mustard on it. She's not supposed to have dairy until she's a year old," I deadpanned.

Scott popped the top on the dressing and poured it into the bowl. "Here you go, baby girl!" he said and deposited the salad bowl on her tray.

I strode to the other end of the table and snatched it away. She already had honey mustard all over her hands and was trying to lick it off, which got it on her nose, cheek, and even forehead. Grabbing a napkin, I got a hold of her hand as quickly as I could and started wiping.

"I thought you wanted me to give her a salad. What are you doing?"

"She's eleven months old, Scott. When you give an eleven-month-old a salad you cut it up into tiny bits so they don't choke, and you put a tiny bit of dressing on it and stir it around so there's enough for taste but not enough to have them painting their face and hair in it."

"I'm sorry, I didn't realize."

"Well, if you were here more, maybe you'd know. It's not rocket science."

I caught Tate's wide-eyed gaze. "Aw you fightin?"

My heart shriveled in my chest. "No, baby," I said at the same time Scott said, "Nope! Of course not!"

Silence stretched across the table as we ate our salads. Even Krista reduced her regular chatter to an occasional "mumumum" when she was chewing the tiny pieces of lettuce I'd cut for her.

When I couldn't take the quiet any longer and my bowl was empty, I stood up. "Who's ready for lasagna?"

"Me!"

"Me!"

"I am."

"Ok, hand me your salad bowls," I gathered the dirty dishes to deposit in the sink. "I used a special recipe I found online. It's so much more healthy than a normal lasagna, and the pictures looked incredible." I peeled back the tinfoil covering the lasagna. The pictures looked nothing like this.

"Abs? You ok?"

A rock formed in my gut as I tried to understand what I'd done wrong. A chair dragged against the floor, and then my husband was next to me. "Why does the cheese not look melted? Was the oven not on?"

Shaking my head, I grasped for answers. "I'm not sure. I used the fat-free version of the cheese the recipe recommended, but I didn't think it would make a difference."

"Looks like it did," Scott said and chuckled like this was funny. Like two three-year-olds would eat unmelted cheese that looked like tiny plastic tubes. "It'll be fine. I'm sure it tastes just as good." He rubbed my back, and I stepped away from his touch, shaking my head.

"I'll just scrape it off. Take a seat. I'll... It'll be fine." I grabbed a metal spatula and used it like a knife to slice a corner piece. Liquid bubbled up as I pressed down to cut the corner. I slid the end of the utensil under the lasagna square to lift a piece out. A thread of zucchini peel that refused to let go dragged an entire slice from the middle of the lasagna. It dangled and started sliding.

I threw the food onto the plate before the errant vegetable fell and made an even bigger mess. When I looked back at the platter, liquid had filled in the space where the square of lasagna had been. Then I noticed a reddish puddle forming on the dinner plate. This was not even close to what the Pinterest pictures looked like.

"Need a hand, Abs?"

I swallowed and then swallowed again. My head started itching, but the last thing I needed was to scratch and get hair in this already disaster of a meal.

"Abs?"

"It's fine. Everything's fine," I bit out and switched the plates for bowls.

"I'm hungry!" Tate announced and Krista, who I'd tuned out until now, babbled louder.

"Here, let me help." Scott grabbed the bread, still wrapped in foil, and set it on the table. As he gave each kid a piece, I noticed a small mound of something white on the table in front of Tucker.

"What's that in front of Tucker?"

"What are you talking about?"

"That! That white stuff!" I pointed, but was it even necessary? Did Scott have eyeballs?

"Oh." He picked up the salt shaker and gave it a shake. "Must be salt. This is empty."

Tucker licked his finger, stuck it in the little pile, and then licked it again. "Sal!"

"And how did this happen, Scott? Weren't you sitting with the kids?"

"Oh, sorry. The Alabama game was about to start, and I was watching my phone. Here, I'll help you bring the bowls to the table."

"Could you please help me cut the kids' food into tiny bites so they don't choke?" I emphasized *choke*. It hadn't escaped my notice that Krista was gnawing on a full-size piece of bread that I would be removing from her hand as soon as she broke through the charred outer crust.

When everyone had their food cut to safe sizes, Scott and I sat down with our own. Feeding a family felt like a never-ending marathon some days. "Who wants to lead the blessing tonight?"

"Meeeee!" Tate raised his hand and lurched into the air. Tucker sat next to him, zoned in on the tiny piece of zucchini he'd pulled from his lasagna. He stared at it like it was a bug and then blew a raspberry at it.

"Tucker," I scolded, realizing everyone needed some Jesus at this moment. "Let's say it together."

Scott's warm hand grabbed mine, and I settled for touching Krista's shoulder with my other.

"God is great. God is good. Let us thank Him…" One voice was missing from the blessing, and I glanced up to see the twin who had previously blown raspberries at his food, sitting with his arms crossed and chin jutted. "…for this food. Amen."

I pinned him with a stare. "Tucker, do you need to say the blessing on your own?"

He narrowed his eyes at me. "I no lie. I'm no thayful."

"Children in Africa are starving right now," my husband said.

"Dey can have it."

"Tucker!" We said it in unison.

"You know, let's just eat." I was tired and my body needed sustenance.

For a moment, the only sounds were forks tapping against bowls and Krista chattering to her food.

"This recipe is interesting, Abs. Where'd you get it?" Scott asked.

"Pinterest. This is a lot more watery than I expected." My lasagna was a vegetable soup, with a nearly flavorless broth.

"You want more bread boys?" he asked and divvied bread to the kids. He held a piece to me. "You want one?"

I shook my head. "Too many carbs." My stomach groaned its displeasure just as my phone buzzed. It was a text from the barn.

Tracy:

> Hey, Oz is having back issues. I think it's the saddle. Can I try Henry's half-pad?

Abby:

> Sure. Hope it helps.

"Who are you texting?" Scott asked. I paused before answering, imagining all the times he'd texted in front of me without sharing who his conversations were with. Was there another woman on the other end of those messages, or was it just work stuff he didn't want to bore me with? "Is it your boyfriend?" he asked with a lighthearted chuckle.

I ignored his joke when I answered. "Tracy's asking to borrow Henry's saddle pad. Her horse's back is hurting. Probably saddle fit, but she can't afford to have a custom saddle for every horse she trains."

"Doesn't she have pads?"

"Yeah, but she doesn't have one like Henry's. And once a horse's back gets sore, you do whatever you can to help it. If a saddle doesn't fit perfectly, which is nearly impossible because a horse's muscling is always changing, then it's like walking around in ill-fitting shoes. Or in Oz's case, cantering and jumping. And the more you do it, the worse it hurts. So, a pad is kind of like a shoe insert to help it fit better."

Scott stared at me like he was calculating a huge math equation on a chalkboard in his head.

"What? Why are you looking at me like that?"

"It just... I know this sounds crazy, but this pad thing sounds like a horse version of what I sell to doctors for their patients."

"I don't know much about what you sell, Scott, but I'm starving. Will you hand me a piece of bread?"

7

Coffee Cake

Krista sat in my lap and we shared a muffin as the book club ladies trickled in. I studied Commanding Cathy from the corner of my eye, trying to figure out what kept her so busy with setup when we bought coffee and brought our books.

Winning Wendy broke the silence. "Hi, ladies! I would have been here earlier, but I got stuck in the worst traffic."

"Hi, Wendy!" Cathy and I said in unison.

"Mumumu!" Krista demanded, and I returned to my little world of a mouthwatering coffee crumble muffin and my baby. Part of me loved that we shared an affinity for the best coffee cake around, while I also regretted having to share one of my favorite things. I could get us each one. Then I scoffed at my ridiculousness. I would not be buying a baby her own muffin.

A chair scraped against the floor, and I looked. "Hi, Sara! How are you?"

"I'm good, thanks! How are you?" Her cheeks lifted with a bright smile, and I wondered what she liked about us. She rarely participated in the discussion.

"We're good. She's hogging my favorite muffin, though." I gave Krista another bite of coffee cake, and she pounded the table with her tiny, closed fists.

We laughed, and Sara took a sip of her drink as Priya dropped her gigantic key wallet contraption onto the table and draped a sweater across the back of a chair.

"Hi, Priya! Do you expect to be cold? It's so hot outside!" Cathy asked.

"Sure, it's hot outside, but we're inside. It's like people crank up their air conditioners extra to be the inverse of how hot it is outside."

My bra was still damp from lugging Krista across the parking lot. This September heat wave killed my excitement for fall plaid and wool hats. I spent ten minutes digging through my drawer for a fall-colored sleeveless shirt. This must be why they make those open-toe booties— when it's fall, but you need some ventilation.

Gabby arrived from the direction of the bathroom, with Gabriella tagging along behind her. I smiled, relief coursing through my veins. Krista babbled, making a sound mysteriously similar to "Ga."

"Oh, my gosh!" Gabriella exclaimed as she came to scoop Krista up. "I think she tried to say my name!"

"See, haven't I told y'all everybody loves Gabriella?" her mom piped in.

The rest of the table said a chorus of overlapping compliments.

"You're so good with her!"

"Of course, she tried to say your name!"

My chest caved in a bit.

"Oh, wow!" I smiled, but it probably came out more like a snarl. "She's not even a year old, so she's not talking yet."

An awkward silence spread across the table before my favorite controlling lady broke it, "Are y'all ready to get started? How was everyone's week? Did you get the reading done?"

The ladies around me chatted again. Gabriella took Krista and all her things, and I turned to focus on adult time. A paper bag landed in front of me, and I jumped, glancing to see where it came from. Lacy Lee nodded to the bag with a huge grin on her face. "That's for you." She took a swig of her drink— an orangish-colored creamy liquid with floating ice cubes. Pumpkin spice even in a crazy heat wave.

The bag crinkled as I opened it, and my face heated at the disruption the noise caused. I reached my hand in and pulled out the contents, the self-consciousness slipping away as I realized what it was. My very own coffee crumb cake muffin, not to be shared with a soul, sat before me. Tears pricked my eyes at the beauty of it.

Cathy started talking, so I picked up my phone and shot Lacy Lee a text.

Abby:

Thank you so much! Want a bite?

Lacy Lee:

NO! That's all yours!

My insides melted. I savored the first bite, getting equal parts crumb, cream cheese layer, and cake. Whoever made this deserved a raise. They should charge triple for this thing. Do they deliver?

Cathy pulled me from my coffee cake haze with a question, "What did y'all think of chapters 3 and 4? Any epiphanies? Disagreements? Wow moments?"

"That lady Janice in the first part of chapter 3 is an idiot!" Wendy didn't hold back.

"Yes, it did worry me," Gabby nodded.

Priya sounded like a commentator in a reality show recap episode when she said, "What was she thinking? She only knew the guy for three weeks and married him? And he'd been married twice already, had three kids, and had gone through three jobs in the past year?"

Lacy Lee piped up, "Maybe she was in love with the idea. Maybe she really wanted to be a mom and felt her clock ticking, and this guy had three kids already. So, it would be like insta-mom."

"Insta-mom?" Cathy gave her a skeptical look.

"Yeah! Marry this guy. Get three kids. No more worrying about running out of eggs or geriatric pregnancies, or any of that nonsense." Lacy Lee looked effortless and carefree, but the words came too easy. I wondered if I was as good a friend to her as she was to me.

"What else stood out to y'all?" Cathy asked.

I stared at a paragraph I had underlined. Sharing it seemed like opening the curtain of my marriage. These ladies were great, but I'm not sure they needed to know my baggage. The first sentence said, *Welcome to the real world of marriage, where hairs are always on the sink and little white spots cover the mirror.* I hated the white spots. I swear the twins purposely fling toothpaste onto the mirror.

Sometimes Scott has toothbrushing parties when he's home for bedtime. It's like he's making it more fun so the kids are more likely to do it. I imagine them flinging their toothpaste at the mirror and jumping up and down.

The paragraph in the book finished with, *In this world, a look can hurt and a word can crush. Intimate lovers can become enemies, and marriage a battlefield.*

Scott and I weren't much on fighting, but if silence was a shield or short verbal jabs were a weapon, we might as well be on war horses galloping at each other, javelins ready. I expected it to be me and him against the world when we got married, but sometimes it felt more like he was the North and I was the South and we were being pulled into something neither of us knew how to get out of.

Could we become Switzerland? Get back on the same page? On the same team?

My mind drifted to the realization that he may have picked another teammate already. What if he found someone prettier who made lots of money and didn't wear a day's worth of toddler stains by the time he came home? I imagined a woman with a battle-ready body instead of this soft mess.

A question popped into my head, and I blurted it out before I realized I was interrupting. "Does anyone here go to the gym? I want to get fit again."

All heads turned to me with confused looks, but they quickly moved to problem-solving.

"I work out with a personal trainer. I'd be happy to send you his info. He's amazing!" Wendy beamed. "I mean, look at this." She flexed her arm like a sixteen-year-old boy showing off his new post-puberty muscles.

I wanted to slap her for the way she showed off to the rest of us. And I kind of wanted to squeeze her arm and ask how she did it. I'd like a muscle like that. Of course, Wendy has the best.

"My friend runs a mommy-and-me workout group," Sara said from the end of the table. "Sometimes I go. Your first workout is free, and we meet this Thursday. Want to come?"

"Wow, Wendy! That's quite a muscle. But I'm not sure if I'm ready to invest in a personal trainer. What time is the workout, Sara?"

"There's a 7 am group and a 10 am group. I normally go to the 10." Her smile reassured me, convincing me I could do anything. Like working out with a group of women I've never met would be fun and empowering instead of humiliating.

"Ok! I'll check my schedule and get back to you." My schedule was empty unless I needed to get to the barn to see Henry. That's how the horse addiction worked. Sometimes, especially when life fell apart, I just needed to get there. It wasn't even about riding, although never getting to ride was a little like baking your favorite dessert and not tasting it.

Either way, something about being there, smelling the horses, hearing them bang buckets and munch hay, smoothed my frayed edges. When Henry stuck his nose in my face and blew a gentle breath across my skin, I got a whiff of Heaven.

"Let me know!" Sara said.

"Do you have to have kids at a mommy-and-me workout?" Lacy Lee piped in. "I can come!"

My chest warmed as everyone at the table laughed.

"Well, some moms don't have kids with them because they're at school, so I guess not! Just show up. They won't tell you no, and if they did, we'll all go exercise on our own. There are some great trails nearby."

Priya interjected, "Back to the book. There was this paragraph on page 32, and I felt seen. Like, did this guy watch my husband and me through the window?"

"What paragraph was it?" Cathy asked.

"The last one. It says, '*He will express his desires, but his desires will be different from hers. He desires sex, but she is too tired. He wants to buy a new car, but she says, "That's absurd!"*' We literally discussed this last night! He was like, 'We need to trade in our car and get the newest model', and I was like, 'No way! Let's pay off the ones we have. They work perfectly fine!'"

"Oh my gosh, I felt so seen by that paragraph, too. My husband always wants to do it, but by the time I get the kids to bed, I can barely keep my own eyes open. Half the time I fall asleep in the kids' bed and don't even make it to my own." Gabby's face turned red as she talked.

"Really?" asked Wendy. "We do it at least three times a week. And some weeks we do it every day! It becomes a challenge to see how many days in a row we can have sex. Sometimes Ray will even come home on his lunch break to hook up. You really should prioritize this, ladies. It's a game-changer."

We all gawked at Wendy. No wonder Scott was texting other women. I was a total failure of a wife.

"Well, Wendy, that's excellent!" Lacy Lee exclaimed, but as her best friend, I heard the bite behind her words. Surely the rest of the table heard Lacy's unspoken reprimand—*You overstepped a line with that statement, in so many ways.*

"Yeah, once he took a day off of work, and we got a hotel room while the kids were at school. So hot. Y'all should try it if you haven't already."

My face was flaming, and one glance around the table showed I wasn't alone. Even Sara's smile dipped at the edges and didn't reach her eyes. Gabby and Priya's colors had moved into a raspberry shade. Lacy Lee's cheeks looked like she'd stepped outside on a blustery day. And Cathy—poor Cathy was paper white.

I could listen to Wendy rave about how her traffic was the worst, her kids were the smartest, her coffee was the hottest, or her personal trainer was the best. But this... she'd just punched me in the gut with her rock-solid arms without even lifting a finger. I reminded myself this wasn't personal. She's not making a statement about me. The reminder wasn't working. All I heard was, *Abby, you're too fat for Scott to want you. You need to suck it up and have sex more. You should want to take Scott to bed. You're not a good enough wife.* I wanted to cry.

"Wow, Wendy," Cathy spoke up. "You've got quite the successful intimate life with your husband. This reminds me of page 37, where it says if your spouse's emotional love tank is full and he feels secure in your love, the whole world looks bright. Ray's outlook on life must be very bright!"

Wendy beamed, and we all chuckled, but beads of sweat dotted at least two foreheads.

"Now, for the part I've been dying to get to. In chapter 4, we finally read about a Love Language! It's called *words of affirmation*, so if this is you or your spouse's Love Language, you'll feel most loved through words—whether it's spoken or written. Who here thinks their or their spouse's Love Language is this?"

Was this one of our primary Love Languages? It seemed like Scott and I had barely talked for years. Surely, if words of affirmation were his thing, he would talk more.

"I'm a words of affirmation person," Gabby shared.

Cathy did the leader thing and asked, "Ok, what makes you say that?"

"Well, when I get cards in the mail, especially ones with handwritten notes, I always save them in a special place. Curtis could do a million things for me, and I appreciate it, but I feel loved when he says things like, 'Dinner was delicious,' or 'Thanks for all your hard work.'"

"Does he say stuff like that often?" Cathy asked.

"Not nearly as much as I'd like, but he gives me cards on special holidays and occasionally says nice things." Gabby's cheeks flushed at the end of her statement.

"Luke is into words of affirmation, I think," Lacy Lee said. "I never thought about it until I read the chapter, but sometimes he'll send me the sweetest text messages. Words aren't really my thing, so I'm always like, that's nice." We all laughed. "But then I thought about the times I've said encouraging words or told him how much I appreciated him, and he seemed happier. Actually, I think the better word would be content? He totally keeps his cards, too."

"Abby, what about you? You've been quiet over there," Cathy said. The entire table turned to me. Oh crap.

"Uh... I mean, I don't know. It seems like ever since the twins were born and then Krista, I'm always chasing kids around and he's at work. We lead very busy lives and don't talk much. It's just a phase." I spoke with all the confidence in the world. "I know once the kids are a little older, we can have regular date nights and get to know each other again." I clung to the hope that this was true and I didn't outright lie to my Christian book club.

Meanwhile, my brain was spinning out of control about whether the other lady in his life said nice words to him. I mean, if there was another lady. I'm sure she was something my mind conjured as a form of self-torture.

But what if there was someone else texting him sweet, uplifting messages? No doubt he'd pick her, when the best I ever did was glare at him with apple juice and ketchup stains on my shirt, when he came through the door.

That image gave me an idea. I'd need to call Lacy Lee as soon as we left the coffee shop.

8

Dragon Slayer

"Hey, Bae!" Lacy Lee's voice came through the car speakers thanks to that glorious invention called Bluetooth.

"Hey, Bae!" I smiled when I returned her greeting. "Hey, I was thinking during Bible study. Or Christian book study. Whatever that group is."

"Wait, are you on your way to see Henry?"

"Eeeeeeee!" Krista cooed from the backseat.

"Oh my gosh, Abs, what if she's saying something? Like, what if she's trying to say my name? I am her favorite aunty, after all."

"Lacy Lee! She's eleven months old! She can't talk yet! The boys didn't talk until they were two, and that's early for most kids."

"Yeah, well, she's a girl, and girls are smarter."

I had to laugh at that. "Ok. I have heard they develop faster. But still, eleven months? Anyway, back to what I wanted to talk to you about."

Krista competed with me for attention, and I had to talk extra loud.

"Scott has been distant, and I just—"

"Yeah, you mentioned this before. You're worried there's another woman. Which there totally isn't because he knows he'd have me to contend with if he hurt my best friend."

"What are you talking about?"

"Well," she explained, "the night before the wedding when you were off with your mom doing wedding-y things, I pulled him to the side, grabbed his tie, yanked him right down to my level, and said, 'Scott Aberdeen, if you ever hurt her, you have me to contend with. And I'm not afraid to go Lorena Bobbit on your jewels, if she won't.'"

A snort of laughter exploded from me. "No, you didn't!"

"I did! I swear! And I can't believe neither of us ever told you this!"

"You definitely never mentioned it. Ok, but hey, let me tell you my idea." I cruised around a curve. As the road straightened out, a ray of sun peeked through the clouds, illuminating a huge patch of the road ahead.

"So, the book talking about words of affirmation got my wheels spinning, and it's hard to speak Love Languages when Scott and I barely spend time together." As I talked, Lacy Lee repeated uh huh's, and the bright patch got closer. A muddy spot sat right in the middle of it—a trick of the light or debris.

"And I'm always running around taking care of the kids. I should try to do something nice for Scott. Like what if—holy mother of a monkey!" I slammed on the brakes.

"Wait, what? You want to gift him a monkey? A real one?" Lacy Lee sounded confused and a bit worried.

"The biggest turtle I have ever seen on land is sunning in the middle of the road! Just freaking sitting there!"

"Well, go pick him up and move him. Save the little guy!"

"Lacy Lee! Did you hear me? The biggest turtle I've ever seen! This is the kind that eats people's hands off with one bite."

"Abs, what are you talking about? Turtles are cute and sweet. You can paint their shells and set them free, and they're like a walking painted rock!"

"Oh my, Lacy Lee. Please don't tell me you've ever done that. The wildlife people would have you arrested. Painting turtles is supposed to be really bad. It, like, makes them a walking target for predators or something."

Silence filled the car, but I could practically see the blood drain from Lacy's face.

"Oh no, Lacy Lee, I'm sure they just say that. You know how they make you think every plastic straw ends up in a sea turtle's nose. Like every time you drink an iced latte through a straw, you're dooming some poor creature in the ocean. But how often does that really happen?"

"But... I... dang it, Abs. I feel so terrible. The turtle was so sweet, and I painted a big sunshine on her back so she was like a walking sunshine, you know? And she probably barely made it past the tree line before something ate her, all because of me."

"No, Lacy, you have no idea. I mean, maybe the sunshine saved her from blending in with the road and getting hit by a car."

"Bububu..." Krista said from the back seat, a constant babble. When that girl learned to talk, she wasn't going to give anyone a chance to get a word in. I better enjoy my chance to speak now.

"So, what are you going to do about the dinosaur turtle?" Lacy asked.

"You mean the alligator snapping turtle?"

"There is no such thing!" she squealed.

"What are you even talking about? Of course, it's a thing. That's what they're called! And they say if you get close to them, those monsters attack like an alligator. That is why I'm going to slowly drive around and hope he doesn't try to bite my tire or something."

The narrow road didn't have much of a shoulder, but I went as far to the right as possible without going in the ditch. I kept my eye on the turtle as I crept by. He turned his head, staring straight back. Then he... "Oh my gosh, Lacy Lee, he winked at me!"

She squealed like a schoolgirl. "That must mean good luck or something. What if he's your guardian angel in turtle form?"

If I'd had a drink in my mouth, I would have spewed it all over the dashboard. "My guardian angel is an alligator snapping turtle that suns in the middle of the road and winks at people as they drive by? I'm putting in a formal request for an upgrade."

"Abs!" Lacy Lee was laughing too hard to talk for a second, but she finally pulled herself together. "I'm just saying maybe your guardian angel, like, took over a turtle's body for a minute or, I don't know, shape shifted."

"You've been reading too many fantasy books, Lacy!"

"Shut up, that's not possible. Fantasy is the best."

"Fantasy is fantasy! It's so weird and so not real!" Honestly. How did she read that stuff?

"Abs, life is hard enough. I don't need to read about other people's real-world problems." The humor drained from her voice. "Besides... it's hard to explain, but somehow the fantasy stories are so inspiring. Like, this little unassuming hobbit takes on the world's biggest burden, doesn't let it turn him into a monster like it does everyone else, and travels to the ends of the earth with every bad guy who ever existed trying to stop him, all so he could save a world who barely knows they're at risk. I love how the most unassuming characters find their greatness and overcome crazy impossible obstacles."

"But half those obstacles are dragons." My argument was dying in my chest, but I had to give one last friendly jab.

"I know, Abs. But sometimes I think there are dragons in our lives. They just might not look like we expected."

"Touché." I wasn't sure how our conversation had become this, but that's why we're friends. The conversation lulled as I processed my friend's words. Krista started clapping, reminding me I had been about to share my plan with Lacy Lee.

"Ok, so the big idea!" I said, bringing our conversation back. "Scott is supposed to be home this Friday, and I was thinking of taking the kids to my mom's, putting on a fancy outfit, cooking him an elaborate dinner, and surprising him with a date night in."

"This sounds like my friend Abby, the dragon-slayer, is picking up her weapons. I like it! How can I help?"

The road turned to gravel as I pulled up the barn drive. I wrapped up the conversation feeling like maybe I could do this. Maybe I could win Scott back.

9

The New Guy

I scooped Krista into my arms right as Jack found us. His nub of a tail wagged back and forth at the arrival of his best friend. "Aaaaaah!" Krista screeched in jubilation.

"Ok, Ok, you two!"

"Hey there, can I help you?" A decidedly un-Tracy male voice with a light foreign accent made the hairs on my arms stand up. His tone was Hollywood hot. I looked up to see dark eyelashes and dimples set into tan skin, and my brain resorted to fifteen-year-old boy crazy Abby. Where did this guy come from?

"You ok?" That gravelly voice tickled my ears as Krista fisted a handful of my hair and shoved it into her mouth like a delicacy.

"Ow, Krista!" I immediately had her off my hip and suspended in the air, trying to pull her away from me. Jack jumped up, booping her toes. She shook her little fists and squealed again, ripping at my scalp. "Krista! Krista! Let go!"

"Here, ma'am, let me help you." Calloused hands were in my face, delicately untangling my hair from the baby torture grip. Krista cooed and giggled, apparently as enamored by dimples as I had been a few moments before. Her chubby hands relinquished their hold on me and reached towards his face.

"Oh, hi, Abs! It looks like you've met Juan!" The guy, apparently named Juan, glanced at Tracy, who was glowing. "We have a professional polo player from Argentina helping out for a few months! He wanted to learn more about our hunter-jumper world in the off-season, and I told him we could always use an extra pair of expert hands."

I almost laughed in Tracy's face, which was turning redder by the second. Did she hear herself? Juan either didn't catch the innuendo or had an incredible poker face.

"Hi, Juan." I nodded. It was probably best a baby filled my arms, so I didn't experience his expert hands against mine. *I am married*, I reminded myself. "It's nice to meet you. Thanks for the help." My face was hot, and my neck itched.

"You too," he smiled, and those dimples made a reappearance. "I was heading to the back barn to tack up Argos. Need anything else, Tracy?"

"No, I'm good. Thanks, Juan!" Tracy said.

He sauntered off, and Tracy and I watched him leave. His jeans were a little snug, and I wondered if that body came from manual labor or hours in the gym. Maybe he won the genetic lottery. "Do all polo professionals look like that?" The question emerged from my mouth unbidden.

"Abby!" Tracy's voice broke the fog.

"Yeah, what's up?" I turned to her.

"You've got a little something on your face." She motioned toward her chin, so I reached up, expecting muffin crumbs or something. Nothing was there. Realization hit.

"Tracy, oh my gosh, shut up!" I squealed as Krista patted my cheeks.

"It sure is nice to have some man candy around here!" She grinned. "But don't forget about poor little Scott waiting for you at home!"

Hopefully, my flinch wasn't noticeable. "You're right. Poor Scott." I paused in thought and then rushed to speak, attempting to cover up any signs of distress. "How's Oz doing? Did the pad help?"

"Oh yeah, it helped a little, I think. I'm working with the vet, but I wish a pad existed that helped saddles fit better. It's impossible to have every horse fitted for a saddle, especially when I have horses come in for short-term training and then leave."

"It doesn't seem like it would be that hard, but based on the number of horses with back problems I've known, I guess it is."

"For sure. Thanks for letting me borrow it. I'll try it a couple more rides and see if he moves better. A saddle fitter's coming out next week." Tracy checked her watch and seemed to remember my time was limited. "I'll run ahead and set up the pack-and-play. See you in a minute."

"K, thanks!" I ducked into the van for the diaper bag with Krista slapping me and babbling.

I readjusted the baby and pulled out my phone to text Scott about dinner while I walked, but words wouldn't come. This was simple. He's my husband. I want our date to be a surprise, but I need him to plan to be home.

"Pack-and-play's all set up!" Tracy called and disappeared into her apartment. A nicker pulled my attention from the phone to all the horses staring at me. What if that was Henry? As the gazes of the beautiful showhorses followed me, I wanted to believe that nicker had been from him to me.

It only took a minute before Krista and I were situated. I pressed the curry comb into Henry's coat, moving it in slow circles, lost in thought. Krista threw cheerios over the side of her pack-and-play, and Jack jumped around to catch them. Henry kept swinging his head around and nuzzling my hip, probably searching for treats.

A black dress hung in my closet that I hadn't worn in over a year. It would be perfect for date night. I loved how it was tasteful, a moderate high-low with the front below my knees and the back reaching ankle length. It was snug around my bust and waist, flaring around my hips, forgiving my mom-bod in all the right places.

Should I do my own makeup? Or have Lacy Lee help? She was great at makeup, especially since she started her side hustle. And what should I cook? Or carry-out? That way, instead of cooking, I could have the house spotless.

Pain shot through my hip, pulling me back to the present. Henry's big eyes peered into my soul. He nuzzled the spot his teeth had clamped down on like he wanted to massage out the pain. "Henry. Why on earth?" He kept looking at me and then glancing at his side. "What is it? Did I...?" Realization finally hit. "Oh. Sorry bud. I guess I was lost in thought and kept grooming the same place."

I moved the brush to his favorite spot on his neck to make amends. He leaned into it, sticking his top lip out and wriggling it from side to side with his eyes half-lidded. "Oh, Henry," I sighed. At least I understood how to make one member of the male population happy.

"Hi, Miss Abby," that gravelly voice from earlier greeted me. "You aren't riding?"

Krista's little hands reached for the newcomer. She found her type already, and I had to admit she had good taste.

"No, I usually just come out and groom him." I switched to a mane brush while I talked and combed through Henry's chestnut locks.

Juan reached down to Krista and let her hold his fingers. She squealed in glee and waved his hands back and forth. "Que nena para más bella." Spit flew from her lips as she babbled back to him, sounding a little like Spanish. Finally, he turned his attention to me. "Why not ride?"

My heart rate picked up as I considered my answer. That question was more personal than asking my age or how much money was in my bank account. "Well, I love to ride, actually." I paused, hoping he would move on, but he dug the chisel deeper.

"That's good. Why not ride then? It's a beautiful day. I can help tack up your horse." Krista still clung to his fingers, and he led her in a sort of dance around the pack-and-play on her unsteady feet.

"My horse, Henry, is being leased out to a teenager. It's a full lease, so he's hers to ride for now. Plus, it's hard to ride with baby Krista. Who would watch her?"

"What about the father?" He glanced at my finger, adorned with a sparkling diamond and matching wedding band. "She's his, too, right? He can watch her so you can ride?"

Henry shifted his weight, and I wondered if my anxiety was bleeding into him. "Yeah, well, he works a lot. He's got to make money so I can stay home and raise kids and have a horse." I nodded towards Henry.

"You don't have much of a horse if someone else rides him." He cocked an eyebrow, and I rushed to defend my husband.

"Scott would watch the kids so I can ride on occasion. It just wouldn't be enough for me to show or anything."

Juan looked up from Krista, his eyes searching my soul. We stood in a semi-awkward silence before he finally said, "You don't have to compete to ride."

"I know. But I was big into showing before having kids. It's my thing." My mind replayed a scene that could have been from a movie, but it had been a regular part of my life. A blue ribbon dangled from Henry's bridle as we cantered a victory lap under the big cypress trees in Florida. Trainers, competitors, and the few spectators cheered and whistled.

I was good at something. I brought something to the table. "It's hard to know what to even do on a horse if I'm not preparing for competition." I chewed the inside of my lip and wondered why I was even telling this stranger anything. It was like his dimples unlocked my jaw. I'd known Tracy for years and hadn't talked to her this much.

"Without a show, you ride because it brings you joy."

This is a lot coming from a guy who makes his living competing on horses. I wanted to say it out loud, but I wasn't brave enough.

"Girls who only love competing don't bring their babies to the barn to groom."

I kept moving the brush through Henry's tail even though the tangles were out—even though over-brushing a tail was a cardinal sin in our horse world. I didn't want Juan to see the emotions welling up inside me.

"It seems unfair to Henry to only be a trail horse."

Juan grunted as Henry touched me with his nose. What was that supposed to mean? I wasn't sure if I should be offended or laugh or shrug. "You and that horse have a bond. He doesn't care if he's showing or walking through the woods. He's happy to be with you."

"You think?" I focused on picking Henry's feet so I didn't have to look at this man. Most days, I wasn't sure anyone was happy to be with me. Henry was a horse. We likely had a bond because I brought peppermints and brushed his itchy spots.

My wrist buzzed and relief washed over me. The alarm that kept me from getting lost in barn time was a nuisance, but today I welcomed the excuse to end this conversation. Saved by the bell.

"Thanks, Juan! But I've got to get my other kids from preschool."

Juan disappeared down the barn aisle as I prepared to leave. I slipped Henry a treat, gathered my grooming tools, fed him another mint, put my grooming box away, and gave Henry three more peppermints and a kiss for the road. *That* is why he likes me.

"Love you, bud," I whispered before scooping Krista up with one arm. I grabbed the pull lever in the middle of the pack-and-play and yanked it up, enclosing all the crusty cheerios and a bottle, before tossing it into the office on my way out.

Today, I didn't have time to make it perfect. With those dark chocolate eyes studying me, like he could see every conflicting emotion and struggle in my chest, I had to escape. How could I plan a perfect date for my husband with another man peering into my soul?

10

Meet Cute

I t was a basic text—to the point, and gave little away. Hopefully, he'd put it on his schedule.

Mom and Dad said they'd love to have the kids for a sleepover. I needed to figure out the perfect meal and wine to show Scott I cared. Because I did, right?

Sure, I didn't get warm tingles around him, but there had been a time when a simple look sent me swooning.

We had lived in the same city for four years, but we didn't find each other until my last semester of college. For most of that time he was just a boy in class. But the last week of school, things changed. I shuddered, remembering the night Scott carried me off into the night, rescuing me from a guy who'd dragged me into a dark hallway at a bar. Then I had finals and was packing up my apartment to move to Florida, and Scott inserted himself into every moment possible.

That night wasn't a memory I wanted to relive right now. But I would relive those first months of our relationship every day, if possible.

Right after college, when I was working at the farm in Florida and he was slaving away at his first real job in Alabama, we carried on text conversations that lasted hours. I remember the rush of hope I'd get when my phone buzzed in my pocket.

One time I was so excited to read his text that I grabbed my phone while pushing a wheelbarrow overflowing with horse manure—the old-school wheelbarrow with a single wheel. With only one hand and one tire holding it up, the entire thing toppled to the side, spilling soiled horse bedding, poop, and old hay across the rubber pavers of the barn aisle. I wasn't even upset when it took me twenty minutes to clean the mess because Scott had texted a picture of his lunch on his desk and said he wished he was eating with me.

I shot him back a snarky response, sure he'd rather be with anyone than alone at his desk. While I was cleaning the mess, he told me he was booking a flight to Florida to have lunch with me. I thought he was joking.

Three days later, we sat at a table outside of a small cafe. I ordered a cappuccino, and it must have been extra strong. For the next half hour, I gripped whatever I could to keep my hands from shaking. Or maybe Scott was getting to me.

We reached for a piece of bread, and when our hands connected, a surge of electricity shot through me. Another human's touch had never made me feel so alive.

After that, he took every opportunity to brush his skin against mine. When the server brought a dessert menu, Scott dragged my chair around the small table, and we sat pressed together as we surveyed the menu. We ordered a glazed donut with fresh strawberries and whipped cream to share.

Sitting next to Scott on a hot summer day, with clouds building in the distance, was something I'd dreamed of since I left him in Alabama. We had spent one week together before I left for Florida, but it was all the time he needed to cement himself in my heart.

Scott wove his fingers between mine. "Is this ok?" he asked while tickling the back of my hand. I turned to look into his ocean-blue eyes but found all the words stolen from me. I smiled and nodded.

"Hey, Abby."

I leaned back so I could face him while he talked, but refused to break the connection of our hands. "Hey, Scott." My voice was breathy.

"I just want you to know," he leaned toward me, staring at my mouth, "that I've been thinking about you." Only a few inches separated us. "A lot."

A speck of water landed on his cheek and another on my head. "Is it—"

The server cut me off, rushing out. "I'm so sorry, y'all, but it looks like our afternoon storm is coming in a little early. Would you like to move inside?"

Rain pattered against our skin and bounced off the table, landing in our drinks and my purse. "Let's go inside." I grabbed my things, and the server held the door, while Scott and I dove for cover.

The rain pounded on the roof through dessert, a thumb war, two glasses of water—to help absorb the caffeine—and a conversation about how many kids we wanted—him: 4; me: 2—and where we wanted to live someday—me: close to family; him: wherever I lived. I knew in my gut that if I chose him, Scott would be my forever. Every cell in my body wanted him.

Time ticked by as rain pounded the roof of the cafe. My boss would understand me being a little late thanks to the storm, but the show horses had a strict schedule. "I've got to get back to the barn," I conceded. "It's time for afternoon hay."

The unrelenting thunderstorm chased us to my car, pelting our skin and soaking our clothes. Just as I dove for cover, Scott grabbed my arm and pulled me back into the rain.

Krista babbled in the backseat of the minivan as I touched my lips, remembering the way his mouth touched mine. Pouring rain had made it hard to see anything, but I experienced it all. Water dripping down the sides of my face, his hands cupping my cheeks, then roving down, tickling my arms. Even with the avalanche of rain, his touch was a fire, consuming me.

The day I stood at the altar and promised my life to Scott Aberdeen, I had a grin stretching from ear to ear. I was imagining a life of kissing in the rain and chasing life together.

But then the twins came. How could I feel so blessed and so ruined at the same time? They were my greatest joy. Yet, with every piece of me that became a mom, I lost pieces of me that were uniquely Abby. Scott probably wondered what happened to the woman he married.

My phone vibrated, pulling me back to the present.

Scott:

> I think I can

He had responded to my Friday night request.
I dropped a thumbs up.

11

I Work Out

My phone buzzed again.

I imagined an exercise class where baby Krista was my weight, and Lacy Lee worked out childless next to me.
I texted back.

And quickly followed up with another message.

The next morning, I dropped the twins at preschool and rolled up to Sara's mommy-and-me class at a local park. I needed all the help I could get to fit into that black dress for date night. So far, I hadn't gathered the willpower to cut carbs.

Lacy Lee's car careened around the curve. She slammed the brakes before turning into the parking lot at a turtle's pace. Her window was down, and she yelled, "Krista!" as she pulled into a spot.

Krista let out a loud, "Eeeee!" and lunged towards the still-moving car, almost lurching from my arms.

"Krista!" I scolded, squeezing her fat rolls so hard she might have bruises, but that was better than a concussion.

"Baby Krista!" Lacy Lee walked towards us with her arms outstretched and a babydoll in one hand. She scooped Krista from my arms and handed me a much lighter replacement.

"What's this?" The onesie on the doll said Baby Kat on it.

"That's my baby for class! She was the heaviest one they had at the store."

"Ok, I call Baby Kat for at least half the class."

"Lacy Lee! Abby!" We turned to see Sara with a baby on her hip.

"Hi, Sara! Who's this?" Lacy Lee asked, bounding over to the pair while I followed, awkwardly carrying Baby Kat.

"This is Stella! My mother-in-law usually keeps her during Bible study and when I work, but I pry Stella from her arms for mommy-and-me class."

The two babies surveyed each other. Krista said, "Uh! Uh!" and reached for Stella. Stella nestled deeper into her mom's arms. We all exploded into laughter over the different personalities.

I turned to survey the workout area. Mats were spaced evenly across the grass, and I tried not to think of the random park goers who would see us exercising. "Ok, ladies! Welcome to class! I'm going to get the music going. Everyone find a place behind a mat. We should have plenty."

All the chatty groups dispersed. Nineties hip-hop blared through the speakers as women and babies formed three rows, facing the leader. The lady with the microphone on her face held a kid so large I wasn't sure he was a baby, and her arm muscles rippled.

"Ok, hold your baby in front of you in a gentle hug, like so!" She supported her kid's bum with one arm and wrapped the other across his chest. "Now march in place!" Everyone started marching, and I held the baby doll to my chest like my life depended on it.

The babies were silent, mesmerized by the movement. I marched and smiled at Lacy Lee, who was getting a much harder workout than me with Krista in her arms.

"Ok, ladies! You know the drill! When he says, 'Let me clear my throat' we're all going to do a squat. Every time he says it, we squat. Only go as low as you're comfortable. No falling with babies. But keep your weight in your heels!"

We marched and marched and squatted and marched some more. It was actually kind of fun. All but one crying baby were either mesmerized by the movement or babbling and giggling. The song ended, and Lacy Lee said, "Switch!" We traded, and I panicked a bit at Krista's weight, but I was here to get exercise.

House of Pain's *Jump Around* came on, and all the ladies groaned. This was not a good sign. The leader laughed, "Oh, come on now! It's going to be fun! We're getting strong! Most of y'all know the drill, but if you're new, during this song, we do sidestep squats during the verses, and when he starts saying, 'Jump around,' you stand up and do shoulder presses with your baby! Go ahead and adjust to an armpit hold. Make sure you have a solid grip below their arms. We don't want to put pressure on their shoulders. Here we go!"

She started us off, stepping to the side and squatting, then bringing her feet together. We tried to go with the music, but it was fast. As I got the hang of it, the song started saying, "Jump!" I lifted Krista into the air, barely able to get her above my chest. After two attempts, we were back to squatting. When I finally got the rhythm, it was time to lift again.

Sweat trickled down my back. This is crazy. One workout won't make me fit in a dress. We should leave.

"You've got this, ladies!"

"I've got a severe lack of muscle," I whispered under my breath. I glanced over at Lacy Lee, thrusting the nearly weightless babydoll in the air like the world's strongest woman. They went into a never-ending repeat of "Jump." My shoulders screamed. This was the perfect time to escape to the car. Except I wasn't sure if I would make it if I tried. A mom yelled, "I hate this song!" A chorus of laughing and groans rose into the air. Finally, blessedly, the song faded away.

"Ladies and babies! To your mats!" the leader yelled.

"Praise God!" another mom piped up, and a roar of laughter and 'amens' followed.

"My turn!" Lacy Lee plucked Krista from my noodle arms and replaced her with Kat.

"We're going to do bridges with your workout partner resting on your lower abdomen. They love this one because it's like a mommy fair ride!" *Love Rollercoaster* came on. "See if you can do it with the beat!"

I laid on my back, placed Baby Kat between my hip bones, and thrust my nether regions into the air to the beat of the music as best I could. I prayed no men were walking through the park while a group of women thrust their crotches into the air. I wonder what Scott would think.

"Runaway baby!" Lacy Lee yelled, and I turned to see Krista crawling away like she was being chased. I cast Kat away, rolled to my hands and knees, and tried to get up. My arms wobbled, before giving out, and I collapsed into an exhausted heap on the ground. "Got her!" Lacy Lee yelled before the sound of raspberries and giggles filled the air. I groaned in response.

12

Preparing for Battle

I woke up Friday morning to Tucker asleep on my arm, his cheek stuck to my skin. Drool? Sugary drink? The next thing to register was how my legs and arms felt like lead, and I wasn't sure if something was wrong with my kidneys or if this pain was from my ab workout. *Oh, Jesus, help me.* Would one class get me into a dress? And now my body may as well be an anvil stuck in bed. I should have started next week.

Krista sounded like Tarzan down the hall, and I warred with getting to her room and scooping her up to stop the racket or leaving her to enjoy her vocal exercises. I wasn't sure dragging my body out of bed was even possible. Maybe one day she'd be a famous singer or actress and buy me the fanciest horses money can buy.

And maybe I could have a personal trainer who worked me out just hard enough to get results without making me two pushups away from death. I extracted my arm from Tucker's face and texted Lacy Lee as much.

Lacy Lee:

> Lol. That's not how it works. Pain is part of the deal with a personal trainer.

She would know since her husband was one.

> Btw. Everything on for tonight?

Abby:

> Yes. Scott has appointments in DC all day, but he promises he'll be home by 7. I'll drop kids with parents at 3, an hour drive home, and then we get ready!

Lacy Lee:

> Perfect! I'll be at your place at 4:30 with our fav coffee and my makeup kit!!!!

She sent a coffee emoji, and I may have drooled.

Abby:

> Hey, Scott. Happy reminder. See you at 7?

Scott:

> Yep. I'll be there. Lv u.

I smiled. This was exactly what we needed.

"Thanks, Mom!" I smiled and tried to duck out the door as quickly as possible, which wasn't quick at all since my legs had cinder blocks attached to them. I needed to leave before my involuntarily controlling mom brain kicked in and I grabbed the kids and ran. The last time they were with my parents, they came home with stories about having a cookie dough eating contest, and it took a week to get the Sharpie "tattoos" off Krista and Tucker.

"Sure thing, honey! We're going to have so much fun, aren't we, kids?" She smiled adoringly at the boys with Krista on her hip, weaving her fingers into my mom's hair. I turned to wave as I booked it for the slightly ajar door. My toe slammed into something soft and a bit squishy. Their terrier mutt yelped, and I sailed through the air, my appendages sluggish from the previous day's workout.

I saw my life and a failed attempt at saving my marriage flash before my eyes. My hands were up in time to grab the doorknob with one and brace against the wall with another.

"Oh honey, are you ok?"

"Mumum!" Tate yelled.

"I'm fine, guys!" I panted, using the doorknob to pull myself up.

"You know, if you weren't always in such a hurry and thinking ten steps ahead, you probably wouldn't be so clumsy. Didn't you say you fell a couple of weeks ago when Scott was out of town?" My mom was sincere, but I dismissed her advice. If the animals stayed out of my way, I'd be fine.

"Thanks for the tip, Mom. But I need to hurry because it's an hour drive home, and I still need to get ready for mine and Scott's date. Love you, bye!" A quick scan said Toto had evacuated the premises, and I finally, blessedly, made my escape.

One hour and twenty-five minutes later, I was home, showered, and doing one more wipe down of the kitchen. I chiseled at a chunk of hardened sweet potato on baby Krista's high chair when the door swung open. "Hey, Bae!" Lacy Lee yelled. A confident grin stretched across her face. "I've got my weapons' arsenal!"

"You're rocking a stylist assistant vibe with all those bags and a coffee in each hand. You could be Anne Hathaway in *The Devil Wears Prada*!" I smiled back at her as I rushed to the sink to rinse the sponge.

"Dang, girl! This place looks clean enough to eat in! I can't, for the life of me, get how you can keep a place so clean with all those adorable kids."

"It's not. There's still some sweet potato on the wall from Tucker's last food-throwing incident."

Lacy Lee made a show of scouring the walls. "I love you, Bae, but you're wrong. This is the cleanest home I've ever been in."

"Well, what do you think of the decorations?" I gestured to the center of the table, where I had set out chunky candles in varying heights over a beige table runner. "Is it too much?"

"Girl, whenever you feel ready, you could start a new career as an interior designer. I'll be your first client. That is so cute. It screams horse girl chic, yet there's no horse in sight."

My cheeks glowed with the compliment. "Thanks!"

Lacy Lee was studying the candles. Most were generic wide pillars, but a couple were in jars. "Oh my gosh, is that the horse breath candle?" She picked it up, took a deep inhale, and sighed appreciatively. "It's like when you give Henry a peppermint, and then he sticks his big soft nose in your face and breathes on you."

"It's my favorite smell!"

"Girl, Scott better be careful or he's going to lose you to a candle." She let out a loud and abrupt laugh. "Ok, let's do this. Operation Woo Your Man is commencing. First step, wash your face."

An hour later, I stared at myself in the mirror while Lacy Lee wrapped my dark brown hair around a curling wand. It had gotten so long since I got pregnant with Krista, and it was thick.

My hair was shampoo commercial level when Lacy Lee helped me with it. Most of the time, I put it in a ponytail or topknot.

My hands drifted up to my face, itching to touch my skin. My eyes looked twice as big as normal, and there was a gentle shimmer on my cheeks. "Uh uh, no touching!" Lacy Lee's hand shot out and slapped mine away.

"How do you do this? Like, do I even look like myself?" I tucked my hands under my butt so I wouldn't touch my face.

"First of all, yes, you look like yourself."

"No, Lacy Lee. Definitely not," I interjected.

"Abs. I put a little glowy stuff on your cheeks and some brown on your eyes in just the right place to highlight the features of an already beautiful face."

"I just... I swear my eyes are normally so tiny, and it's like you made them twice as big." I paused in thought. "Do you think Scott will like it?"

It had been so much fun getting ready with Lacy Lee that I'd momentarily forgotten what we were getting fancy for. Anxiety hit like a punch to the gut.

"Abby." Warm hands pressed against my cheeks as she came to eye level. "I'm pretty sure Scott Aberdeen loves you, and this whole other woman thing is your worst fear, creating untrue stories in your mind. But either way, one look at you, and he will forget everyone else exists. You are kind and beautiful and a great mom. You are a blessing to everyone around you. We're pulling out our weapons and fighting to save your marriage, like Frodo fought to save the world."

Tears threatened to spill over as I stared at the face of the girl who knew me better than anyone except God himself. My teeth worked on the inside of my lip while my mind spun with a million responses, most of them rebuttals. She sees the world with rose-colored glasses, which is why everyone loves her.

A voice whispered in my mind, *But you tend to see the world through a lens so dark it's hard to find the good parts.* I had to swallow the lump in my throat before I responded.

"Ok, Lacy Lee. Thank you. Let's get my marriage back on track!"

"Whoop!" She squealed as my phone buzzed on the counter. I picked it up, and the floor dropped from beneath me.

Scott:

> I'm so sorry, babe. I'm stuck in D.C. Raincheck?

13

Warrior Princess

Emotions washed over me like ocean waves.

"Raincheck?" Confusion and denial. "Raincheck!" Disbelief.

"Raincheck for what?" Lacy Lee grabbed my phone from my hand to read the text.

"Our date." The blood drained from my face as the wave absorbed back into the ocean, taking my fight with it.

"Nope. Text him back," she said, matter of fact.

"He can't make it. He's stuck in D.C. for work."

"Abby Aberdeen. Text him back now or I will."

"Lacy, he said he can't make it. That's it! I'll just have to try another time!" My voice was rising, the anger washing out the sadness.

"Pick up your sword, Abby. Fight for your marriage." Her eyes blazed. A shiver swept across my skin, and I grabbed my phone.

My fingers hovered over the call button, but my eye snagged on my husband's photo over his number. He had the five o'clock shadow in the picture that had always been irresistible, and the corner of his mouth turned up into a shy smile.

When he wasn't posing for photos but genuinely happy, his smile lit up his entire face, exposing slightly crooked teeth. Sometimes, he even snorted when he laughed. I missed it. I was always so uptight, but when Scott was happy, I breathed easier. Funny, I couldn't remember the last time I breathed easy, and I couldn't remember the last time I saw that carefree smile, either.

"Hey, Abs," Lacy Lee's voice was soft, like she was dealing with a scared puppy, "hold my hand, and let's pray over it." Warm fingers wrapped around my own, pulling them away from the phone screen.

"Ok," I said with a watery smile.

"Dear God. Hey! It's me and Abby. I guess you know that." I chuckled at the intro to Lacy's prayer, which caused a tear to squeeze out and land on our joined hands. "God, please guide us here. Abby really wants her marriage to be good and full of love. And maybe we're onto something with this whole Love Languages thing we're reading about. But it's hard for them to show each other more love when Scott's always gone. God, guide us and help us. Tell us what to do. Help Scott be home more. Love you. Amen."

"Amen," I repeated and grinned, swiping at a tear before it ruined my makeup. "That was the most mumbly prayer."

"Shut up!" Lacy Lee shoved my shoulder.

I reached out and squeezed her hand one more time. "Thank you," I whispered. My phone buzzed in my lap, and my momentary calm was gone. Scott's photo filled up the screen, and Lacy Lee squealed. "Answer it! What if God's bringing him home?"

Hope warmed my chest as I slid my finger across the bottom of my phone screen to answer and put it on speaker.

"Hey, Scott," I forced cheer into my voice.

There was a slight hesitation before Scott's voice came through, urgent and apologetic. "Hey, Abs. I wanted to make sure you got my text. I'm real sorry, but Doug was supposed to be our company's representative at this banquet tonight, and his wife went into labor two weeks early. I was already at a GW Hospital meeting with clients, so they called me to take his place. Can we do a raincheck? Next week?"

The balloon of hope deflated, taking the fight with it. Another week of distance. Another week of wondering if my husband had another woman. And who knew if my parents would keep the kids next weekend? Or if Scott would actually show up?

But who was I to argue with someone when a lady was in labor? "Yeah," I mumbled. "We can try again next week."

Lacy Lee started acting frantic, mouthing something to me. Scott was talking, but I missed whatever he said, trying to figure out what she was miming. I shrugged to Lacy Lee, then put my hand on my ear, but she kept mouthing.

"Ok, well, I gotta go get ready," Scott said.

Lacy whisper-shouted, "Where? Ask him where he's at."

I shook my head at her. It didn't matter. We'd pig out on fancy wine and food and have a girls' night. I didn't want to think about whatever overpriced hotel he was staying at with whatever other ladies may or may not be scoping out my husband while I sat at home.

Lacy snapped her fingers in my face, grabbing my attention, and said, "*Ask!*" just as Scott said, "Did you say something?"

"Uh, yeah, I was trying to ask, where's the banquet?"

"Oh. It's at the Four Seasons downtown." Lacy Lee shoved my arm and then made a circular motion with her hand for me to keep asking, so I asked the only questions that came to mind.

"Are you staying the night, too?"

Scott seemed confused that I was showing interest, but his voice warmed. "I'm not sure. The company booked a room for Doug. I haven't checked in, though. I didn't pack a bag because I thought I'd be coming home. It'll depend on how late everything goes. I don't want to make the hour drive home if I'm already exhausted."

My mind conjured an image of a beautiful woman leaving a banquet with him, a little too much alcohol in both their systems, a quick walk, and a heated elevator ride to a gorgeous hotel room overlooking the D.C. monuments and glowing lights of the city. "Well, that's convenient!" I snipped.

"Yeah." He paused. "It is. Hey, I really need to get ready. I've got to grab a tux from this rental place, and I'm supposed to meet with a couple of other sales reps before the banquet. But I'm sorry. I promise next week."

"Ok. Next week," I repeated, my face heating with frustration. I imagined all the work I put into tonight. Could I make this happen again? And if I did, would he find another reason to skip?

"Bye, Abs. Love you."

"Love you," I said, the line going silent before I finished. A tear streaked down my face as I threw the phone on the bed.

Lacy Lee was a whirlwind. She grabbed things from drawers, the closet, and the bathroom and flung them into my favorite weekender. Bax's eyes followed her from where he lounged on his dog bed in the corner. "What is going on?" I kind of laughed as I said it, then wiped a tear and thought longingly about the bottle of wine on the counter. "I'm not sure what you're doing, but I'm going to grab the wine," I announced, and as I turned towards the door, a clothing item pelted me. "What the...?" I bent over to pick it up and realized it was the dress I had planned to wear for our date. Looking up, I caught a gleam in Lacy Lee's eyes. "Should I be running away? That look can only mean..."

"No wine, Abs. We've got a bit of a drive," she announced.

"Lacy. I love that you want to take me on a getaway or something. That's real sweet and all. But it's probably too late to book a room somewhere, and we have the house to ourselves and tons of food arriving in an hour. Let's just stay-cay." I walked towards the closet to hang the dress up, and then I was going to pour myself a very hefty glass and find the cheesiest chick flick on TV. Hopefully, Hallmark had a Christmas movie running, even though it was fall.

"Abby Aberdeen. Put that dress on. We're not going on a girls' trip. We're going to D.C."

I stopped, and for the 37th time that evening, the blood drained from my body. Where does the blood even go when that happens? How did I have any left?

"Lacy, he's got a work thing. It's important. We can't interrupt."

"You're important. Your marriage is important. And besides, we're not interrupting. We're just..." she paused. "We're going to strategically place ourselves in the same hotel. At the same time." Her grin was devious. "I have a sudden craving for a cocktail from that bar at the Four Seasons."

"Lacy, I'm not..."

"*I love you, now get that dress on*!" she shouted.

I inhaled and prayed in my mind, *God? What am I supposed to do?*

Lacy Lee's voice piped up, "The dress, Abby. You need help?"

"I've got it," I growled back at her through clenched teeth and started pulling off clothes. "What are you going to wear? I'm assuming you're coming with me since this is all your idea?"

"I have that pink dress and heels in my trunk that I never unpacked from my last fancy event. It'll be nice enough, I think, if I put my hair in an updo and keep it simple. I may need to borrow jewelry."

I stepped into the black dress and pulled the thin straps over my shoulders. Lacy Lee zipped the back and helped me get into shoes and choose a pair of earrings. They looked like a cascade of silver vines dangling from my ears. The diamond from my Grannie's simple necklace rested at the base of my neck.

I walked to the full-length mirror in my closet, Lacy Lee behind me. My eyes trailed from my strappy black heels to the high-low skirt draping over my hips, the cinched waist, and finally my face and hair. Inhaling a deep, cleansing breath, I pulled back my shoulders and tilted my chin up.

"Whoever thought a hot dress could be battle armor?" Lacy said with a spark in her eye. "You're a warrior princess, Abs, and Scott is going to forget his own name when he sees you."

"Let's hope I can still walk in these warrior princess heels." I grabbed my friend's hand and squeezed it. "Let's go get my husband back."

14

Sustenance

"Sweet! My neighbor said she'll take care of Baxter and grab the food when it arrives!" A sense of adventure was easing its way into my chest. There's something about a road trip, even a short one.

"Perfect! You told her to eat it, right? Fancy meals are always better fresh."

"Oh dang, I assumed she knew. I'll text." The car careened to the right, and I grabbed for the door. "Lacy!"

"Sorry, figured we needed some sustenance and there's no line! See?"

My heart was still beating out of my chest as Lacy rolled down the window.

"Welcome to Chick-fil-A! How may I serve you today?" A kid with curly brown hair and an unfortunate case of acne peered over a red iPad.

"Yeah, I'll take a number 1 and a cookies-and cream-milk-shake." Lacy turned to me. "You want the usual?"

"Uh, no. I'm getting a fruit and yogurt parfait. I'm not hun-gry."

The teenager started pecking on his iPad and Lacy leveled a glare my way. "I don't think so. You've got a big night, and you need some calories."

"Like you said, I've got a big night. I'm not feeling up for food at the moment." And I want to look as skinny as possible in this dress.

The kid shifted as he listened to our argument.

"How about you get the wrap?" She looked sympathetic.

"Need any help over there?" A female with blonde hair and dimples shouted over to our guy. His cheeks flushed and his forehead glistened with moisture.

"You need more calories, Abs."

"Uh, I'm—" the boy stuttered as the girl arrived at his side, shoulder-bumping him and giggling.

"How can I serve you? Is there a problem?" Her smile was radiant.

Lacy and I both stared for a second, awestruck at the scene unfolding in the Chick-fil-A line. "We're good! Just add a chicken ceasar wrap and a water!" Lacy held up her credit card.

The guy—his name tag said Connor—stared at his iPad, gripping it until his fingers were a bloodless shade of white. His other finger hovered over the screen, searching for the button. "Connor!" The girl sang his name and then hip-checked him and giggled again. Connor stumbled to the side and regained his footing, his face beginning to resemble a red onion.

"Are you ok?" I asked. "You know what? Don't worry about the wrap and water." I didn't want them, anyway.

"Don't worry! We'll get you those for you, ma'am. Here, let me help!" The girl leaned over Connor's iPad, brushing her shoulder against his as she pressed a few buttons while the poor boy stared at her. "All set!" She lingered close enough for their arms to touch as she turned and smiled at us.

"Thank you," Lacy Lee said, and I could hear the smile in her voice even though she was facing away from me.

Connor's mouth moved like whatever words he wanted to say weren't coming. The girl glanced at him before turning to our car, her perfect teeth gleaming as she responded, "My pleasure."

When we had our food, Lacy Lee gunned it. The car felt like an overfilled balloon, and as we hit the main road, the tension deflated into an explosion of laughter. "Oh my gosh, did you see that poor kid's face?" I squealed as I dug a fry out of the bag and stuffed it into my mouth.

"He sweated through his shirt in 3 seconds flat. I literally watched the stain appear at his pits." Lacy Lee held her hand out for a fry as she talked.

"Was he thrilled or mortified when she hip-checked him?"

"That was epic!" Lacy Lee said, and she wiped under her eyes.

"Are you crying?" I couldn't let this go. It was too good. Crying over teenagers at a drive-through?

"No! It's my allergies," she said as she tapped under her eye to protect her makeup.

"Uh-huh. A kid with bad skin and a blonde with dimples, and your waterworks are in the on position. I'm supposed to be the emotional one in this relationship."

"*Shut up*," she said with a weak laugh. "These hormones I'm taking have my emotions all over the place."

I reached out and grabbed her hand, squeezing it. "Let's be sure not to watch any soldier homecoming videos or we'll both need a pint of ice cream and a box of tissues." I squeezed her hand one more time before pulling the food out of the bag. "Let's eat."

"You want sauce on your sandwich, or do you want to dip it?" I asked her as I dug for the foil bag and cracked open a buffalo sauce.

"On the sandwich, please."

I emptied the buffalo sauce onto the chicken breast and set the bun in place while she drove us toward the interstate.

"*Holy crap!*" Lacy screamed as I flew forward, and my seatbelt locked. The empty sauce packet and food bag hit the dashboard and fell to the floor, but I saved Lacy's sandwich.

"What in the world?" I panic-scolded, eyeing the bag with relief that it hadn't spilled all over the floorboard. When I looked up, it took a moment to comprehend the scene before us. I set the sandwich down and rubbed my eyes. A gigantic, very familiar turtle sat in the middle of the road.

"That's him, Lacy! It has to be!" I said, hardly believing myself. I mean, I'm sure there's more than one gigantic alligator snapping turtle in the world, but they were the same size. The way he looked at me was too familiar, and chill bumps erupted across my arms.

"Abs, are you sure that's a turtle? That thing is uuuugly."

"Put on your flashers. I'm getting out of the car!"

"What if he eats you? What if he, like, laser beams you to another dimension? What if this is some big cosmic trick?" she pleaded, clinging to the safety of the car.

"You can stay inside, but I'm checking it out."

He was facing the other side of the road, so I tiptoed up behind him. How was something so ugly related to those adorable little boxer turtles I see at the barn? The monster craned its neck around and moved its feet like it was turning to face me. A squeal came from inside the car, followed by a hand slapping the dashboard.

I laughed at her freakout and then realized I was on the road with a turtle that, according to rumors, was capable of biting my toes off if I couldn't get out of the way in time. And I definitely wouldn't be moving quickly in these high heels. Maybe it was the animal lover in me, or because I swear it was my second time seeing this guy, but I couldn't bring myself to be too afraid. "Hey, bud," I mumbled like I was talking to Bax. "What are you doing over here? There's way too many cars. It's not safe."

The creature moved toward me, and I danced back a couple of steps. It peered at me with endearing eyes, and I melted a little.

He reminded me of a hairless cat—ugly but cute at the same time. That is, if you overlooked the stuff growing on its shell.

Lacy Lee honked the horn, and I backed closer to the curb. Big, Cute, and Ugly followed suit. A jolt of excitement shot through me as I realized he might follow me to safety. "Get out of the road, ok?" I said as I stepped up onto the curb and into the grass, praying I didn't ruin my shoes. "You can't camp out where cars can run over you. Although you're so big, the people in the car might be in more danger than you." I was rambling.

He edged toward the curb some more, and I let out a "Whoop!"

Lacy Lee yelled from the car. "What is it? What's happening?"

"He's following me!" I yelled and took another step back. The turtle edged toward me, stretching one of his scaly dinosaur-looking legs up onto the curb and pulling himself up. "That's it, bud! You're almost there!"

Another car zoomed around us in the left lane, but I ignored it. Lacy Lee beeped the horn again. "Abs, we've got a marriage to save!"

"Oh, right. We're going to try to win my husband back." The turtle edged into the grass, and I smiled, full of hope. "Wish me luck, or better yet, pray for me!"

I hurried to the car, trusting that the beast was safe from traffic and wouldn't chase me. "Have a good night!" I called and slammed the door, questioning my sanity at wishing a turtle a good night. He turned his head and gave me a wink as a loud noise sounded ahead, something between a pop and a bang. Tires squealed on asphalt, and there was a crunch of metal. A burned rubber smell filled the car, even more powerful than the French fries.

The car that had flown past us a few seconds before now sat cattywampus on the road. The right tire was reduced to a strip of rubber and a metal rim, and the bumper was crunched into a road sign.

"Abby, did you see that?" Lacy Lee exclaimed. "That car hit something in the road."

She threw it into drive, easing onto the gas with an eye on our turtle friend and searching for what caused the accident. About halfway between my new friend and the crashed car, a garden hoe sat, blade up. It almost blended with the road in the evening light. The driver, a hulking guy who appeared to have come from the gym, was inspecting the damage with a phone pressed to his ear. Deflated airbags hung from his steering wheel.

We rolled to a stop and Lacy lowered my window. "What are you doing?" I whispered.

"Hey! You ok?" she asked, and instantly I was ashamed of myself. What kind of Christian didn't help stranded people on the side of the road? *A self-preserving one*, I lashed back at myself, which Lacy Lee was not. She cared more about others than her safety or comfort. Which is also why we're on our way to Washington, D.C. My cheeks heated at the realization.

"I'm good. Help's on the way," the guy waved, muscles rippling in the glow of streetlights. "Hey, aren't you Luke's wife?"

"Yeah! Oh, hey, Toby! I didn't recognize you with the..." she gestured towards her chin to reference his short beard. "You sure you're good?"

"My roommate's on his way. Thanks! Tell Luke I said hey."

"I will. Sorry about this mess. Since you're good, we're going to keep going. Have a good night. Hope you can get it worked out!" We waved our farewells and hit the road to the Four Seasons in D.C. to find my husband, hopefully not with another woman on his arm.

15

D.C.

"Let's roleplay what you'll say to Scott when you see him!" Lacy Lee said as we drove.

"Um, ok. But what if he's with another woman?"

"Good point! What are you going to say if he's with another woman?" she asked, like it was no big deal for this to happen.

"Honestly, I'll just go home." My breath was getting short at the mere idea. "And then, I don't know, file for divorce?"

"Abs, you realize there are women in the workforce, right? And just because there's another woman with him at the banquet does not mean he's cheating." From the passenger seat, I spied her lifted eyebrow.

I took a deep inhale, trying to calm myself. "You're right. I'm pretty sure there's a salesperson on his team who's a woman. But what if he prefers her to me? What if she's beautiful? What if they...?" I couldn't finish the statement. "Take the exit. Let's turn around."

"No, Abby! We are not turning around. What if she's beautiful? Good for her! So are you! Scott chose you, remember? What if Scott tells her what a hero his wife is for taking care of three kids while he's out working?"

Now it was my turn to lift an eyebrow.

"There are a million possibilities, Abs! You may as well focus on the great ones. Ok, so this is what you say if there's another woman with him. Are you ready?"

"Ready," I said, with more resolve than I felt. "Teach me, Sensei."

"You say, 'Hi, I'm Abby Aberdeen! Scott's wife,' and you reach out your hand to shake hers. Then you step close to your husband because he's yours, Bae. Claim that man candy. Now, it's your turn!"

My face flushed at the audacity of that statement and the silliness of practicing, but I obeyed my friend. "Ok, so I walk in, and Scott is standing with a woman."

"Or a man. I mean, whoever he's with."

"Ok, whoever he's with. I'm going to walk up and smile and say, 'Hi, I'm Abby Aberdeen. Scott's wife!'" I stuck out my hand for an invisible shake.

"Great! You've got this, Bae!" Lacy Lee cheered me on as we crossed the bridge into D.C. The sun was setting, reflecting pinks and oranges on the river. The Washington Monument looked like a beacon to Heaven as we entered the city.

"You got any deodorant in here?"

"Girl, my husband is a personal trainer. Of course I have deodorant! Check the glove box."

The blinker clicked as we followed the GPS to our destination, and my heart pounded with it. "I may need to put deodorant on my hands, too. Is that a thing? And maybe my face while I'm at it." The stress was hitting hard.

"Take a deep breath and count to ten, Abs. You're gonna be good. We can powder your face if need be, but it'll be fine. Once we get outside, the cool breeze coming off the water will dry that sweat right up."

The disembodied robot lady guided us through the city. We hooked right following her instructions, and a short pull-through drive framed by men in fancy uniforms came into view. My stomach soured. "Lacy Lee, I'm not sure about this."

"We've got this, Bae." She cut me off. "What's that Bible verse that was on your journal last year? *If the Lord is with her, she cannot fail?*"

"I'm not a fan of those cheesy and sometimes misquoted inspirational sayings," I complained.

Lacy Lee pulled into a parallel spot and threw it into park before spinning in the seat to talk eye to eye. "Abs. Receive it. If the Lord is with you, you cannot fail. God wants you and Scott to have a marriage that honors him. Some mistakes have been made, but we're going to go out there and do our best and trust God with the rest, ok?" She reached out and squeezed my hand. I took a fortifying breath before responding with a voice that sounded resolute. "Ok."

"Ok, let's do this!" Lacy Lee checked for traffic before hopping out of the car and rushing to the sidewalk. I grabbed my favorite bag that held all life's necessities—except deodorant—and stepped into the chilly night air in front of the hotel, feeling like a little girl playing grownup. The click of her shoes and the warmth of her body told me my friend was by my side. We stared at the magnificent building together.

"So, uh, do we just go in?" My hands were clammy. I should have put deodorant on them.

"I guess we march between the toy soldier men?" Lacy Lee chuckled, but there was an edge to it. She was nervous, too.

We shared a glance, her eyes asking if I was ready. I nodded, abrupt and confident. "Let's do this."

Twelve seconds later, the heel of my right shoe jammed between the bricks on the sidewalk. "Lacy! Help!" I lifted my foot, tugging. It didn't budge.

"Abs, what in the...?"

"I'm stuck!" I bent down, hoping to pry it with my hands. My formerly beloved mom bag slid off my back and whacked me in the face. I squeaked and stumbled sideways as firm, gloved hands grabbed my arms and steadied me.

A man spoke. "It's ok, ma'am. Relax. We'll get you fixed right up."

My face flushed as I looked around at all the people gawking at me—from tourists strolling down the sidewalk to a businessman who must have stepped out of the pages of a billionaire romance novel. His hair was gelled back, and a phone pressed against his face. Mr. Romance Hero cocked an eyebrow at me before climbing into a jet-black limo. The driver closed the door behind him. His book must be enemies-to-lovers if that's how he handles a damsel in distress. Or he's the villain of the story.

Lacy grabbed my formerly favorite mom bag, a hand covering her mouth, but it didn't hide the lurching of her shoulders.

Warm hands still steadied me, as I stood with my high heel buried between two bricks, glaring at my best friend. "Is something funny?" I asked.

"Not at all!" Lacy Lee said, turning away. When she turned back, she lost control, laughing so hard she leaned over and braced herself on her knees. "You should have seen yourself! You looked so panicked. I'm over here thinking you're being kidnapped or run over, and when I turn, you're trapped in the sidewalk. And then your gigantic mom bag!" She paused to catch her breath. "It attacked you! I don't even know why you have it. A little clutch would look much better with the dress and would have hurt much less when it clobbered you in the face."

"You better be glad I don't have a clutch because I'd be throwing it at you if I did! Some kind of friend you are!" I declared, but when I paused and imagined what I looked like, Lacy's laugh became contagious. The bellman smiled at us, which only made me laugh harder.

"I heard someone needs a gallant rescue," another toy soldier said as he strode toward us. Lacy Lee and I quieted ourselves, but the hysterical laughter left my eyes watery and underarms even more damp than before.

"Yes, please," I said, wiping the tears. When I saw what was in the guy's hand, I wasn't sure if he was here to save me or cook me dinner. "I'm really looking forward to freedom, but why do you have..." My voice trailed off as the man bent down and gripped my foot with one hand.

A brief shhh sound came from the bright yellow can he was holding, and then he pulled up on my foot. When it didn't budge, he changed angles and sprayed some more before lifting my shoe out of the tiny gap between bricks in the sidewalk. He is not my Prince Charming, I reminded myself. But he was a hero.

"Thank you so much! I can't believe that worked!" I gushed.

"Did he rescue you with cooking spray?" Lacy Lee eyed the can. "That was amazing! Abs, I thought your mom bag had everything, but you need to add a can of cooking spray."

The two men smiled graciously. "We buy it by the case. You would be surprised how many heels we have to unstick. You were lucky the sidewalk didn't chew up your shoe."

The second bellman nodded. "Last week a lady had a brand new pair of Louboutins, and once we got the heel out, it looked like a three-month-old puppy had spent an hour with it."

"Ouch." The mere idea made my heart hurt.

"Ma'am, come right this way. Let's get that shoe cleaned up for you. The cooking spray is great for escaping cracks in the brick walkway, but we wouldn't want you to slip once you get to the marble floors."

A few minutes later, we strode into the Four Seasons, and warmth wrapped around my bare skin. People milled about, most in business attire, but some dressed formally. A man in a suit greeted us from behind a podium with a "concierge" sign on the front. "May I be of any assistance to you, mesdames?"

"Uh..." I gripped the strap of my bag, hoping more words would flow before Lacy Lee piped up, "Yes. We're here for a cocktail!" She smiled like we came to fancy hotels for cocktails all the time.

"Delightful!" The word sounded strange coming from this man's mouth, but he pointed us to the bar, and I chewed my lip as we walked.

"We made it!" Lacy nearly squealed in her excitement.

A buttery, warm voice that I recognized all too well sent my pulse running. I panicked, glancing around the room, and found Scott walking off the elevator in a tux with a man and a woman on either side. The woman was thin, with brunette hair that held a curl better than mine ever would. She wore a long royal blue dress with an empire waist and fabric that flowed as she walked. She was everything I'd never be.

A vice grip on my arm yanked me sideways. I yelped before I could stop myself and floundered in my heels like a baby fawn learning to walk. Scott glanced in our direction. Just as Lacy Lee and I ducked behind a column, a confused expression crossed my husband's face.

16

Four Seasons

"**D**id he see us? Oh crap, Lacy. What are we doing?"

Lacy peaked around the column.

"He'll see you!" I grabbed at her, but she ignored me.

"He's walking in the other direction. I think we're safe." She returned to our hiding place, and we both leaned against the pillar, allowing the coolness of the marble to calm us.

I turned toward my best friend, crossing my arms. "So, what's your plan? What happened to 'Hi! I'm Abby Aberdeen'? like we practiced in the car?"

For a moment, all I got was a rare but classic "oh crap" expression. Finally, she shrugged. "It didn't seem right in the moment. We've come to the Four Seasons. Let's get a drink at the fancy bar."

My heart dropped to my stomach. "That's it? We need more of a plan than that!" I scolded.

Lacy peaked around the pillar again before standing tall and sauntering out of hiding. "Let's get a drink, and we'll figure it out. I'm sure it'll come to us."

We claimed spaces at the bar, sitting with our knees toward each other so we could talk while we nursed our drinks. Lacy ordered a side of fries.

"Ok, so what's our plan?" I prodded again. Sure, I was a smart girl with a college degree, but this spur-of-the-moment stuff was so out of my depth.

"Well," she ran her finger through the condensation on her glass before taking another sip.

"Lacy."

She laughed, a bit nervous, and started to talk when something bumped against me. I turned, my heart in my stomach, sure that Scott was here to confront me for following him.

Dark brown tweed was inches from my face. Scott didn't own any dark brown tweed. Then I smelled the cologne. It reminded me of my high school boyfriend. Was it called Cigar? A list of these facts lined up in my head when a throat cleared. Tilting my chin up to follow the sound, I found myself looking at a guy about an inch taller than Scott with dark brown hair. It looked like the updated version of the nineties butt cut.

An elbow jabbed me from the other side and I realized I'd been staring. Crap. I needed to say something. "Uh, hi. Can I help you?"

The tweed guy laughed. It was schmoozy and entitled, like he knew his place in the world, in life, in this bar, with women, and he could tell I didn't respect it.

"You mind if I sit here?" he asked before flicking his hair out of his eyes.

"It's a public bar," I said with a smile somewhere between my appease-a-toddler look and stab-a-stranger-in-the-eye face.

"Well, I'll take a seat then. There's no better spot than next to two beautiful ladies." I eyed the plethora of vacant seats down the row, but didn't comment.

This guy was good-looking, but so over the top I was barfing in my mouth a little. Do women like this kind of thing?

"Can I get you a drink?" He slid the menu towards us. I crammed a handful of fries in my mouth, eyes wide, while Lacy responded for both of us.

"We've got drinks, thanks! Besides, we're driving home later and I'm a lightweight!"

I swallowed my mouthful of fries, relieved that Lacy could think on her feet.

"What'll you have?" the bartender asked the stranger.

"I'll have a rye Manhattan, rocks. And go ahead and get these girls a second round of whatever they're drinking."

The bartender nodded, but I interjected, "That won't be necessary. Thank you, though."

"I insist," the guy said, winking at the bartender, who scurried off.

I took a deep, steadying breath.

"Where are you ladies in from?" His eyes roved Lacy's body as he talked, pausing on her chest.

I waited to see if she wanted to respond, but when she didn't, I figured I could answer a question with a question as I grabbed my drink with my left hand, flashing my diamond. "What makes you think we're not from here?"

"We're at a hotel. Aren't hotels for people traveling?"

"We live in the suburbs of D.C., so we're basically from here," Lacy Lee deadpanned, and I considered kicking her. Too much information! "We're here for the banquet." She smiled.

The bartender slid another round in front of us, and I questioned whether I should drink it or let it go to waste. I needed to have my wits about me when I confronted Scott, or whatever the plan was.

"What banquet?"

I slurped the last sip of my margarita through the tiny straw. Maybe I'll have a few sips of the other. Lacy's toe connected with my calf, and I jumped, ready to yell, when she caught my eye. "Abs! Tell him about the banquet!"

"The banquet?" It was a statement and a question in one. I moved the straw to the fresh drink, stirring and trying to buy time while I decided what to say. "It's an award thing." Duh. Facepalm.

"Oh! What kind of award are you picking up?" the guy asked, refusing to take a hint. Heat crept up my neck as I took a long swig of the second margarita, hoping the guy would forget about me.

"It's a surprise!" Lacy exclaimed, and I laughed into my straw. The tequila was making my brain fuzzy, which made me care a little less about being perfect. Or kind. Using my left hand again, I grabbed the glass and licked the salt off the rim.

"Hey, thanks for the drink," I lifted the glass toward him in a toasting motion, "but we were having a really important, really intimate conversation, and we need you to give us some space."

Lacy's face was turning red from containing her laughter.

"Oh, I didn't mean to intrude," Sleazeball said with a smile that told me he definitely did mean to intrude. "I see my business partner over there, and we need to catch up on some things."

He stood and stepped into me. The heat of his body was making me sweat and his hand touched the small of my back. My skin crawled.

"I hope to reconnect with you after your intimate conversation," he winked, and I considered throwing an elbow to his neck. This started out fun, but my head was fuzzy and he was making my skin crawl. I needed to focus on the reason we were here. Scott Aberdeen.

As if drawn by my thoughts, a very familiar voice—the most familiar voice—broke my too-much-margarita fog.

"Abigail?"

17

Cocktail Hour

And there went all the blood in my face, again.

Mr. Can't Take a Hint's hand pressed against me as Scott traversed the seating area. "Abs, what are you doing here?" His eyes followed the hand on my back up to the face of its owner before traveling back to me. Ice stole over his features. "And who's he?"

I froze. My throat stuck, my tongue wouldn't move, and my hand was glued to the drink. I could only blink at my husband.

"I'll hopefully catch up with you later!" Mr. Wannabe Nineties Boy Band Star gave a quick bow as if we were royalty, smiled at Scott, and exited stage right.

"Abby, who is that?"

His words sent an image into my head of him standing next to that gorgeous lady in blue. Then I remembered his phone call earlier, and the date he had canceled. My body thawed and words shot out of my mouth, "What do you care? You can't even make it to our date."

It wasn't what I had planned to say, but my mouth got ahead of my brain. This was supposed to be a storybook moment. I should be seducing my husband, sashaying over to him while his eyes roved over me in the only dress I owned that made this blubber of a body look sexy. I'd trace the lapel of his tux from his shoulder down to the button, inhale his cologne, and just as my body nearly combusted with the need to feel him, he'd grab my face with his warm hand and tilt my lips to his.

Instead of closing the divide, my words and tone created an even larger chasm.

"Abs, I said I was sorry. Really, I—"

"Scott!" a sharp female voice carried across the room. "We're about to start, and your stage call is one of the first after the video."

My eyes searched for the source of that powerful voice and landed on the woman in the blue dress. Her accent sounded French to my untraveled ears, and she had an elegant black clutch tucked under her arm. I groped for the handle of my favorite bag. It wasn't a black-tie appropriate purse, but it held everything I needed except deodorant and cooking spray. I had been so excited when Scott gave it to me three weeks before Krista arrived. It had been the trending mom-bag on all the baby blogs.

"Wait a minute, Auri," he said and stepped towards me, reaching his hand out.

"We don't have a minute, Scott." She enunciated his name.

Scott looked at her and back to me. "Abby, don't leave. I want to talk as soon as I can step away, but I've got to go. Stage call."

"We'll see," I stammered, heart in my throat. He nodded and turned away, hustling in what must be the direction of the ballroom. My heart pounded in my fingers, ears, and even my hair.

"Dude, you were harsh."

I spun around to face Lacy Lee and inhaled a deep, defeated sigh. "I know." My words came out in a moan. "It just happened. He was here, and he looked so shocked to see another man interested in me. And that sleazeball had his hand on me.

And then she yelled." I took a swig of my drink. "She's so perfect. She even has a freaking accent. I thought I was beautiful until she showed up in that goddess dress. It was like angry word vomit."

Lacy Lee's brows furrowed during my monologue of shame, and when I finished, she gave me a sad smile. The pause seemed to linger, building space between who I want to be and the person I really am. I replayed my harsh words and tone in my mind and chewed my lip.

"Abby, you have a right to be upset," she said. "And I think Scott knows you well enough to know that when you feel out of control, you kind of bark at everyone." Her shoulders lifted into a shrug and a genuine smile crept onto her face. "Ok, now I'm imagining you as a papillon whose favorite toy got taken away."

"Oh my gosh, Lacy Lee." I wanted to keep having a pity party, to drown in my self-condemnation. "It's not funny!" I shoved her shoulder half-heartedly. "I mean it! This is serious! I'm supposed to be Love Languaging my husband to win him back, but instead, I bit his head off!" My shoulders started to shake as Lacy's laughter spread to me.

"Did you see his face when he realized Mr.—what did you call him? Sleazers?—had his hand on your back? Poor Scott!" The entire bar watched us as Lacy Lee's laughter crescendoed. She doubled over, dabbing at tears.

She took a long sip of her drink, and I realized I needed to eat more if I wanted to finish this margarita. I dipped the cold fries in ketchup and got to work.

I took a moment to figure out what fast food chain these reminded me of. They weren't smooth-edged and they didn't have the brown "real potato" edge like Wendy's. "Hey, who else has fries like this?" I asked Lacy and shoved three more into my mouth.

"They're kind of like Burger King, I guess? Yeah. Like a high-end Burger King." She leaned over the bar, mushing the fry into a mound of ketchup, when the thunk of a glass hitting the bar and the clank of ice spilling hit my ears. Lacy Lee leaped to the side and backward off the barstool, but she wasn't fast enough. Her neighbor's drink waterfalled over the edge, soaking her dress in what appeared to be bourbon and coke.

"Oh dang," we said in unison.

"I've got the mom bag. Let's find the bathroom and try to fix this." I took one last sip of my margarita, grabbed the gigantic but beautiful rose-colored bag, and scanned the area for a sign pointing to the bathroom.

A chorus of "I'm sorry," "We'll get that cleaned up for you," and a few more "I'm so sorry!" sounded behind me.

Lacy Lee put on her winning smile. "It's ok. But could someone point us towards a bathroom?"

We stood at the sink, the front of Lacy's skirt under flowing water. Pink was a gorgeous color. Pink and bourbon? Not so cute. We rinsed and squeezed and rinsed some more.

Heels clipped on the hard floor, and two women in elaborate gowns rounded the corner. The four of us made eye contact, and I saw them glance at Lacy's exposed rear end. The girl loved a thong, and the skirt didn't hide much since a large part of it was in the sink. "Hi!" Lacy said with a confident smile.

The ladies smiled back and continued whatever conversation they'd been having while they dug through their clutches. "I can't believe the Texas branch won the big award," one of the girls said.

"Well, it's almost unfair. I mean, there's so much money in Texas and the state is gigantic. Have you seen the hospitals?"

"Good point. Did you hear that Cassidy girl's flight got delayed? I guess her and her plus one will be coming in late and missing the banquet."

They kept talking, and I kept rinsing, but now my wheels were spinning with a plan. If Cassidy isn't coming, there must be two spots available in that banquet room.

18

Plans

"I have a plan," I told Lacy as the women slipped out, and we rung the water out of her skirts.

"Does it include a fairy godmother and a new dress?" she moaned.

"No, but it does include a hand dryer and a seat at the banquet."

"Wait a sec. A seat at the banquet in Heaven or a seat at this awards thingy? It's probably easier to get a seat at the table next to Jesus."

"Tonight!" I exclaimed as I pushed the button on the hand drier, ending the conversation for the moment.

Ten minutes later, Lacy's dress was dry, but we were both dripping from our temples and armpits.

"I can still see a waterline." Lacy sighed as she spoke. "Did you see how fancy these girls are?"

"Hold on." I dug into my bag. "I have the perfect thing!"

A delicate piece of fabric with blues, pinks, and purples in a watercolor flower pattern spilled out of my hand.

"I love this bag!" Lacy smiled. "It's like you're a mom Macgyver with that thing."

I smiled and shrugged, getting to work, tucking it into the slim belt at her waist. The scarf draped artfully over one side.

"Dang, Abs! Where did you get this? I need one. It took this dress from a 7 to a 10!"

"Scott's mom gave it to me for Christmas. It lives in my bag. It's nice to have around. If it's raining, I can put it over my head; if it's cold, I can throw it over my shoulders or wear it like a scarf; and if my best friend has a drink spilled on her, I can tie it around her waist!"

Tugging it around so it covered the water line, I stepped back and admired our work. "It was a happy accident!"

"Ok, now we need some wet wipes. Standing in front of the drier heated me up, and not in a fun way." Lacy Lee started fanning herself with her hands.

"I got you." Reaching into the side pocket, I brandished a travel-size pack of wet wipes. "Can I even be considered a mom if I don't have these on me at all times?"

"Is that all it takes? Maybe I need a case from Costco." Lacy laughed, but there was a hint of pain in her eyes.

"If you're anywhere near as good of a mom as you are an auntie, you'll be incredible. It'll happen, probably when you least expect it."

Her eyes filled.

"Emergency!" I hollered. "Squeeze your butt cheeks! Squeeze 'em hard! It'll keep the tears from falling!" I gave her butt a pinch. "Dang, girl, you've got a tight butt!"

"Hey, if you were married to a personal trainer and let him train you, you'd have a pretty tight butt too." She laughed, the tears drying up. Mission accomplished.

"If I was married to a personal trainer, I'm pretty sure we'd never make it more than four minutes into a workout before we'd be doing our own kind of exercise, the kind magazines say burns 5000 calories. Although there's no way that's true."

"Well, it probably depends on how crazy you get," she snorted. "And it's a good thing the gym is in our garage for sure." Her cheeks were pink.

"Lacy Lee!"

"That workout bench isn't just good for bench pressing."

I gasped. "The one his clients use?"

"Don't worry. We wipe it down," she snorted, and I shook my head.

"Speaking of." I handed her a couple of wet wipes and grabbed one for myself. "And my secret weapon." I set a travel-sized bottle of baby powder on the counter. "Cucumber melon scent, so we don't smell like an actual baby."

"I appreciate the offer, but I don't need butt powder," Lacy said as she tossed her used baby wipe in the trash.

"No, girl. Have I not told you? You can use it for basically anything. Boob sweat? Put a little powder under the girls. Stress sweat? Powder up your pits. Oily hair? It even helps with that! But white powder and a black dress is a dangerous combination, which is why I went for deodorant earlier. Baby powder is my best friend, though."

"Hey now! You better not be replacing me with a tiny $2 bottle of powder."

I shook my head. "It was at least $3. Inflation and all." I smirked before I sprinkled a little in my hand and carefully patted it on my armpits, trying to keep it from getting on my dress. Lacy copied.

"Friend check," she declared, and we turned to each other, each spinning and eyeballing the other head to toe. "Passed! A+. You're looking hot and smelling lovely. Scott will be drooling like a labrador when you walk in!"

I rolled my eyes at her. "Thanks, Lacy! You too!" I paused for a moment, taking in my reflection in the mirror.

"What's on your mind, Abs?" Lacy Lee prodded, and I wondered if she even needed to ask. Sometimes she knew me better than I did myself.

"It's hard to put words to it. I feel more beautiful tonight than I have in a long time, thanks to you." I smiled at her. "This is the most I've looked at myself in years. Normally, I avoid mirrors and reasons to dress up fancy."

"Aw, Abs—"

I plowed forward, cutting her off. "You're going to tell me this body carried my beautiful babies and blah blah blah, but when I see that hot, skinny lady in the blue dress, or I remember what I used to look like, it's hard to like this version of me, and I'm not surprised at all that my husband doesn't either."

She grabbed my hand, and we stared into the mirror, looking into each other's eyes. "Abby, first of all, you don't know that about Scott. That's a story you've created that has yet to be proven. And you're right. I'm going to tell you, your body did grow three babies. Two of them at once, even! But I also think, as women, we tend to obsess over what we don't have or what we aren't. You're beautiful. And you'd be beautiful if you lost 30 pounds or gained 30 pounds. With makeup or without. Because you're Abby."

"Ugh. I know. Beauty comes from the inside. But it's like I obsess over things."

"Really?"

"Yeah!"

Lacy Lee smiled and cocked an eyebrow, and I realized this was a fact she was quite familiar with. "Anyway," I kept going, "it's something I have a really hard time with. I wonder if Scott could even be attracted to me now."

"You've heard that comparison is the thief of joy, right?" She raised an eyebrow at me.

"Yeah, yeah. I know. I compare my worst to other people's best."

"But have you ever thought about comparing yourself with past versions of you? Like, you get obsessed with how you're a bigger size now because younger you was so thin. Well, I can tell you now, I loved younger you, but she was not the superhero that current you is. It's not even a fair comparison."

"What do you mean?"

"Younger you basically had nothing to do back then except ride horses and work out. Think about all that you currently tackle in a regular day. You're keeping three kids under four alive and well. That in itself is like three full-time jobs. Plus, you keep that house immaculate. You actually read before book club. You visit Henry a couple of times a week. You cook healthy meals—like three meals—every day. Luke is lucky if he gets three home-cooked meals in a week, and I don't have kids to chase around."

"Yeah, but I should—"

"Uh-uh. Nope. We're not shoulding ourselves." Her tone was gentle but unapologetic. "Also, would you be friends with me if I talked to you the way you talk to you?"

That question sucked any words right out of my mouth. Lacy Lee grabbed my chin with her hand like a great-aunt about to give a little kid a stern talking to. "Stop talking to my best friend like that!" She mock scolded in the worst impression of an old lady voice I'd ever heard. "Or I'm going to make you clean all the floors!"

"I already clean all the floors," I deadpanned.

"Ok, I'm going to make you wash the curtains!"

"Done."

She broke character at that. "Dang it, lady, see what I mean! Old Aunt Lacy can't even come up with a punishment for you. You do so much!"

"How about doing two of those mommy-and-me workouts in a day?" I laughed. "I am still hurting. It's making walking in heels even more difficult than normal."

My phone buzzed, and I checked it.

Scott:

> Banquet is about to start. I'll come see you at the bar after my stage call.

"Oh crap, we gotta go! It's about to start!"

Lacy Lee picked up my bag and swung it to me. "You with me?"

I nodded and grabbed the bag from her as we walked to the door.

"Then let's do this!" She slammed the bathroom door open as she said it.

"Did you quote Ratatouille?"

"Well, yeah! It's only one of the best animated movies ever made."

"Ok, Lacy Lee. I love you, but I disagree. Also, we have to act super mature now because we're about to walk into a fancy banquet." I glanced at her. "I'm not sure I said it before because you were busy giving me an incredible pep talk, but you look boiling. There's no one else I'd rather crash a banquet with!"

I grinned at her, and then the reality of what I was about to do hit me. My feet slowed of their own accord until I was no longer moving down the hall. "Oh crap, Lacy. Maybe we should wait at the bar. This is crazy. What were we thinking?"

She strutted forward through the double doors of the banquet hall before I could turn around. "Smile! This will be fun!"

"What's your name?" A lady sat behind rows of nameplates with table numbers.

I scanned them hurriedly, looking for Cassidy's so I could add a last name, but the lady was looking at me expectantly and I wasn't seeing it.

"I'm Cassidy," I smiled. The lady scanned a name list and Lacy whispered into my ear, "You're from Texas!"

My eyes finally landed on Cassidy's nameplate. There was a small gold medal on the side. What on earth? But I had to plow forward, this time with a Texas accent. "Cassidy Templeton," I declared in my best Friday Night Lights Tammy Taylor impression. It was a little more twangy than my mild northern Virginia accent.

"Oh, here it is! Wow, congratulations! Here's your name plate and your guest's, Steve Templeton." The lady glanced at Lacy Lee and her smile faltered for a second. Lacy wasn't pulling off "Steve" very well.

"Thank you." Lacy gave her a nod. "It's Stevie. We're best friends and do everything together!" She beamed and grabbed our name tags.

"Oops!" I said, my face flushed. "It must have auto-corrected to Steve when I filled out the RSVP. Anyway, thank you!" I turned, hoping to escape before any suspicions arose.

"You're welcome, dear! We heard you weren't going to make it. I'll be sure to let them know you're here." The lady pointed us toward our table, and Lacy led the way.

I couldn't decide if I should laugh or panic. We were in. That was way easier than I expected. I scanned the room for Scott and found him sandwiched between the man and woman he was with earlier, lost in conversation.

Lacy Lee and I found our table. Three people were on the left side and two to the right. Our seats sat waiting, facing the stage. It appeared every table had a vacant spot so no unlucky person got stuck with their back to the stage.

"Hi, I'm Stevie and this is Cass," Lacy Lee greeted the people sitting at our table, and I had to contain my eye roll. She was way too good at this stuff. I'd have to let her carry the conversation, or I'd definitely slip up.

Lacy Lee pulled out my chair for me with a mischievous grin, while I smiled and nodded to everyone.

"We thought you wouldn't make it!" someone said.

Biting into a roll as he spoke gave me the perfect opportunity to let Lacy Lee talk for us. "We had some flight trouble, but we're here!" She took a deep breath like she was so relieved. "And boy are we hongry." The twang she added to *hungry* was terrible. We were screwed.

"So, Cassidy," a lady said, and I noticed her name plaque had a silver medal on it. "Tell us about your success this year! And being so new with the company, too! How did you do it?"

I chewed my roll slowly, trying to buy myself time. "Oh God, please forgive me," I whispered in my head. I was so focused on my ploy to get into the banquet that I didn't realize so much lying would be involved.

Lacy touched my arm and smiled. "Yeah, Cass, why don't you share? It's been quite remarkable."

The bite of bread felt like a rock going down my throat. Channel your inner horse girl, I told myself. Riding an unruly horse in a judged class makes this look like nothing. Which gave me an idea.

"I owe it all to what I learned from my horse." I took another, larger bite of my roll, so they had to wait for me to chew. Slowly. And deliberately. This is a room full of medical salespeople, not doctors. I wasn't sure if anyone could save me if I choked.

The speakers screeched, causing a unified jerk across the room as everyone turned to see what was happening. On the stage, a woman in a purple gown that clung to her curves stood next to a man in a suit. The guy leaned forward across the podium. "Is this thing on?" He tapped on the mic and I fought the urge to roll my eyes.

The room chuckled, and I took a second to thank God for getting the spotlight on someone else. As everyone settled, I turned for a second to glance at Scott. His sky-blue eyes, like a cloudless afternoon, were pointed right at me, and his mouth was set in a firm line. I tilted my head and shrugged. He lifted his eyebrows and shook his head.

I poked Lacy to get her attention and pointed at Scott. A smile stretched across her face. She lifted her hand in a small, hopefully unnoticeable to everyone else, wave.

Scott shook his head again. My insides were a turmoil of panic over what we'd done and what Scott would think. A few hours ago, I was cleaning food off the high chair, and now I was sitting at a banquet at the Four Seasons with a little gold medal on my, or Cassidy's, nametag.

19

Celebrations

“I know y’all are hungry.” The lady on stage spoke into the mic. “We’ve prepared a presentation for you to watch while you eat. It’s been a phenomenal year at MedDev and we want to share a video so you can see all the good you’re doing. This isn’t just medical sales, this is life-changing. People’s lives are better, more full, every day because of you. Enjoy the video and your dinner.”

The couple walked arm in arm off the stage, and a video started playing. A server set a plate in front of me and removed the cover, revealing a lobster tail, a mouthwatering cut of steak sitting in its juices, what appeared to be a twice-baked potato, and asparagus. My mouth started watering. This. Was. Incredible. No wonder Scott skipped our date. I turned to him with a face that said, *is this how you eat all the time?*

His cheeks turned red, a small smile on his face, and he shook his head. As if he could read my mind, and answered, *no, Abs, I don’t eat like this all the time.*

Which I didn’t believe, so I glared at him.

He laughed and shook his head, and a moan sounded next to me. I turned to see Lacy Lee with her eyes closed, savoring a bite of something.

"Oh my gosh, Ab—I mean Cass. It's so good. You've got to try the lobster."

The video started playing on the big screen as I dove into my steak.

I didn't know much about what Scott did other than travel a lot, fill our bank account, and then stress that there was never enough money. I knew he did medical sales and something about prosthetics, and he often met the patients.

A voice from the video said, "MedDev—making your prosthetic fit into your lifestyle, not the other way around." I glanced up at the screen and was mesmerized.

Pictures told story after story. Smiling, happy people posed for photos, doing things like riding bikes, holding golf clubs, or wearing running clothes with a medal around their neck. Hospital photos followed—they looked terrible, with wires and machines everywhere. Then, there was rehab with crutches and rails, exercise balls, and other struggles. After the pain, the video returned to joy. People were doing the things they loved before their accident or illness, with one obvious difference—a prosthetic limb.

An older lady wore golf shorts that showed off both legs. One of them looked like it came from a science fiction book. Her photos showed her posing with a friend on a golf course and bowling with grandkids. Then an article popped up with a headline that read, "*When a Barrel Race Becomes a Race for Life*." There was a photo of a rodeo arena and a body strapped to an orange board surrounded by EMTs. They even showed the life-flight helicopter with cowboys and cowgirls holding hats over their hearts in the background, and my heart dropped to my stomach.

The last picture was her barrel racing again, a huge smile on her face. Then a picture of her hugging a horse that looked like a smaller version of Henry with a longer mane and a stripe down his face. A young girl, hardly older than the twins, sat on the horse, beaming.

Lacy Lee dabbed at her eyes. A lump filled my throat, making it hard to enjoy this mouthwatering meal. I shoveled potato into my mouth, determined to do my best.

The video closed with a clip of each featured person thanking MedDev. They said things like, "Before MedDev, my prosthetic was painful. I thought I'd never be able to do what I did before the accident. Because of your you-fit technology, it doesn't hurt. Sometimes I even forget that part of me is missing. It's like I found a new part of myself." The people in the video had wet streaks on their faces. Across the room, you could hear hiccupping and sniffling. Napkins dabbed at faces.

When the screen went dark, everyone sat, entranced. Awe settled over everyone like a blanket. Someone behind me started clapping, followed by a second and third person. Soon, the elegant crowd in formal gowns, tuxedos, and multi-piece suits stood and cheered.

I couldn't help but think, all that time Scott was leaving us, he was helping people like those in the video. Maybe some of those were his actual clients. Lacy Lee and I shared a glance and stood together, clapping and whooping for MedDev and all the developers and salespeople who changed lives.

The couple reappeared, strolling across the stage, arm in arm, until they reached the microphone. "Let's hear it for all the hardworking people in our company. We don't just sell medical devices. We change lives. We make prosthetics fit into our clients' lifestyles!"

The crowd roared, and I wondered if confetti would fall from the ceiling.

Daria, as she had introduced herself earlier, leaned into the mic. "Now it's time for what you've all been waiting for. The awards presentations! Please have a seat."

Everyone complied as servers buzzed around the room, depositing cheesecake and chocolate mousse and filling coffee cups. I made sure to flip my cup upright so they filled it. The idea of coffee and dessert was making me giddy. If Scott isn't cheating on me, he better think twice before he leaves me home with the kids during another banquet like this.

Dan, the man on stage, announced they would start with team region awards and move from west to east. "The Pacific Northwest Region winner is The Rainy Day Warriors team!" A tall, thin guy stood up from a table on the far side of the room, and ran up to claim the prize while his table cheered extra loud.

Oh no. What if Cassidy was supposed to accept an award? I mean, there was a gold medal on her nameplate.

And what region was she in? Was Texas a region by itself?

"In the southwest region—"

Southwest has to be Texas, right? Oh crap, oh crap, what was I going to do?

"Our winner is team—"

Oh God, what do I do? Help!

"Phoenix Rising."

Uhhhh, is that me? I looked at Lacy Lee, panic written all over my face. Her expression matched mine.

"Would the representative from Phoenix Rising please come to accept the award?"

I have a freaking gold medal on my nameplate, and the check-in lady congratulated me. I turned to look at Scott, hoping he had answers, but he shrugged his shoulders.

"Oh! That's my team!" The lady next to us with the silver medal on her name card giggled and pushed away from the table to claim the award.

Lacy Lee leaned into me. "Dodged that bullet!" she whispered into my ear, and we both giggled as we took bites of dessert and sipped coffee.

More regions and awards were called out, which I clapped politely and alternated between a bite of my cheesecake, then Lacy's chocolate mousse, and then a sip of coffee.

"And now for the eastern region, our highest sales team is The Patriots, based right here in DC, Maryland, Virginia, and Pennsylvania!" I had a mouth full of cheesecake when I realized this was my husband's team! My fork clanged to the table, and my chair toppled behind me as I stood to clap.

Lacy Lee yanked on my dress, and I glanced down to see people staring up at me like I had three heads. When I looked around the room, there were more eyes focused on me than on the recipient of the award, my husband. It hit me—to Cassidy from Texas, he was a stranger.

Lacy Lee righted my chair and Scott leaned into the microphone. Daria and Dan both stage-laughed. "You don't have to say anything!" Dan said, and you could tell from his face he didn't want Scott to speak.

But as I got myself settled back into my seat, Scott's voice rumbled through the speakers. "I want to thank my team, who's worked hard this year. We've all put in endless hours to help MedDev get to more patients. And I know they're not here," Scott was staring right at me, "but I'd like to thank all the families. Being married to a medical salesperson isn't always easy. None of those patients would have their success stories if we didn't have support from home. So thank you."

With one last glance in my direction, he strode off stage, and the room broke into applause again.

I watched Scott step down from the stage, walk around the edge of the room, and make his way back to his table, where the stunning lady in the blue goddess gown gave Scott a kiss on the cheek.

20

Speeches

W hat the...?

Daria and Dan were talking on stage and I stared at them, but I wasn't there.

I was a garment in a washing machine. Probably something boring and frumpy, like a bathrobe. And I was going through the cycles. First, I filled with water, and I thought, *hey, that's not so bad*. And then it started the agitation thing, and I was like, *you know what? It's ok. It's going to be good*. But now the machine is spinning, and I'm spinning. I'm stuck to the side, and I can't breathe.

And I'm so empty. I'm wrung out.

A hand clasped mine, and I jumped, wishing it was Scott's but knowing my best friend's hand. "They called your name," she whispered into my ear. I looked at her, blank, confused.

"Cassidy Templeton, winner of the MedDev Gold Medal, the highest achievement for salespeople, sources say you did indeed make it to the banquet. Please come up and accept your award and share a few words with us!"

Lacy squeezed my hand and whispered with an undercurrent of sarcasm, "Congrats, Cass! You better bring us a great speech!"

I almost laughed. It was hilarious, really. It would be funnier if we could crawl under the table. We'd eat our dessert and drink coffee and laugh about how we snuck into a banquet, and I almost outed myself when Scott got his award. But accepting an award as Cassidy Templesomething for work I know almost nothing about... crap. Crap crap crap.

Lacy stood up and pulled on my hand. She smiled for show and gave me a big hug. "Do you want me to go up with you?" she whispered into my ear. "I could pretend to be your supportive plus one."

My face turned red. "No thanks. I'll fly solo," I muttered.

I walked to the stage, and the room roared with applause. My mind flashed to Daniel in the lion's den. Would the lions eat me? They threw Daniel into the pit for staying true to God. Here I was a fraud. What if someone in the crowd knew Cassidy? They'd know I wasn't her. Would they call the cops?

My legs were numb. I was levitating to the stage. I was pretty sure I was smiling, but I couldn't feel anything other than a slight tremor in my hands. "God. I'm so sorry." I mumbled. "But please help."

Somehow, I made it up the stairs and across the stage. Even though it was a banquet room and not a vast concert hall, the lights blinded me to anything beyond the edge of the podium.

Daria handed me a trophy that resembled a prosthetic leg built for an infant dipped in gold. The base said,

Cassidy Templeton

Gold Medal

#1 in US Sales

I closed my eyes and took a deep breath. The realization I was taking Cassidy's moment made lead settle in my chest.

But she's not here, a voice whispered in my head. *Bring her honor. Make her look good.*

Dan's voice piped up as my thumb caressed the smooth lines of the trophy. "So, Cass, you're new to the company this year, yet you've come in and blown everyone out of the water. We would love a few words from you. The secret to your success!" His teeth glimmered when he chuckled, and a low rumble of laughter filled the room.

The secret to my success. Ha! I'm a broken housewife whose husband is probably cheating on me because I'm not enough. I'm not sure I've seen success since the moment I said, "I do."

But that's not true. Scott and I were happy for a while. Really happy. I kept our home immaculate and always had dinner on the table when he came home. We had a lot of good sex, and I was beautiful and wanted.

Scott was getting started in sales, and I was riding professionally at the time, winning pretty big classes with Henry and bringing a few other young horses along. That was before I stepped back from riding to have the kids. I know I'm supposed to think my kids are my greatest success, and I do love them so much. But the last time I truly felt good about myself, it was on the back of a horse.

I stepped into Dan's spot behind the podium and gripped the edges, grateful it was smooth as my knuckles turned white. Looking into the crowd and through the bright haze, I saw Lacy Lee. Scott was out there, too. Probably annoyed and a little nervous, but he was there.

A story came to mind as I looked at the people I loved.

"The secret to success for me comes from my horse." I smiled, and I felt the crowd smile, too. There may have even been a few chuckles. "I know that sounds silly. Most people imagine horse girls as spoiled girls spending Daddy's money. But most of us aren't like that. Most of us are driven by a passion deeper than we know how to explain, to love and care for an animal that becomes our best friend, our partner in crime. And every day we put our lives into their hands, or I guess you might say hooves.

"It's not lost on me that my thousand-pound horse could kill me any second if he really wanted to." I paused, knowing these people who work with doctors and prosthetics had seen a lot of injuries and accidents. They were aware of the dangers of life.

"I grew up obsessed with horses, and if I wanted to ride, I had to work. I learned what it meant to work day in and day out. Did you know horses eat and poop every day, including on Christmas?" I glanced up, hoping the line would draw a laugh, and it did.

"I learned what it felt like to soar over obstacles, to be the best rider-and-horse combo of the day, to take home blue ribbons and trophies. And, I learned what it was like not to be the best, to have a bad round, to make a bad decision that affected my entire team, or for my horse to just have an off day. Horses taught me passion, work ethic, and drive. Grace and humility."

I imagined myself as a salesperson at MedDev. My speech was a combination of truth and story, what I imagined a horse girl would say if she became part of this company. "Horses are also expensive." My mouth twisted into a smile and everyone laughed openly, now.

"I applied for the job because it sounded interesting and I needed to pay for all my horses. But once I got started I realized, maybe not everyone is passionate about horses, but there's something they love. MedDev helps me help other people get back to what they love after tragedy.

"Like the girl in the video, I've always wondered what I would do if something terrible happened to me. I've always vowed I would do my best to be in the saddle if physically possible, because that's where I feel joy. That's where I feel most complete."

I swallowed a lump of grief as I realized that leasing Henry out to another person, all the duties of being a mom, Scott being gone all the time—it was a lot. I think I need to find my way back to that place of joy. Maybe I'd be a better mom if I did.

"Anyway, I love helping people." As the words poured out of my mouth, I realized that would be the secret to any outstanding salesperson's success, so I declared it. "That's the secret. I want to help a lot of people get back to the things that bring them joy."

I stepped back, and the room broke into a roaring applause. For a moment, I was lightheaded and had to take a deep breath and center myself. The spotlight shifted to the crowd, and I sought Scott, knowing he would ground me. Dan stepped toward the podium as my gaze clashed with my husband's, and I stepped back to the mic, cutting Dan off before he spoke.

"One more thing." The crowd quieted, leaning forward to catch what I would say next. "When Scott from the Eastern region accepted the award and said it couldn't be done without the support of family, he was right. Everyone here is having an incredible meal, staying at a fancy hotel in a historic city.

"Are people at home caring for kids and holding down the fort so you can be wined and dined? Yes, you've worked hard, and yes, you've earned it, but so have they. Don't forget to give them an award as well. Thank them. Take them to a fancy restaurant, get them a massage. Because I know you work hard, but I'm guessing there are other people behind the scenes who make your work possible."

I tried not to look at Scott, but I couldn't help it. Our eyes snagged on each other, and he nodded as he stood from his chair and started clapping. Soon, the entire room stood and applauded. A cool burst of air hit my skin, and I rushed off the stage, mortified I'd accepted an award as someone else. What if I got busted? Would they send me to jail? And what did I just say? Now, I was second-guessing it all.

The room continued to roar as I walked to the table. I was ready to grab Lacy Lee and run. Maybe we could hide in the bathroom until this was over and I found Scott. The smartest idea was to go straight home and try to have a date night next week. This had gotten out of hand.

Lacy Lee wrapped me in a warm hug as I got to the table. "That was insane! You did amazing!" she squealed into my ear.

"I feel like I just stole Cassidy's moment," I moaned, wanting to run but being held in place by my friend. "What if they find me out and arrest me?"

"Girl, she's not even here. You made her look amazing. And you can't run now or they'll suspect something." She smiled and squeezed my hand as the crowd calmed down and reclaimed their seats.

"We have one thing to do!" Dan spoke into the mic and smiled at Daria, who leaned in and finished his statement. "Toast to our winners and a new year!"

Servers appeared from doors, pouring into the room like we'd kicked a fire ant bed. They handed out filled champagne glasses and left open bottles on every table for refills.

The hum of chatter escalated as people grabbed their flutes, ready to toast and end the evening. A throat cleared into the microphone, and a ting-ting-ting reverberated through the room. Daria held her glass high and spoke into the mic, "MedDev, thank you for an incredible year of changing lives and helping prosthetics fit into people's lifestyles! Cheers!"

Dan and Daria tapped their glasses together, and clinking and "Cheers!" filled the room. Our table all turned to one another with twinkling eyes and well wishes. I knocked back half the glass in one gulp, thankful for a drink after that time on stage. The people at our table congratulated me and my tablemate from Phoenix Rising. They zoned in on me, attacking me with multiple questions at once.

Lacy Lee flung out her arms and declared, "The lady needs a drink! Give her a moment!" They all laughed and turned to one another for conversation.

A warm hand touched my arm. I turned in shock that a stranger would touch me, dreading the guy from the bar. But when I saw the person, it was no stranger. "I wouldn't want to offend..." he paused and checked Lacy Lee's nameplate, "Steve Templeton, but that speech was deserving of a kiss. It's quite impressive what you did, selling more than anyone else in your first year in the company." The light hit his eyes, and I wanted to melt into him.

"Really?" I blushed. "I guess I'll have to get one of those from Stevie, then."

Scott growled, "I couldn't take my eyes off you all night. All I wanted was to have you to myself, but instead, I had to share you with this entire room."

My chest warmed, which only ignited the crack going through the center. "Well," I said, buying time, unsure what to say. "I had planned for you to have me to yourself."

Lacy Lee nudged me, "Hey, I hate to interrupt, but do you have a bottle or something in your mom bag?"

"Yeah, it's in there somewhere. Maybe a side pocket. Dig around."

She rummaged through my purse, and Scott touched my elbow, pulling my attention back to him. "I'm sorry. I wanted to be there. It's just..." He looked around, and I followed suit.

The room was clearing, and only a few of us were left. "We might need to break this up or find somewhere more private," I said. "Otherwise, people are going to be very skeptical of Cassidy chatting up a married man."

"MedDev booked everyone rooms. I wasn't planning to use mine since home is close, but I can check in, and we can go there." His face was getting closer to mine as he spoke, and heat slowly climbed up my body. I wanted this, but did he want me or the girl he saw on stage? The girl on stage was a fluke– me channeling who I imagined the number one sales girl who lived in Texas would be.

She wasn't Abby Aberdeen, tired mom of three. I could never be successful, hard-charging, and so full of passion and love like her. That Abby was in the past.

Lacy Lee's voice broke the cacophony of roaring voices in my head, "This party has been great and all, but I think y'all could use a night to..." she paused for emphasis, *"talk."*

I laughed and nearly cried because we did need to talk. Our marriage needed this more than anything. But now that I had this opportunity, I wasn't sure if I could say all those words that had so confidently whirled around in my head. I wasn't even sure if I'd be able to remember them.

We both glanced at Lacy Lee. "Thanks, Lacy," Scott said.

We arrived together, and I felt like the worst friend letting her leave alone. But I could ride home with Scott in the morning.

"Abby. This is why we're here, is it not?"

Scott looked between us. "Wait, why are you here? And how did you get into the banquet?"

"Long story. I'll tell you later." A small laugh escaped me. "Lacy, thank you so much." I wrapped her in an embrace, and we clung to each other for a moment.

"I'll go check in," Scott said. "It sure would look fishy if Cassidy and I walked to my hotel room together, so I'll text you the room number and see you in a minute, ok, Abs?"

"Ok!" I said over my shoulder and watched him saunter off. "Lacy, what am I going to do?" I whispered. I had this big idea of a date night setting everything right in my marriage, but now I can't for the life of me remember how that was going to fix anything.

She backed away so we could see each other while she spoke. "Be honest with him. Tell him what you're worried about and how you feel. Maybe y'all could talk about *The 5 Love Languages* because I have a feeling y'all are just speaking the wrong language to each other."

"Ok." It came out more as a mumble. "Easier said than done."

"Yeah, well, maybe pray about it, too. We get all wrapped up trying to fix things ourselves when really we need to depend on God." She cocked an eyebrow. "I think I'm the worst at that one, but it seems like that's what God's been trying to tell me lately."

With a deep sigh, I gave her one last hug and grabbed my bag. "I don't know what I did to deserve you as a friend, Lacy. Thank you. I'll walk you out."

21

The Hotel Room

A ping sounded from my phone as I walked with Lacy Lee.

I got her to the door, and the toy soldier who saved me from my shoe debacle promised to walk her to her car. Once Lacy Lee left, I dropped Cassidy's award at the front desk for her to pick up when her plane finally arrived in DC. The concierge gave me some stationery, so I included a quick note.

Hi Cassidy,
Welcome to DC! I've got a funny story for you...
Call me when you can.
~Abby Aberdeen, aka Scott Aberdeen's (DC area sales guy)
wife, (aka Cassidy 2)

Hopefully, this girl had a sense of humor. I'm not sure how I'd feel if someone spoke on my behalf without my permission. It wouldn't be good.

The elevator dinged before the doors opened. No one was inside, praise the Lord. I prayed as I stepped inside, pressed the button, and watched the doors close. My stomach dropped when I launched up fifteen floors.

Every breath, every step, every thought, was a prayer. *God help me. God help us. Help me. Help us.*

I wanted to get butterflies when Scott walked into the room. I wanted to feel safe in his arms. I wanted to want him and for him to want me. I didn't want to feel like I raised three kids on my own. I didn't want to worry that he was sleeping with another woman when he left our house. Did I want too much? *God, am I asking too much?*

It didn't seem like it.

I tapped on the door labeled 1508. Almost immediately, the double clack of the latch echoed throughout the hall. Scott stood there. He'd shucked his jacket, and his bowtie hung from a loosened collar. Blue eyes pierced me, devoured me, as I stepped into the room. My heart pounded in my throat. I felt like I was doing something wrong, meeting a man in a hotel room.

Except he was my man. Maybe this is what we needed—a night away from the house that constantly reminded me of how alone I was.

The door tapped again as it closed, and my husband stepped towards me. The heat from his body made me feverish. Mere inches separated us, and I wondered how long it had been since we were this close. My heart rate kicked up a notch. I wanted to be right here with him, but what if he didn't like what he saw when the dress came off? I should go.

I took a half step back, and Scott's hand touched my thigh, holding me in place. A firework went off right where our skin connected, sending a flame of need through my body. For a moment, the world spun. I closed my eyes, taking a deep, centering breath, and when I opened them, Scott's mouth had moved closer. His hand trailed up my thigh, lifting my dress with it.

Heat pooled at my core, and my brain went haywire, on the verge of short-circuiting. Our noses touched, and we shared the air as his hands explored my body, grazing the skin under my dress. Everywhere he touched, he raised goosebumps and sent fire through my veins. I had never wanted my husband more. I wanted his mouth on mine, and I had no intention of stopping there.

I was paralyzed with need and desire and a bit of panic. We needed to talk first. We were supposed to discuss things. What if he does this all the time? He seems so... so... good at it. I don't remember Scott Aberdeen ever making my body react like this. Like everything in me wants to jump into bed with him. But that can't be right.

Isn't this what you wanted? I heard a small voice say in my head.

Yes! I wanted to love his touch. I did love his touch. And I feared it. What if my fat rolls repulsed him? He lowered his mouth to mine, his warm breath caressing my lips before he ever so gently kissed me. It was so subtle I wondered if it was my imagination. Finally, heat seared my lips as Scott kissed me fully, and in a moment of resolve I didn't know I had, I turned my head so that his mouth dragged against my cheek.

"We need to talk." It came out hoarse, barely above a whisper. If only hoarse from me could be sexy like Janice Joplin, but it was more like ET dying.

"Ok, then talk," he said into my hair, his hand back to the top of my thigh, stealing most of my working brain matter.

I slipped to the side, needing to break his touch so I could think. "Sorry, Scott. I just... I can't yet," I stuttered. Pressure built behind my eyes for what must be the hundredth time that day, yet I had a feeling it wouldn't be the last.

The muscles in his jaw tightened before he spoke. "Why not, Abs?"

"I just..." I trailed off when the words didn't come to me. We stared at each other; a gaping silence filled the room as we both waited. Was he really so clueless? Did he not know what we needed to talk about?

And where should I even start? What do I say? *God, help me.* I repeated my earlier prayer. *Help us.*

Words spilled out. "That thing you said tonight, when you picked up your award, about the families sacrificing. Thanks for noticing."

The muscles in his jaw tightened again, but the hard, defensive glint in his expression softened. "Yeah, well... I know I'm gone a little too much. And you take on a lot having the kids alone when I'm out of town."

We took a moment to soak in what we'd both said. It was a start, but it was a tiny hammer and chisel to a huge iceberg.

"Scott, this isn't working."

He jerked like I'd slapped him. "What do you mean? Like, we aren't working? Did you come all the way here in that dress to tell me that?"

Flames lit my face. What in the world? "No!" I shot back. "At least, I wasn't planning on it. Unless..." I paused, unsure I wanted to voice this worry that had gnawed at my insides for weeks.

"Unless what?" Scott bowed up, ready for a fight, and the tightness in my chest eased the tiniest fraction. If he cared this much, surely...

"Unless you're cheating." I know I said it. I felt the air push through my vocal cords, and my mouth moved, but blood was rushing through my ears, and all I heard was a roar.

He stood there, feet rooted to the ground, his face turned white, and the confidence I'd had seconds before left with the color in his face.

"Abby, I thought you trusted me." His voice was low, and I couldn't figure out if hurt or anger caused it. I felt guilty for the accusation if I was wrong. I felt ripped in half if I was right.

This wasn't like an argument on TV, whipping back and forth. Each statement took a minute to form in our mouths before we unleashed it into the room. It was my turn, and when the words rolled off my tongue, there was a hollow in my gut, and likely a punch to his.

"I thought I did, too. And I tried. I did. But the way you stare at your phone instead of me. You're always gone and staying in hotels. And I started to wonder who you're really meeting for happy hour and if you spend all those nights alone."

Scott stood there for a moment. I watched the emotions pass over him. Frustration, anger, then sadness and guilt. "Abs, I'm so sorry."

What was that supposed to mean? The room started to spin. What was he sorry for? I walked to the bed and set down my purse. It fell over, and a baby bottle rolled out, filled with what appeared to be sparkling grape juice. I don't know. Nothing made sense. I melted onto the bed, unable to maintain any sense of composure as the pressure behind my eyes released.

"Scott. How?" A hiccup shook my shoulders. "Why? How could you?"

I couldn't look at him. He was supposed to be my ride-or-die. He was supposed to be *it* for me. 'Til death do us part. I buried my face in my hands. "I mean, I realize I'm not skinny and pretty like I used to be, but..."

Gentle fingers grabbed my wrists. He crouched in front of me, a wet streak on his face. "Abby, no, you misunderstood. I never slept with anyone else. It's just me in the hotel rooms, and all the texts are work-related. It's non-stop and maybe I need to set boundaries, but it's all work." He stared into my eyes like he wanted me to see the truth in the depths of his soul.

"But what about that lady tonight? She kissed you! I saw it!"

"Kissed me?" He looked genuinely confused before realization dawned on him. "Oh, Auri. She's..." he shook his head, "just a coworker, Abs. She's the only woman on our team, and she's French. It's a French thing, I guess. She does those cheek kisses to greet people or celebrate them."

I chewed the inside of my lip, trying to process all of this. I stared at his chin, unable to make eye contact. "Ok."

"I'm sorry, Abby," He pressed his forehead against mine and cupped my cheek. "If you're wondering this. If you're asking these questions, then I've sucked at being a husband. And I'm sorry."

I chuckled at his wording, because he had sucked at being a husband.

"Did a snot bubble come out of your nose?" Scott asked in disbelief. The disgusting pop of moisture on my face, coupled with his question, sent me into a laughing fit. It must have been contagious because he joined me in what felt like a manic episode of humor. The bubble of tension had exploded, and we laughed hysterically. And then, for some reason, the humor of the moment morphed into sobs that wracked my body.

Scott's going to run, I thought. Anyone with half a brain would escape a wife as crazy as me. But Scott chased away my worry as his arms wrapped around me, cocooning me against his warm body. "Scott," I hiccupped, "I'm going to ruin your shirt."

"I don't care," he said. "It's rented anyway." He held me tighter. For the first time in recent memory, I relaxed into my husband's embrace and cried like a blubbering fool.

"I'm sorry, Abs," he said again into my hair. "I work too much. I wanted to provide a great life for y'all, but then..." He paused like he didn't know what to say next. "I'm going to find a way. I've been brainstorming ideas and even talking to our CEO about taking more of a management role so I can stay home more."

My phone quacked, and I peeled myself away from his warm chest. "That's probably Lacy Lee. Let me check it real quick." Scott's hand drifted to my hip as I reached for my phone.

Lacy Lee:

> I'm home safe. Go get 'em tiger. Love you.

"What'd she say?" Scott asked.

"She's home safe."

I glanced back up at my husband, cold now that space stretched between us. His eyes looked hungry and a little lost, and my mind drifted to *The 5 Love Languages* book. I wondered if touch was one of his Love Languages.

I replayed in my mind how he tried to touch me when he came home from work, and I always ducked away, afraid the kids would see. Which was silly. It was good for them to see us love each other, right?

But I always felt so gross. So untouchable.

"Abby, where are you right now? Your mind drifted."

I looked at my husband. Even with a big wet spot on his shirt, half his tux strewn over a chair, and hair mussed from frustration, he was so dadgum handsome. His blue eyes were liquid, and the blond scruff on his chin begged me to touch his face.

"I was thinking about this book we've been reading in our church book club." My face heated. This isn't what most people imagine talking about in a hotel room with their husbands.

"Yeah?" he said. "Tell me about it. It must be good if you're thinking about it while looking at me. Is it one of those steamy romances?" He grinned.

"Scott! Ew, no! It's my *church* book club. We don't read steamy romances." I crossed my arms and leveled him with a glare, not sure what to do with my body. Why did talking to my husband feel almost unnatural? We really needed to do this more often. Like, practice talking or something.

"Ok, what's the book?" Scott mirrored me by crossing his arms, but it looked more mocking than anything.

"Well, it's called *The 5 Love Languages*." I looked to see if he would roll his eyes, but he didn't, so I kept going. "The guy basically says that a lot of times, the reason a husband and wife are distant from each other is because they have different Love Languages. So they speak, or act, the language they need instead of what their spouse needs."

Scott crept toward me. "Maybe we feel distant from each other because we need a night to ourselves without the kids," he muttered as he reached for me.

"You have a valid point," I said, smiling, but a little frustrated. He was listening, but not hearing. And he wasn't wrong. "I just... I feel like..."

Scott's right hand started at my knee again, trailing up under my dress.

"I feel like you were the most beautiful woman in the room tonight." He kissed my lips and then pulled away, his left hand now trailing up my other side, and I couldn't seem to breathe. "And you gave the best acceptance speech," he kissed me again, "and you made the Cassidy chick look really good," his mouth pressed against mine. He tilted his head so our fore-heads touched, and my eyes drifted closed.

Scott leaned into me, and I allowed myself to fall back, hes-itantly excited. Maybe my date night wasn't such a failure after all? Something plastic and cold broke my plush landing, and I pulled away from his kiss, "What is this?" I held up a baby bottle, and it hit me. "Lacy Lee put the leftover champagne in here!"

"Let me see," Scott said and stuck the nipple into his mouth, sucking on it. "Yep, definitely champagne. This is quality stuff, too!"

"Scott!" I squealed, "Take the top off, you weirdo!"

He tilted his head back for another drink, and I had no idea what was happening to my insides, but I needed his attention back on me.

"Give it to me," I demanded. I took the bottle, twisted off the cap, and chugged. The bubbles tingled in my nose, forcing me to pause. Scott grabbed it and downed the rest in one gulp.

"We'll have to thank Lacy Lee for that," he said and tossed the bottle to the side. It was enough champagne to make my body warm and my mind not worry about silly things like Scott not liking me.

His lips found my neck, and I launched into a fit of giggles at the tickle of his facial hair. Scott persisted, and my giggles morphed into a low moan as I enjoyed the perks of being married to Scott Aberdeen.

22

Good Morning

The sun peeked through the window, a much more gentle alarm than my normal wake-up call of Krista screaming. Scott was still asleep, and I took a moment to study him. How could he sleep when light streamed into the room?

I remembered the way we drifted off, hand in hand. Neither of us liked snuggling at night. It was way too hot. But our fingers touching was a way to stay connected, even in slumber. It was the first time we'd slept like that since before Krista came. I reached out and wove my fingers between his, wanting to feel his warmth again, to know this was real. Scott Aberdeen hadn't gone to some other woman.

He was still mine, and I was still his, and we'd get through this.

His fingers squeezed and yanked, and I yelped as he pulled me on top of him. My husband smiled up at me, tickling the palm of my hand. "Caught you staring!" he smirked.

"How on earth? Your eyes were closed!" I objected.

"Abby Aberdeen, don't doubt me. I have my ways."

He tugged me toward him, closing his eyes and expecting me to close the distance. "Ew, Scott, your breath is awful!" I pushed away, laughing.

His face flushed before a grin stretched across it. "Ok, good point. Yours isn't great either."

His wandering fingers stole the air from the room. "I don't want to kill the moment, Abby," he whispered, those hands seeming to have a mind of their own. He brought my hand to his mouth, "How about...." he kissed my knuckles, "we just," his warm lips pressed against the delicate side of my wrist, and tingles shot through my body, "don't kiss," his mouth found the inside of my elbow, and need overwhelmed me, "on the mouth."

He looked into my eyes: a question, a plea, a hope.

I paused, dying on the inside over my self-restraint. I wanted to scream, *YES*! But I pretended like I had to think about it. I cocked an eyebrow. "Shower and room service after?"

His voice was husky when he responded, "Anything for you, Abs."

The shower water massaged my shoulders, and I smiled to myself. I couldn't remember ever being so satiated in every way. Waking up in a hotel with Scott fulfilled a fantasy I didn't know I had. All that cheating stuff had been in my head. Lacy's and my plan had worked! Now, to figure out this Love Language thing.

It had been a long time since I stood under the stream and didn't worry about what the boys were getting into or if Krista was awake.

"Hey, babe! I'm running to get some coffee from across the street. Want a caramel macchiato?"

I peeked around the shower door and smiled. Scott crossed the steam-heavy room, meeting my lips with his own. "Yes, please," I smiled and then ducked back into the hot water.

"Be back in a few," he said, before leaving me to my solitary, as-long-as-I-wanted, bottomless hot water, amazing shower.

This was the life.

Wrinkles formed on my fingers, and I reluctantly turned the shower off. The steam was so thick I could hardly breathe, and I might pass out if I stayed in much longer. That would be traumatic for Scott. I chuckled.

The lotion from the Four Seasons smelled like grapefruit, and I made sure to stick the tiny bottle in my mom bag so I wouldn't forget it. I'd have to snag an extra one for Lacy Lee. She loved fancy travel-sized lotions and shower gels. I went ahead and packed the toothbrush and toothpaste the hotel had given us into a side pocket.

Wrapping myself in the Four Seasons robe brought a smile to my face. I slipped into the complimentary slippers and walked out of the bathroom, channeling my inner diva. Scott and I should purchase the robes. It felt like wearing a hug.

I surveyed the room, trying to decide what to do. Scott had draped my dress over the back of a chair so it didn't have too many wrinkles.

I smiled to myself. A friend had called it 'the walk of shame' when you sleep with a man and have to wear the previous day's clothes. I'd had a tryst in a hotel room with my own husband. No shame here. We should definitely do this more often.

Picking up my shapewear, I folded it and packed it into the side pocket of my bag when a knock sounded on the door.

Scott probably had his hands full with coffee. "Coming!" I sang the word as I danced across the room in my robe and wet hair to open the door. I could almost smell the caramel and coffee, and my mouth started watering. The brushed copper of the door handle was cold against my pruned skin as I pushed it down and pulled, a smile already on my face.

The first realization that hit me was the smell of old eggs, so different from what I expected. A tray covered in dirty dishes sat against the wall two doors down.

It took a moment for my brain to cycle through what I was seeing. Standing in front of me was not my husband holding two coffees. It was the woman I'd seen with him the night before— the one who had worn the goddess dress and sat next to him all night and kissed him.

She stood across from me now, her perfectly manicured eyebrows looked like those stamps advertised all over Instagram a few years back. The arches were lifted, yet I couldn't see a single wrinkle on her forehead. Was she an alien made to look like the perfect female specimen? Were her eyebrows drawn on like that? Or maybe she'd been seeing the Botox guy I'd heard the preschool moms talk about.

Her joggers looked like they'd never been jogged in. They must have cost $200 from a small boutique, but then I realized I shouldn't judge. I never did yoga in my yoga pants. In fact, maybe these pants we all wore should be renamed. Her hair was slicked back into a tight, jet-black ponytail.

It took me a second, but I finally pulled myself together enough to paste on some semblance of a smile. "Uh, hi! Can I help you?"

The lady smiled back, but with her sharp features, it reminded me more of a cat on the hunt. She lifted a folded sweatshirt towards me, one I recognized well. It was Scott's favorite Yale sweatshirt. He took it everywhere. One of the doctors from the university gave it to him when Scott helped fit a prosthetic on the doctor's daughter.

"Yes, sorry to bother you," she declared in her lilting French accent. "I was returning this to Scott. He left it in my room yesterday."

She deposited the sweatshirt into my arms, winked, and left.

23

The Exit

I backed into the room, numb. The door closed on its own, double clicking like the hammer of a gun being pulled before slamming into the frame. The bang echoed into every corner, and I fell to my knees like I'd been shot. I would rather have a bullet to my chest than this. Surely, this hurt worse.

The back of the door loomed over me, and the carpet offered a cradle of comfort. If only it would suck me into its fibers and I disappeared. I saw my world through a new lens. The disheveled covers told a story of infidelity, like the web of a spider I'd been lured into. The tux jacket thrown over the chair was a costume he put on to make me believe he was someone else, someone polished and trustworthy.

I wanted to cry. I expected to sob uncontrollably, to be a blubbering mess.

Instead, I sat in a void. My personal black hole.

Time stood still as I grappled with this new reality. Scott lied. What I thought was the best night of my life was a lie. My marriage was dead.

Images from the night before replayed in my mind. Scott pressing me against the wall. The way his eyes bore into mine. His hand grazing the skin under my dress.

I replayed the way he responded when I asked if he'd been cheating, the way his face turned white. His guilt was on display right in front of me, yet I believed his line about being a sucky husband. Sucky husband didn't even begin to describe it. He was the worst—a cheater.

Nausea hit me like a punch to the gut, and I scrambled to the bathroom to empty my stomach. Tears finally squeezed out, but I didn't have time to cry. I needed to escape before Scott returned. I couldn't face that cheating liar right now. I needed to get away.

Rinsing my mouth, I threw off the robe, wishing for an incinerator to burn it. Donning yesterday's dress, I grabbed my mom bag and shoes and ran. The sweatshirt lay on the floor where I dropped it. It reached out and grabbed me as I sprinted over it, and I yelled in shock as I soared for a moment. My foot disentangled from the shirt and I was able to get my feet underneath me before hitting the ground.

I turned to glare at the offending garment before escaping through the door, down the hall, and to the elevator. *God, please. God, please. Don't let me run into Scott.* The elevator doors opened like they were stuck in molasses. Had they been this slow yesterday? I stepped into the empty box and pressed the L, just as a ding sounded from the neighboring elevator. *What if Scott's on it? What if he sees me?* I frantically banged the door close button like an SOS signaler on a sinking ship. *Close, close, close. Come on, close!*

The two doors crept towards each other, and in the final sliver of light, I saw two cups of coffee held by strong hands.

Don't stop. Don't stop. Don't stop, I pleaded with the elevator. I pressed my body into the back corner, trying to look normal in case the small box stopped for another passenger. The numbers of each floor lit up as we passed them, and I begged the lights to keep moving.

God must have had some level of mercy because the elevator continued until the little light on L brightened. Before the doors opened completely, I dove into the lobby, refusing to look up or make eye contact with anyone. I needed out before someone recognized me from that insane stunt on stage.

I rushed towards the exit. What if that wasn't Scott upstairs? What if he's walking across the lobby now?

"Hey, Miss!" someone called, but I kept my head down. The fuel and marijuana smell of the city turned my already uneasy stomach, but it pulled me forward. Toy soldiers parted like curtains at a show. I was the show. *Everyone knows,* a little voice whispered in my head. *Everyone knows and you're just a big joke, a big fat ugly joke.*

A tear hit my cheek, and I wiped it with the back of my hand as I strode through the doors. Three taxis waited by the curb. The driver for the first one leaned against the car, and I lifted my eyes enough to make contact. He nodded, stepped away from the sedan, and opened the door to the backseat.

"Where to, ma'am?" he asked in a thick foreign accent.

"Gainesville." My voice sounded raw and unused.

"Virginia?" he clarified.

"Yes."

The door closed, and the driver rounded the car to the driver's seat. I hunched over, pressing my head into clammy hands.

"You ok, ma'am?" he asked.

"Just... please..." Even now, I couldn't lie. "3203 Rogers Way in Gainesville. Thank you."

The sound of fingers tapping a touch screen filled the silence, and eventually, the car lurched into motion and pulled away from the hotel. I stayed low in case Scott was outside. He may be anywhere between the coffee shop and our room. Based on the way he'd lied, he could be anywhere with anyone. He might have used coffee as an excuse to go to someone else's room. The churning in my stomach started back up, and I closed my eyes and took a deep breath. *God, help.*

"You have a music preference, ma'am?"

"No." My voice rasped into my hands. "Thank you," I added, disembodied. Was this even me? Was this real? Maybe I'm still asleep in the hotel, and this is all a nightmare. Maybe Lacy Lee and I had a wreck on our way to DC, and I'm in a coma and dreamed up all of last night. That had to be it because it had been too good to be true. And this. Now. A living nightmare.

The driver slammed his brakes and my bag went flying, some of the contents spilling onto the floor. I braced into the seat in front of me. For a moment, I wished I had flown forward, spilling onto the asphalt. Then I would have a problem people could help with. An ambulance would show up, and they would carry me off to a building filled with helpers. But no one could fix the actual problem at hand. The damage was done. It was like losing an appendage. There's no reattaching a leg once it's severed. MedDev would not save me.

"It's a yellow light, keep going!" he yelled at the car in front of us before turning his head to talk to me. "Sorry, ma'am. Crazy city drivers. Please put your seatbelt on."

I obeyed, realizing the hotel was far enough behind us. I didn't need to worry about Scott seeing me. Historic buildings surrounded the car as we drove, and I wondered how on earth they lasted so long? How did governments not crumble? How were monuments still standing?

I, Abigail Aberdeen, Suma Cum Laude, president of my college's equestrian team, favored working student at a top hunter and jumper barn in Florida until I got married, a mom who'd pushed three babies out, two of them in the same night, cannot save my marriage. Yet a government put together by a bunch of rebels still existed.

Something rolled across the floor and hit my foot. I glanced down to see the baby bottle Lacy had filled with champagne and had to bury my head in my hands again. What would she say?

How did we get from there to here? My cheeks flamed at the memory of Scott drinking from the bottle, and saliva flooded my mouth. I swallowed it down and wiped stinging tears off my cheeks.

I needed to get to the barn. It was the one place things made sense. I just needed barn time.

24

Running

"This is it." I pulled the door handle before the car stopped, but the lock held. The air in that tiny sedan was stifling. I needed out now. The taxi crawled for ages before finally coming to a complete halt, the doors unlocking. "You take credit?" I asked, handing the driver my card before he answered and practically leaping to the curb.

The driver processed payment on a little hand-held thingy before offering it to me with a tip screen. I punched the highest number, mumbled a "thank you", took my card, and ran to the door. "Ma'am!" I heard him yell as I typed in the unlock code that, praise the Lord, worked on the first try. Even if the house was on fire, I wouldn't turn back. Whatever he needed couldn't be that important.

I opened the door enough to duck inside, slam it closed, lock the deadbolt, and slide to the floor. I melted onto the cold hardwood, my body lurching with sobs. Baxter appeared, nosing my face before settling onto the floor beside me. I reached out and buried my hand in his soft fur, an anchor.

A knock sounded at the door, and I nearly screamed. What if it's Scott? What if he's chased me here? He was the last person on earth I wanted to see. I held my breath and tried not to make noise; part of my body pressed against the solid oak door. Baxter looked expectantly toward the commotion, but didn't get up. The knock sounded again, followed by, "Ma'am! Ma'am?" The taxi driver.

Oh God, I prayed, *please make him go away*. Holding in the sound of crying turned my eyes into rivers. Between that and the snot, there was no way on Earth I'd open the door. Something tapped on the ground on the other side of the door, and then it was silent.

"Thank you, God," I whispered. But what if Scott was on his way? What if he's trying to track me down? I had to get out of the house. I ran back to our bedroom, and for a second, I thought about grabbing the sharpest knife in the kitchen and running it through our mattress and sheets, the curtains, and his favorite dress shirts. I wanted to destroy everything because he ruined what mattered.

But more than that, I wanted to get out of the house before he got here, and I wanted to ride off into the sunset on Henry and gallop until my mind cleared and I knew what to do next.

It had been so long since I used horse riding pants that it took a moment to dig them from the depths of the drawer. I had tucked them away safely, thinking I was happy to put my family before my horse. It seemed like the right thing to do, but the more I unraveled, the more I realized how much of myself I gave up for Scott and the kids.

I found my favorite Tailored Sportsman riding pants. They made me feel like a professional, and the four-way stretch fabric was so comfortable. As I slid them up my thighs, they got stuck midway. I tugged again, confused for a moment, wondering if Scott had put them in the drier and they shrunk to a kid's size. Then it hit me. I haven't worn them since before Krista—maybe even before the boys, and my body was quite different. Until this moment, I didn't realize how long I had gone without doing the one thing that brought me the most joy.

I screamed before ripping the pants off and throwing them on the floor. I dug into my drawer for another pair and pulled them on. The zipper stretched wide, and there was no way the button would reach the hole.

Hot tears of rage streamed down my face. How dare he make me give up a piece of myself and then screw around? How dare he leave me in this house thinking we're both sacrificing when he's out there hooking up with other women? I gave up my horse for this. My future. I could have chased my dream, but instead, I'm a suburban mom, trapped at home, and overweight. I carried our babies and gave up the life and the body that I knew, and he gave up nothing. Marriage is all about mutual sacrifice, but I'm the only one who knows anything about that.

I dug through my drawer, hoping to find my stretchy riding tights. Surely, I could still fit this embarrassment of a body in those. I yanked the drawer out and dumped everything to the floor. They were nowhere. Another drawer with barn clothes was dumped on top of the first, and I finally found what I was looking for.

Staring at the mess I'd made, I struggled to fill my lungs with air. The realization hit with shocking clarity that I failed. Sobs wracked my body anew.

I'm a failure.

I, Abby Aberdeen, am a failure.

My knees hit the beige carpet of my closet, where I slumped over. Liquid poured from my eyes and nose and even my mouth. I thought it might even be coming out of my ears, and then I cried harder because I'm Abby Aberdeen, who's supposed to have her crap together, but now I'm wondering if tears can come out of my ears.

Enough, I told myself.

"Enough," I yelled out loud this time, to the empty closet and to the faithful dog who stood sentinel at my door. I needed to pull myself together and get out of there. I needed a tissue, stat. Actually, I needed a box of tissues, but when I looked around frantically, I realized I didn't normally keep them in my walk-in closet.

Liquid dripped from my chin, and I was pretty certain this wasn't a tear. Grabbing the closest garment, I wiped my face and unloaded the plethora of mucus that had built up in my nose. It was then I realized that my previously favorite Tailored Sportsmans had been demoted to a snot rag. Maybe I should blame Scott for that, too. I would. It's all his fault. Me not having a reason to wear my riding pants, me not fitting into my pants, and me crying right now and needing an urgent snot rag.

All. His. Fault.

I wriggled into the tights that were like the yoga leggings of riding clothes. While they'd never been my favorite, sometimes you need some good stretchy pants with a side pocket. I was a mom, and it was time to embrace these and promote them to favorite pant status.

Quickly, I dug to the back of my sock drawer and got actual boot socks. Sure, any socks would do, but for some reason I couldn't explain, this stuff mattered. I needed my actual riding clothes. These overpriced boot socks made by an equestrian clothing brand were helping me reclaim a tiny piece of myself, and I needed every part of the real Abby Aberdeen that still existed.

I threw on a polo shirt, grabbed a jacket, and hurried to the mudroom for my paddock boots and helmet, making a pit stop at the guest bathroom to pee and get a box of tissues. If I was going to cry on my drive, I would be prepared. Before leaving, I let Baxter out back to do his business.

My phone buzzed. Lacy Lee. I silenced her call and kept going. The boots felt good on my feet. They were superhero armor that locked into place, making me a better version of myself, a version that could overcome anything, even a cheating husband. Another buzz told me a text came in, so I glanced down at my phone to find I had missed a lot of notifications.

9:37am

Scott:

Where are you? I've got your coffee!

9:42am

Earth to Abby…

10:20am

Hey I'm getting worried.

10:25am

Really hoping you didn't get abducted. I've got a couple of client appointments at Georgetown Hospital at 11 and 1. Should I cancel? Call the cops?

10:35am

I'M CALLING LACY

10:40am

Your location tracker says your home… you'd tell me if something's wrong, right? I'm on my way to my appointment.

10:43am

Lacy Lee:

Hey how was last night?! AMAZING I hope!

I ignored Scott, but hit reply to Lacy.

I turned my phone to *do not disturb* and walked out the door, nearly tripping over my mom bag and a baby bottle sitting next to it. I reared back and kicked the bottle into the yard, slung my bag over my shoulder, and strode to the van. On my way, the annoyance over litter in my yard forced a detour. I grabbed the bottle and threw it in the trash can. I never wanted to see it again. If I needed to replace it, I'd get a different brand.

I made a beeline to the barn. The only person I wanted to see wasn't a person at all. Henry was waiting.

25

The Barn

It normally took twenty-five minutes to get to the barn. Today, with my insides ripped out and my hope gone, I found I didn't care about silly things like yellow lights and speeding tickets. Nineteen minutes after leaving the house, the gravel of the parking lot crunched under my tires. I made sure to slow down for the safety of the dog who brought so much joy to Krista.

The windows of the horse stalls faced the parking lot, and I sought Henry out. From the rhythmic dropping and rising of a dark form, I assumed he was munching hay. Quick movement in the stall next door caught my attention, and I stared until the form stood tall and paused. Even from the shadows, I felt Juan's gaze, and imagined the flop of messy brown, nearly black hair and a grin that made me sweat.

Today, instead of shifting my eyes, I raised my hand into a wave and smiled back. If Scott wasn't ignoring all the undress-me looks of the opposite sex, neither would I. Two could play this game.

Juan nodded toward me and went back to cleaning the stall. I dropped the visor down to check myself in the mirror. Boogers on the side of my face from one of my many meltdowns in the last hour sure would be an instant turnoff to a certain Argentinian hottie.

There wasn't much I could do about the puffy eyes, but I kicked back half a bottle of water I'd grabbed from home to try to rehydrate. I'd need this water for all the crying that would inevitably come later, even if that was the farthest thing from my hardened heart at the moment. I knew these emotions came in waves, and currently the only thing I felt was a desire to hurt Scott.

Rage fueled me. I imagined destroying Scott Aberdeen every bit as much as he destroyed our family. A twinge of my conscience said that may not be the most holy or productive way of thinking, but at this moment I didn't care. I swiped on some sheer pink lip gloss to draw attention there instead of my eyes. My lips were the only feature of mine that I loved, so I may as well play them up.

Helmet in hand and phone in my tights pocket, I slammed the car door and strode into the barn.

Juan stepped out of a stall and looked me up and down, leaning against his pitchfork. "You riding today?"

I cocked an eyebrow. "Yeah. You were right before. The girl who leases him is in the middle of soccer season so she probably won't be out." I knew she played soccer, and I figured any sport like that meant Saturday games, but I was just guessing. It hit me: the barn was quiet for a Saturday. "Where is everyone?"

"Tracy took a trailer to a local show. Be back this evening. I'm heading over when stalls are finished."

Good. Right now, I didn't want to face anyone beyond who was already at the barn.

"Need help?" Juan started toward Henry's stall before I answered. He grabbed the halter and slid it over my handsome boy's head.

"Thank you," I said with a sigh, my breath catching in the middle.

"No problem," Juan clipped Henry into the cross ties in the aisle of the barn. "It makes cleaning his stall easier." He looked into my eyes a moment longer than etiquette called for. The flirty smile that was so easy to send his way a minute before refused to surface. My world became thick sludge, and it took every effort to wade across it to get Henry's brushes from his box.

My body trembled with the effort, reminding me of when you've had the flu and the fever is gone, but you're still wiped out and useless. I grabbed a peppermint from the box and fumbled with the wrapper until it came free. The process had Henry going crazy. My reserved, well-behaved horse had his left hoof stuck straight out in the air like he had started to paw but didn't finish. His brain got stuck on the need for candy. His antics broke away a bit of the sludge weighing me down, and I held the mint to his muzzle.

His lips grazed my palm until the mint disappeared. The grind of the peppermint between his teeth soothed me, ironic since the sound of humans eating made me want to jump out of a window. Henry stretched his nose toward me, hoping for more and blowing a gust of peppermint breath into my face. I smiled, and my eyes watered. More weight fell away, and I took advantage of the momentary reprieve of pressure to groom him.

I concentrated on the withers, where a horse's neck and back meet. He stuck his nose in the air and swayed back and forth. At least I was enough for one male in my life. I made sure not to linger too long in one place. A driving fear that Scott would track me down kept me moving. I needed to escape before he showed up.

It had been a long time since I'd saddled Henry. The tack room door sat ajar, so I slipped in and inhaled the scent of leather and glycerin soap. This would have been the aroma that defined my career if I'd chosen a path without Scott, but instead, poop diapers and rotten milk were my daily perfume. The thing was, I loved my kids, and I mostly loved my life aside from Scott being gone so much.

But right now, I really missed this. The leather, the horses, and even cleaning stalls. I could spend hours doing chores at the barn and listening to my favorite podcast or the sounds of horses around me. Did it have to be one or the other? Because I'd never give up my kids.

"You ok?" Juan's voice came from across the room, but he walked toward me, trapping me in his gaze. My hand clung to the doorknob, an anchor as Juan stepped close enough that I smelled pine shavings and men's cologne.

He was a few inches taller than me, enough not to be too imposing. He stood so close our breath mingled. "Abby?" The Latino accent when he said my name sent me into a spiral.

I gripped the doorknob tighter, leaning into it, which sent it careening away from me and slamming closed. My body followed, and I flailed for a second before finding myself propped against the closed tack room door. I closed my eyes and took a deep breath, trying to gather my thoughts, but the scent of leather and man overwhelmed me. I sensed a hand next to my head.

"Abby." Juan had followed me, stepping into my space. He consumed every logical thought and replaced it with things I knew shouldn't be there. "Everything ok?" He paused, furrowing his brows as if doing so helped him see what was happening in my mind and heart. Then he rephrased his question. "Are you ok?"

His hand hung in the air, inches from my face. Like he wanted to touch me, to comfort me, but something kept him from moving closer.

A rogue tear streaked down my face, and I jerked my hand up to wipe it. "I'm... I'm fine, Juan." I peeled away from his five o'clock shadow, soul-gazing eyes, and scent that made my brain short-circuit. "Rough morning is all." I stepped to my saddle, which was blessedly where it had been over six months ago when I last looked at it.

Say something, I scolded myself. *Say something!* Scooping the saddle into my arms, I finally came up with words. "Hey, do you know where Henry's bridle is?" It may be right where it's supposed to be, but I feigned ignorance. Maybe it wasn't. I needed Juan's mind off of me and this come-apart I was having.

"Tracy has him in a different bridle. I'll grab it." Juan rushed to the other tack room that held Tracy's personal gear. I was grateful I asked the question and that it gave Juan a reason to give me space.

While I waited, I grabbed a clean black saddle pad off the top of the stack. The color matched my mood perfectly. The saddle, girth, and square pad were balanced on my right arm, so I reached up with my left to grab the half pad that provided extra cushion between the saddle and Henry's back.

Grabbing the edge, I tried to gently jiggle it free from the center of the stack. It was a game of saddle pad Jenga, and the entire tower threatened to topple.

I wiggled it side to side and lifted a tad to tilt the stack in the other direction. So close! My breath was shallow, and I worried that even the slight wind coming from my mouth would send them tumbling. The pads tilted away from me, and my heart did a little victory leap. Almost there. A couple more inches.

With one last tug, I realized the saddle pad below mine was sliding out. The entire stack teetered, now leaning towards me. I wanted to scream more curse words. Why couldn't something simple go right for me? I stood helpless, a pile of gear in one hand and every half pad in the barn launching a personal assault on me.

Before I released a wild banshee scream of frustration, two tan arms snaked up in front of me, balancing the Jenga tower.

A desperate laugh escaped as pressure filled my eyes. "Thanks," I told Juan as my heart sank. I couldn't even gather gear by myself. It was like victorious, excellent at everything

Abby was version 1.0. The current Abby 2.0 struggled to get a saddle pad down without help. 2.0 was glitchy and could use an update.

Juan's tan skin crinkled as he smiled, "You're welcome, Abby. I'm here to help."

I nodded. "Thanks."

Images of a younger me played through my mind when I could carry everything—a saddle, both pads, bridle, jumping boots, and a grooming box—all in one go, plus open and close the doors on my own. I was so independent, and I never needed help. Now look at me. My younger self would be so disappointed. I'm disappointed.

"Hey," Juan interrupted my spiraling thoughts, "It's ok to get help. That's why I'm here." He winked, and my heart fluttered like a dying butterfly.

"Thanks, Juan." I made the most fleeting eye contact to be polite and ducked towards the door.

"I've got the bridle!" He grabbed the door and opened it for me. This poor guy must deal with emotional women all the time at the barn. He could probably pass whatever test counselors have to take to get certified without cracking a book.

When we got to Henry, waiting patiently in the aisle of the barn, I plopped my gear on top of the saddle holder, sighing in relief. Abby 1.0 rode six horses in a day, pushed overflowing wheelbarrows through the mud, and never even batted an eyelash at the weight of my tack. Now Abby 2.0 was nearly done in from carrying a single little English saddle for four minutes.

But you have to start somewhere, the voice in my head said, and I knew today was the beginning. It was time to reclaim my horse girl self and my horse girl muscles. I wasn't sure how I would do it with three small kids to take care of, but if Scott showed me anything today, it was that I needed to put my needs first, too. And I needed more horse time.

26

Back on the Horse

Juan grabbed my saddle pad and started tacking up Henry, and I tugged on the half chaps that would protect my calves from getting pinched by the saddle. I zipped in, whispering a prayer of gratitude for elastic and that they still fit. We worked in tandem, not talking, as I geared myself up, and he helped get Henry ready.

Soon, the clips from the cross ties clanked against the wall, a sign that he was nearly done with Henry. I smiled, watery and weak, but still a smile. It was pretty clear why Tracy hired him. Henry dipped his head into the bridle, opening his mouth for the bit like he was looking forward to our ride.

"Ready?" Juan asked, looking towards me.

Having someone tack up for me was strange, but nice. Plus, the process moved faster with an extra set of hands. I'm not sure five minutes had passed since our little moment in the tack room, and my horse and I were both ready to go.

"Yeah," I nodded, my insides a turmoil of gratefulness for Juan, fear that Scott would show up before Henry and I escaped, and anger and sadness over what I knew about him and us and our marriage. My world was crashing around me, and the only way to remedy it was riding off into the sunset on my horse. I needed to be on his back.

I tried to stay calm. Juan led Henry out of the barn, and I walked next to them. He led Henry towards the riding arena, and I knew what he was thinking. Surely, I'd want a safe ride in a fenced enclosure for my first ride in who knows how long.

"Juan, I'm going on a trail." I kept my voice resolute. No one would talk me out of this decision.

Juan paused and looked at me, his eyebrows raised. "How long since you rode?"

"Not too long." If we're comparing it to how long the Israelites waited on Jesus.

"I thought you said since having kids." He looked me up and down, clearly calculating in his mind. "At least a year?"

"I'm going on a trail, Juan. Thanks for your concern, but I'm good. I used to ride the circuit. I may not look like it anymore," my cheeks heated as I pointed out the obvious, "but I can ride."

His face darkened. "I don't know what you're talking about, looking like something. You look like a rider to me. The best riders start in the arena when they haven't been on for many months."

"Well, thanks, Juan. I'm ready to get on."

He nodded and led Henry to the mounting block we kept in the yard.

My heart raced, and my palms grew clammy as I climbed the three steps and gathered the reins. I stuck my left foot in the stirrup and swung onto the saddle, lowering myself onto Henry's back. Henry took a few steps forward, even with Juan holding his bridle.

"It's ok, you can let go," I said while I checked my girth and fixed my stirrup length. He looked at me with a questioning lift of his eyebrow, but I knew part of my horse's anxiety was a reflection of my own. Once we got moving, I would relax, and so would he. We needed to move.

"It's fine, Juan," I tried to steady my voice, but I'm pretty sure he heard the shake. I used to be so at home on a horse. This was like going back to your parent's after being away at college. It was a warm hug, a safe place, but still a little strange. Like you're trying to figure out where you belong.

This is Henry, I told myself and sat up tall. *We're fine. He will always be home. It's like riding a bike.* Juan stood to the side and watched me get settled. "Hey, Juan," I called, "Can you open the back gate?"

He speed-walked to the gate in question, unhooking the chain and swinging it open in time for us to stride through. His expression was clear—he didn't like this, but wouldn't stand in my way. I offered him a grim smile. "Thanks."

He looked up at me, once again peering into my soul. "Be careful, ok? I won't go until you return." It was nice to know someone was looking out for me.

"Thanks, Juan," I said, giving Henry an inch of rein and letting him move into a trot as Juan sauntered to the barn.

A plethora of trails snaked through hunt country and all around Henry's barn. Turning left led to hills that were great for conditioning. If you tracked right, it led across the road to a resort and winery that allowed equestrians to ride on their property.

We were free entertainment for the guests. I mean, how cool would it be to sit on your fancy resort balcony, drinking wine, and watching horses traipse across the lawn?

Straight ahead, the trail took you to a field that was full of crops for part of the year, but the farmer let us ride on the edge.

Past the first field, an old carriage path cut through the next neighbor's woods. A couple of the local foxhunting groups used it on occasion, and I'd always dreamed of chasing the hounds with them. There were gates and places to jump the stone wall. As long as we were respectful of land and livestock, they allowed us to ride on it.

Most people from the barn chose the hills for conditioning or took a little jaunt to the winery. They loved tying their horses to the hitching post and grabbing a glass of vino. For a moment, I considered drowning my sorrows in a bottle, but what my heart really craved was a gallop.

The trail opened up, and Henry moved into a ground-covering trot, stretching his legs out with each step. I lagged behind the motion, struggling to find the rhythm. Would I even be able to do this? Do I still have the muscles I need to hold myself on his back without bouncing around like a sack of potatoes?

After a few steps, it started to come together. I stood as his momentum flung me up and sat on the next beat until we floated together. Up, down. Up, down. We became a single unit, moving as one. This body that had carried and fed three babies started to remember how to do this, too.

Henry swung his legs from his shoulder when he trotted. I remembered why I loved this horse. He rounded his neck as if proud, even excited, to have me back.

With each beat of his hooves, I heard,
This
Is
Where
You
Belong.
This
Is
Where
You
Belong.
The trail narrowed as we entered a small patch of woods. I thought, *we should slow down*, and Henry dropped his pace to a walk without me pulling on the reins. We followed the path around some trees, and I leaned forward to keep from being brushed off. Yellow leaves fluttered through the air around us,

drifting to the ground. *This,* I thought. No more words came to me. I didn't need more. *This.*

We dropped down a bank into a small creek, all of which Henry did with ease. I smiled, imagining myself in a foxhunting tweed coat and surrounded by other riders. He sure had the brain for it, unlike a lot of show horses.

It was kind of funny how some horses were so sheltered they couldn't mentally handle the things that should be most natural to them—creeks, trees, small animals. It was sad, too.

We take an animal that should be in nature, teach it to be incredible at jumping manmade sticks in manmade arenas, and then the horse can't fathom hopping over, or even getting close to, a real log. They'll jump a water jump in an arena but won't dip a toe into a babbling creek.

We love these animals so much and become so focused on making them amazing show horses, that they forget who God made them to be.

Something tickled my cheek, and I reached up to rub it, pulling a damp glove away from my face. Wow, what is happening? I'm crying over horses living in stalls too much?

And then I realized what my subconscious must have been working through. I was a little like a show horse, cooped up and becoming something new, which really I was happy to be. I loved being a mom. My kids were my greatest blessing, and I loved being a wife and keeping a house. But becoming a mom had cut me off from another thing God made me to be. Horses were a part of me.

Henry picked up a trot, and we glided along, my rising and sitting with the rhythm as effortless as... well... nothing compared. Absolutely nothing else in my life felt this right.

But what if I get hurt and can't take care of the kids? And should I be spending money on a horse when there were so many other important things, like the kids' college funds?

Guilt gnawed at my chest.

Something shuffled in the trees next to us, and in a blur of motion, a bird swooped across the trail. Henry dipped to the left, spinning nearly a hundred eighty degrees. It happened so fast I didn't have time to hold on or get scared. I instinctively pulled on the reins, and almost as quickly as it happened, Henry relaxed again. My heart raced, but a tiny smile forced itself onto my face. I was still on his back. I could still sit a horse.

Promising myself and Henry to stay present, I got him heading back in the right direction. The entrance to another field lay ahead. Henry felt my intention, picking up a trot and pulling on my hands a bit. The idea of galloping across a field was starting to sound really dumb and dangerous. What if a bird flew out of the trees again and I can't ride it out? What if he steps in a hole and we flip? What if...

But before more worst-case scenarios could roll across my mind, Henry trotted to the edge of the field and, without waiting for my blessing, rolled into a slow canter. For a couple of strides, I tightened the reins, wondering if I should let him keep going or slow him down and walk home. I didn't really need a good gallop, did I? Was it a smart decision?

What would Scott say if I got hurt?

And on that thought, I stood in the stirrups, grabbed some mane, and clucked my horse forward. He shot off like a bullet.

27

Wings

The wind whipped my face and sent tears streaming into my helmet. The speed gifted to Henry from his champion sire stole my breath. As we careened across the field, memories of our early days together, when he was a young and silly retired racehorse, played across my mind. I didn't quite trust him in a romp across the field back then, but we were both older and more mature now.

The woods approached, so I leaned my weight back and squeezed the reins. Henry pressed into my hands at first, asking to keep going, but I pulled again and he checked his speed.

We dropped from a blistering run to an exuberant canter before entering the woods. It was still fast, but if I needed to duck from a tree branch or make a quick turn or stop, we could handle it at this pace.

A log laid across the trail up ahead. I considered slowing and finding a path around it, but Henry's ears perked forward. The natural obstacle drew him forward. Hoofprints in the dirt leading to it were proof other riders had been enjoying going over the log. I decided to put my heels down, grab some mane, and let it happen.

We reached the base in three breaths, and as he launched forward, a huge smile broke across my face. Henry hung in the air for a moment, and I imagined wings sprouting from his shoulders. We landed on the other side, and he kicked his back heels up in celebration before perking his ears and continuing down the path.

I laughed and scratched his neck in front of the saddle as we cantered on. Up ahead was a break in the trees, and a coop jump, designed for foxhunters to be able to jump into the field, stood, solid and threatening. Henry's head went up, and our pace slowed as he took in this new obstacle.

We could slow down and go through the gate. We probably should choose the safer option, but I craved the freedom of flight. I shifted my weight back and gave him a loose rein, allowing him to decide. A few paces from the jump, Henry's energy shifted, and he powered towards it. The coop looked a lot bigger up close, and my heart pounded in my throat.

Maybe I shouldn't...

Henry's hooves found the perfect takeoff spot before launching into the air. Crouching over his withers, I buried my fingers in his mane. I wanted to tuck into the fetal position and cower. I wanted to hold my arms out to the side and feel the air and freedom against my skin while I shouted for joy. How could I want two completely different things at the same time?

We soared, momentarily weightless, a picture of the girl I always thought I'd be. Thanks for ruining it, Scott.

Henry landed and cantered forward. His breathing grew louder with each stride, and his pace slowed. My boy was finally getting tired, but he'd probably never stop unless I told him to. He loved a good run even more than I did.

We made our way across half of the field before I slowed him to a walk. He needed to catch his breath. Plus we had a long ride back if we moved at a more sensible pace.

Back... did I have to? I let my reins dangle at the sides of his neck and reached forward to rub under his mane.

"I love you, Henry." A hiccup escaped in the middle of his name. He was such a good horse, my best friend.

How did we end up here? Another girl leasing him. Me trapped at home changing diapers and chasing toddlers. Which I loved. I really, truly did. But I loved this, too. And Scott.

"Henry, what do I do? Scott's cheating and we have three kids and I can't support them on my own. But I won't stay with Scott if he's seeing other women. I won't."

Henry continued meandering forward, his ears swiveling toward me, listening. "Why would he do this to me?" Sobs shook me. "Am I... am I not enough?"

My body lurched every time a sob stole my breath. Henry's steps slowed, smaller, and safer, until he stopped. It was hopeless. Why did Scott have to ruin everything? Why am I not enough?

Henry turned his head enough to see me with his left eye, like he wanted to check on me. Like he wanted me to know I'm enough for him. My sobs became wails as I melted into nothing, leaning on Henry's neck for support and wrapping my arms around him. He stood there, patiently absorbing my tears into his mane.

"God, what am I supposed to do?" I cried. "How could he? How could he do this to us?" I dug my fingers into the wiry mane hairs under my face until they cut across my fingers and my knuckles hit the softness of his coat. Henry stretched his head down and tore the grass at the roots, coming up with a mouthful. The rhythm of his chewing soothed my frantic heartbeat. Every few seconds, his head dipped while he got another bite.

"Why am I never enough? I'm not enough for the kids." Henry's body lurched as he kicked at a fly on his belly, and I wiped my nose on my sleeve. "I'm not enough for Scott." My insides were an empty cavity. "I'm not enough for me." Maybe that was the source of all our problems. I wanted more from myself. Expected more, like to be skinny and smile like those homestead moms on Instagram who do literally everything and make it look so easy.

A breeze blew across the field, and the pieces of my hair that escaped my helmet tickled my cheek. "God," I whispered, taking a deep breath and closing my eyes. I felt every shift of Henry's weight as he took a step and dipped his head again. The sound of grass being torn from the ground filled my ears, and wind tickled my arms. Birds chirped to each other in the distance, and a nearby bee buzzed.

I cracked my eyes open to see the bee hover over the center of a purple wildflower about ten feet away. Multiple blooms sprouted from a single stem, and the insect struggled to decide which one to forage from. He took to the air and landed on a different cluster of buds nearby. I sat up in awe, untangling my fingers from his mane, as my eyes and mind finally expanded beyond me.

Henry and I waded through a sea of purple blooms. A Bible verse immediately came to mind:

Why would you worry about clothing? Look at all the beautiful flowers of the field... Even Solomon, in all his glory, was not arrayed like one of these.

"Ok, God," I whispered. "I hear you. If you take care of the flowers, surely you're taking care of me."

The blanket of fear that had melted into my skin when that lady came to the door vanished. In its place was a covering of love and peace like only my Father in Heaven could provide.

Another time came to mind when an all-consuming fear had been wiped away and replaced with peace—the night Scott became more than the cute guy who sat three seats over in class.

Lacy Lee had talked me into going out one last time before school ended. Bars were not my scene, and I was so uncomfortable. Lacy Lee had gone off to get drinks when some creep dragged me into the dark hallway by the bathrooms. He pressed me against the wall, and I was trapped. People walked past, ignoring us. Probably, they assumed it was consensual, but I was seconds from—I still couldn't admit the word to myself.

Even remembering the moment made my stomach churn with vomit. But then a door slammed, and the voice of that boy from class who always borrowed a pencil was asking if I was ok. There was a blur of shouts and fists, and strong, safe arms swept me off my feet, cradling me and rushing me to fresh air.

He set me back on my feet and leaned down until his face hovered right in front of mine. "Abby, are you ok?" he asked. My tongue was stuck, unable to respond because of what just happened. And because this boy had saved me. I had this un-explainable knowing that even with all my big plans to move to Florida and ride horses with top trainers, this boy would always be the one to save me.

I remembered the way my body trembled as I nodded, lean-ing towards him, and Scott wrapped me in his safe, warm arms.

I trembled now, as I took a deep breath, and a fresh tear spilled down my cheek. "God," I pleaded. "He was supposed to be the one to save me. Why did he break me like this?"

As I said the words, I heard a big part of my problem, and my heart shriveled at my own mistake. God didn't make husbands to save their wives. Only Jesus could do that. Even on his best day, Scott was still human. My cheeks flushed in shame. "I'm sorry, God." The breeze tickled my cheek and lifted Henry's mane, and I knew I was forgiven.

"But God," I pushed. "How could Scott do this to us?" A thought came to me as if placed there. *What if things aren't how they appear?*

I rolled it around in my mind along with the vision of that lady holding Scott's sweatshirt out. What if it's not how it looks?

"I don't know. It looked very incriminating." Why was I arguing for the thing I wanted least?

Faith.

"Faith?" I nearly laughed. "Did you see that lady? She's every-thing I'm not."

Faith.

I pressed my fingers into Henry's mane as the word filled my mind and soul. I closed my eyes and took a deep breath, letting faith fill me on the inhale and sending out fear and suspicion and everything else bad on the exhale. "God, help me have enough faith to give Scott a chance to explain himself."

I gathered my reins and pressed my leg against Henry's side to get him moving. It took a few attempts before I convinced him to stop eating and head home.

"Thank you, Henry," I whispered, "and thank you, God."

It was time to face Scott and figure out the truth.

28

Heading Home

We walked towards home, and Henry was content to take his time. I debated over hopping the coop or pausing to unlatch the gate at the edge of the field. The gate would take effort and time when we could just go over a jump. Several strides out, I shortened my reins and gave Henry a squeeze with my calves. He trotted a few steps before his head lifted, and he rolled into a canter. The jump drew him, and I sat up tall and let it come to us, giving a little pressure with my legs for reassurance.

We landed with ease on the other side, and I let him continue his forward pace for a bit. This ride was everything my heart needed, but it was time to get back to my husband.

Peace had settled on my heart in the field, and I knew it was God's way of telling me to trust. The situation wasn't what it seemed. I'd run out on Scott after such an incredible night. What was he thinking right now? Maybe I should text him before I get back to the barn and let him know I'm ok.

Something rustled in the woods ahead, catching Henry's attention. He perked his ears, but nothing else happened. I slowed him to a trot, just in case.

What do I say to Scott? Where do we go from here?

The noise in the woods drew my and Henry's attention to the right. As I turned my head, Henry stumbled. He tried to recover, but his front foot stuck on something. The momentum of his body kept going, shooting me towards the hard-packed dirt and a cluster of stones in the ground.

The ground moved towards us in slow motion. Who would take care of the kids if I got hurt badly? What did his hoof get stuck on? I hope Henry's ok.

What will Scott say?

29

Juan Takes Over

Answer, Tracy. Answer.

"Hey Juan, what's up?" Tracy's voice came through my phone. I could hear the announcer in the background and at least three people having a conversation. Something about jump number six, but right now, there were more important things.

"Hey. Abby's horse came back with no Abby."

"I'm sorry, Juan. I don't understand. Came back from where?" Tracy asked as the other voices faded into the background. She must have stepped away to talk to me.

I gripped the phone tighter as I tried to explain. "A trail. She rode."

"Abby took Henry on a trail?" Tracy sounded excited, and I wanted to yell at her because she was missing the point. But I took a deep breath and explained.

"Yes, Abby was upset. Said she was riding on a trail. I said to ride in the ring, but... anyway, she left an hour ago. Henry came back, but no Abby. He pulled a shoe and scraped his knee." I paced back and forth in the barn as I talked. Henry was safe in his stall, and I'd pulled his tack. I kept watching for Abby, hoping she'd walk up to the gate she left from.

"Crap. Ok, I'll send you her husband's number. Can you call him for me since you're there and know what's going on?"

A stab of anger shot through me at the mention of a husband. Something told me her tears this morning were his fault.

"Yeah," I conceded. "Send the number."

"Keep me updated, Juan." The excitement from before was replaced by concern.

"K. Bye."

As soon as the husband's number came through, I tapped it and waited. The shrill ringing sound added to my anxiety.

30

Scott's Turn

I took one last glance at my phone before knocking on the door. My chest had been hollow all morning. Something happened when I was getting us coffee, but I had no clue what. A nagging sense of unease filled me when I saw my sweatshirt on the floor.

Things were looking better between me and Abby, so why did she pick up and leave? All I could come up with was she wanted barn time while her parents had the kids. Sometimes it felt like a competition for Abby's attention, and today—based on the location of her phone—the horse was winning.

On the screen, underneath a smiling photo of Abby lying in a hospital bed with a baby in each arm, was a map with a blue dot on it. She was still in the area of the barn, so I may as well go forward with my appointment. It would be nice if she'd answer her calls or text back, though.

I tapped on the door before striding in. This client deserved my full attention. God knows she's been through enough. "It's so great to meet you, Jen, and—" I looked to her husband, hoping he'd offer his name. They didn't put family names on the chart.

"Ben," the man said and grabbed my hand.

Jen shook my hand and gave me the smile of a fighter, down on her luck. It didn't reach her eyes.

"I'm real sorry about your accident, Jen. The doctors wanted me to speak with you. They're hoping MedDev can help. Can you tell me how the transition has been to having a prosthetic?"

"Well..." Her long pause was a statement in itself.

I glanced to her husband. "Have you discovered any perks?" I asked with a half smile, hoping to get her talking. Most people mentioned the close-up parking spots.

"I get half off pedicures now!" Her smile stretched up into her eyes.

Ben cut in, "I told her she should do them all the time now that she gets such a good deal on them!" A laugh filled the room. We toed the edge of a cliff where one tiny step would plummet them into the abyss.

"Life with a prosthetic is a huge adjustment." I gave Jen my most comforting and heartfelt smile. "What are some of the challenges you're having? Is there any pain?"

Jen and her husband made eye contact. He gave her a nod, and she started into a long list of problems. I'd found that most people just needed a listening ear from someone who cared. While Jen talked, I settled into a chair against the wall.

Occasionally, I'd make a note on my clipboard. A buzz from my pocket sent shockwaves through my body. What if it's Abby?

"Do you need to get that?" Jen's husband nodded toward my pocket.

I glanced at the couple, torn. The vibration stopped just as my hand was going to the pocket. Checking the number, I saw it wasn't Abby. Probably spam, but I'll check messages when I leave.

"No, it's fine," I said. "Keep going. Tell me about the pain."

"Ok," Jen went on, "I know the scar is healed and probably isn't—"

My phone buzzed again, and blood rushed to my face. "I'm sorry, I need to get this." I grabbed my phone and rushed for the door. Glancing at the screen, I realized it was the same strange number.

The unease that had pestered me all morning morphed into nausea. I pressed the green button. "Hello, this is Scott."

"Hey, this is Juan," a man's voice with a thick accent came through. Spam, I thought, but decided to give him ten seconds before hanging up.

"Hi, Juan, what can I do for you?" I was prepared for him to tell me about the tax relief act or an extended warranty for my car.

"I'm at Heaven's Orchard Stables. Abby had an accident." The hallway began to spin. "She took her horse on a trail. He came back, but not her. I'm on my way to find her."

Abby had an accident? I leaned my head against the wall, grappling with what this guy was telling me. What was she even doing on a horse? I wanted to punch something. I needed to find Abby. What if she was really hurt? What if...? I couldn't go there. "Thanks, Juan. I'll head right out. Coming from DC, so it'll take me a bit, but I'm hurrying."

"K see you. I'll call if I have an update."

"Thanks." My voice was hoarse as I clicked the end button. I ducked into Jen's room.

"Hi, Jen. So sorry, but there's been a family emergency. I need to go. I'll follow up soon or have someone else from the team follow up." Jen and her husband sat with gaping mouths and matching looks of concern as I jetted out the door. It didn't matter. There were more important matters at hand.

I raced to the elevators and slammed my hand against the button. Nothing opened. I looked from one to the other, wondering how long it would be. After ten seconds, I ran for the stairs. Sweat beaded on my head as I descended them two at a time. At ground level, I found the exit, pushing the door open so hard it hit the wall. The valet guy stood by the curb, half asleep.

I handed him my tag and slipped him an extra $50 bill. "I'm in a hurry."

"Yessir," the kid said and rushed off. I checked my phone. No texts or calls in the four minutes since I rushed out of my appointment on the seventh floor. I pulled up Abby's name and pushed the call button, hoping against hope she'd answer.

"Hi, It's Abby. Leave a message." It beeped before I hung up, and I stood there listening to the silence.

A car door slammed and the valet kid walked towards me, sweat dripping from his sideburns. "Your car, sir."

"Thank you." I hung up the call and checked the time. It had been seven minutes since Juan's call. Seven minutes could be an eternity if Abby was hurt, lying in the woods with no one to help her. I imagined the pictures of some of my amputee clients. So many had nearly died from blood loss and had to be medevacked. Would Abby last that long?

I pulled onto the street, and a long string of brake lights filled my vision. I didn't have time for traffic. Abby didn't have time. I punched the steering wheel, sounding the horn, and screamed, "GO!" I needed to get out of the city where I could pick up speed.

The light turned green, and everyone moved like a line of ants. If only I could kick the ant bed and wake them up. Get them to scramble out of my way. "God, please," I begged. "Please take care of her and get these cars to move." A DJ rambled on the radio, and I turned it off before I got angry enough to slam my hand against my console, wishing it was the guy's nose.

Finally, I pulled onto Interstate 66. There were an insane number of cars for a Saturday, but I swerved around them, gunning it every time I hit a rare, traffic-free space. I needed to be there for Abby. She was probably lying somewhere in the middle of the woods. How would I find her? Maybe she wasn't hurt. Hopefully, she was walking back to the barn. Plenty of people fall off and don't get hurt, right? But fear consumed me.

I glanced at my phone screen. Abby's blue dot hadn't moved. Had she dropped her phone somewhere? Or was she not moving, either? I would follow the GPS to that spot.

Juan might find her before I get there. A bolt of anger shot through me at the thought of another man with Abby.

The way she left this morning with no notice gnawed at my insides. If something happened, there was one person she'd tell. I needed answers.

"Hey Siri, call Lacy Lee."

The phone rang twice before a voice that could cut glass answered.

"Hello?"

"Uh, hi Lacy. It's Scott."

"Hi, Scott." Anger poured through the phone.

"Hey. There's been an emergency. Abby's missing."

"Of course, she's missing, Scott. What did you expect after what happened this morning?"

"Lacy, what are you talking about? We had a great night. I left to get coffee this morning, and when I got back, she was gone." I squeezed the steering wheel until my knuckles turned white.

"Must not have been that good."

I ignored her jab. "Do you know why she left and has ghosted me all day?"

Lacy paused before finally grounding out, "Maybe you should talk to her about it."

Words flew through my mouth, "I would have if she answered her phone!"

"Well, she must not want to talk to you then. You should give her space."

"She surely didn't want space last night or this morning." She would know all of Abby's most intimate secrets if she didn't already. I accepted that long ago.

"Was that before or after your girlfriend stopped by the hotel room?"

Lacy Lee reached through time and space and stabbed me in the chest. I glanced down, sure a knife protruded from my heart. I should pull over before I crashed the car and took innocent lives with me to the other side.

But there was no knife or blood—only an invisible wound threatening to kill me.

"My girlfriend?" They were the only words that came. My world was crumbling.

My girlfriend came by the room?

"Yeah, Scott. And I don't know if you remember what I told you when you married Abby, but you better watch your back. Nobody hurts my best friend like this."

The word *hurt* brought me out of my spiral and back to reality. "Do to me what you want, Lacy, but first, we worry about Abby. Someone from the barn called. She took Henry out on a trail, and he came back without her. I left a client when I found out and am heading there now."

"What? Why are you just now telling me?" I had to turn down the volume on the Bluetooth to keep my eardrums from exploding. There were shuffling sounds, followed by a slamming door. "I'm heading there as soon as I can get dressed. Let me know if you hear anything."

Her sense of urgency was starting to match my own, and I finally had an ally since we both cared about Abby.

"But Scott?"

"Yeah?"

"You need to know this is all your fault."

31

Scott's Search

My fault. My fault. My fault.

I've not been the best husband, but didn't we make steps in the right direction last night? And who is my girlfriend?

I needed to talk to someone. Too much was happening that I didn't understand. I want to be a good husband. My parents were still happily married after forty years. I want Abby and me to be like them.

Checking the clock, I knew I had time to make one more phone call before I got to the barn, and it felt like the most important call of my life.

The phone rang on Bluetooth. "Please answer. Please," I mumbled under my breath.

On the third ring, there was a click followed by, "Hullo?"

His voice gave me hope.

"Hey, Dad!"

"Hey, there, Scottie! Whatcha got going on? How are those adorable kiddos and that gorgeous wife of yours?"

In my mind's eye, I saw his bushy gray mustache and the crinkles by his eyes. I didn't call my dad nearly often enough, but in moments like this, I realized I should. He was a wealth of wisdom and my closest friend. Apart from God himself, no one loved me more unconditionally than my parents, except for possibly Abby. But that's up in the air at the moment.

"Hey, uh, I need to talk to you about something. Do you have a few minutes?"

"I've got as much time as you need, son. What's up?"

"Well, I really screwed up..."

Dad listened quietly as I told him everything—the way Abby and I weren't on the same page anymore, how cold she was, how hard I worked to provide for the family, and that sometimes I traveled too much. But shouldn't she appreciate the lifestyle I provided her and the kids?

And then I got into the events of the last 24 hours, how she crashed the banquet, and we had the most amazing night. She disappeared when I left for coffee, but when I remembered I could track her through my phone, it showed her location at the barn.

I told him about Juan calling and then talking to Lacy Lee.

"Dad, what if Lacy's right? What if it is all my fault?" As I finished my story, my heart pounded double time. The shopping centers I zoomed by were blurs in my peripheral vision while I ran my hand through my hair and waited for Dad to talk.

"Scott." His voice was full of emotion. "The first thing I want you to know is that me and your momma love you and your family, and we pray for you every day. I think... no, I know that this may be a turning point in your marriage. It could be the beginning of the end, or, I reckon if you let it, God could use all this for good. But, I need to know, and I need you to really think about your answer, are you committed to making this marriage work? Are you committed to loving Abby, even when she's mad and barkin' at ya like women do sometimes? Or when she's a mess? Or when she does things you don't understand or agree with?"

"Well, yeah." A hint of defensiveness filled my words. "That's why I work so hard. I want to provide for her and the kids."

"Son, I hope you can hear me when I say this, but sometimes us men have a way of hiding from the hard stuff at home or in our hearts and calling it work. Do you remember when you were ten or eleven, I used to work all the time? And then one day I started showing up for dinner and didn't hardly miss a meal with my family after that?"

"Yeah, I hadn't thought about it in a long time, but I remember."

"Your momma and I had a similar thing happen. Like father, like son, I guess. The more work asked, the more I gave. It felt good at work, like I was making a difference, and you could say I was addicted to that feelin'. And honestly, raisin' little kids is hard, and your mom made it look so natural, so I thought I'd just let her do it while I provided. But one day I realized—yer momma helped me see it—that the most important work I had was at home. She said, 'Do you wanna be married to me or that job? Because I ain't playing second fiddle to no corporation.'"

I chuckled, imagining my mom saying those exact words. She was a force. "I do remember how you started eating dinner with us every night, but I never thought much of it. I knew I loved having you there. We started feeling more like a family then."

He didn't say anything to acknowledge my statement, but there was a smile in his voice when he kept going. "And women, the good Lord made them emotional creatures. Now, we don't all fit into the same mold, but what I've seen is that when a woman doesn't feel loved, she turns a little mean. That Abby you married, she's a spitfire, and I bet she about cuts you in half with her words sometimes."

"Ha! Tell me about it." I ran my hand through my hair, remembering some things Abby had said in the past, but even worse was the way she said it.

"Now, Scottie. Do I need to ask about that girlfriend statement you said Lacy Lee made?"

"Dad, I promise I've been faithful to Abby. I would never…"

"That's what I figured," he cut me off. "Just needed to make sure. What it sounds like is you need to show your wife you love her."

My face got hot, and I gripped the steering wheel so tightly my hands turned white as paper. I didn't want to make excuses, but I had always tried to show her love. Always.

"You there, Scott?"

"Yeah, Dad. I'm here. Look, I try to show her love. I work to provide for the family, which I know you said, and maybe you're right. I might be going a little overboard in that area. But whenever I get home, I always try to say nice things and give her hugs and affection. She just…" I paused for a deep sigh. "She just dismisses the nice things I say and ducks away when I go to kiss her, saying the kids are watching or whatever. What else can I do?"

"Scott, I'm going to guess those are the things that make you feel loved. But what makes her feel loved? It's a little different for all of us."

Something about this conversation reminded me of what Abby said in the hotel room. She'd tried to talk about Love Languages or something.

"Dad, have you heard of a book about this? I can't remember what it's called, but Abs mentioned it last night."

The smile returned to my dad's voice, and I imagined the corners of his mustache turning up. "*The 5 Love Languages*! Yes, your mom and I read it together a few years ago. It's exactly what I was trying to explain."

I realized with a start that the barn was close. "Hey, Dad, I gotta go. I'm close. I've got to hang up so I can find Abby." The words sounded so calm to my ears, but my insides were a turmoil of fear, regret, and hope. I tried not to imagine the worst, but my brain kept cycling back to all the bad things that could happen with such large animals.

"Ok, Scott. I'll say a prayer for you and Abby. Trust in the Lord, ok, son?"

"Ok, Dad. Love you."

"Love you, too."

We both hung up, and I immediately pulled up my message thread from Abby. She still hadn't responded to anything. My mind raced through scenarios where Abby couldn't text, and all of them were terrible.

I needed to focus. I clicked on Abby's name, and the map popped up with a dot that was supposed to be her cell phone location. A button underneath the map said "directions." I clicked on it and a route popped up. Six minutes away.

I picked up speed. If a cop got behind me, he'd have to follow because I wasn't stopping until I found Abby.

Two turns and one long winding country road later, the GPS said to take a right. The entrance to the barn was ahead, and my heart threatened to beat out of my chest. I ran my hand through my hair for the hundredth time, trying to decide if I should follow the GPS or go to the barn. An image of Abby hobbling back to the barn and me not there to help her filled my head. But another of her lying on the ground in the woods, broken and bleeding out, chased the hobbling one away.

That last vision had me following the directions on my phone. The dot was to the left of the road, a good bit up ahead. I passed a field with recently harvested crops and a dense forest lined by an old stone wall.

A few hundred yards from where the GPS dot flashed, I slowed the car, straining to look into the woods. I glanced back to the road and had to slam the brakes. Papers from my passenger seat smacked the dashboard before spilling on the floor, and the sweat on my hands made it difficult to grip the steering wheel. Up ahead sat a gigantic turtle.

The creature appeared to be dormant, and I wondered if it had already been hit. To get this big, you'd think it had some self-preservation. I looked back at my phone. According to the

GPS, I hadn't reached her location yet, but it probably wasn't exact. The turtle blocked the road, and I refused to wait anymore.

I opened my door and stepped onto the gravel, glancing at the creature. He had the creepy beak of an alligator snapping turtle and looked at me from head to toe. I stopped for a minute and stared at this beast, who might be prehistoric. Animals supposedly can't reason, but he clearly judged me.

It started to come my way, and I jumped backward, jolting back to reality. Abby.

I took off towards the ancient-looking stone wall, climbing over and pausing to take in my surroundings. From where I stood, it looked like a thick forest. My hands shook as I went into my call history, found Juan's number, and sent a text.

Scott:

Hey, it's Scott. Have you found her? I'm following her location from my phone.

As soon as I clicked send, three dots appeared under my message. I stared, hoping he had good news; hoping my wife was ok and taking care of Henry. And hating the idea of him finding her first.

Juan:

Been on the south trails. No trace.

Nausea hit me and I swallowed the urge to vomit, reminding my body that I needed to keep it together and find my wife.

"Abby!" I yelled, hoping she'd hear me. I walked deeper into the woods, away from the road and that monster in the road. "Abby!"

32

Awake

Hair tickled my nose, and I reached up to scratch it. Hard chunks of dirt ground into my skin when I rubbed, startling me. I jerked my hand away from my face and opened my eyes. Pain shot through my head at the blinding light as the realization hit—I was lying on the ground with a rock poking my hip.

"Ow."

The sounds of the forest assaulted my brain like I was at a death metal concert. It took me a minute to realize I was on the carriage path close to the barn. Apparently, I'd taken a spill, but remembering it was like grasping at rays of sunlight.

Scott's never going to let me on a horse again.

My eyelids were heavy, like bags of sand sat on top of them. I wanted to let them sink into my brain, but an internal warning system blared every time I considered a quick nap. Not that the ground in the middle of the woods was the ideal place for an afternoon snooze.

I wracked my brain for the incident that landed me here. Scott and I had an incredible night together. My cheeks flushed when I remembered waking up next to him. And I took a hot shower in the hotel, and someone knocked on the door.

The frantic escape rushed back to me—the need to be on Henry. Our reckless gallop across the field. The bees and the flowers and the peace that filled me.

The last memory I conjured before waking up was knowing things weren't how they looked and wanting to talk to Scott. The word *faith* was a rain shower drenching my thoughts.

I had been heading home to talk to him. But now I'm on the ground, and Henry's nowhere to be seen. Pain shot through my head, and I battled with the need to close my eyes. My body hurt. Everywhere.

A thought hit me. They say the day after a fall is the worst. Someone will need to put me out of my misery tomorrow if it's worse than this.

I wondered what the kids were doing. Was little Tucker being mean to Tate? Had Krista made my parents crazy with her screaming and drop-the-cup game? Had they fed my kids all the junk food and let them stay up all night and watch TV? They were probably feral at this point, and my soul yearned for hugs from my babies. This was the longest I'd ever been away from them, and every cell in my body craved their chaotic, joy-filled presence.

Maybe I can let my eyes close for a minute. It won't be a big deal. A memory of Scott's hands tickling my bare skin tugged me into unconsciousness. Could we get through this mess and have a do-over? He may never want to talk to me again after I ran out on him. If only he knew what happened.

I wanted to tell him—to laugh and cry at the absurdity, pain, and fear that lady caused. I wanted him to explain it away and hold me. I wanted him with me now.

"Abby!"

Ok, apparently, this was a severe head injury because I had hallucinated my husband's voice.

"Abby!"

I opened my eyes again and fought the urge to squeeze them closed when the sunlight pierced my brain. Had I been asleep? Or did I just close my eyes? A wave of panic swept over me, making me slightly light-headed. How can I not know? What's wrong with me?

"Abby!"

It's really Scott. It's his voice! How? Why?

"I'm here!" My attempted yell came out in more of a whisper. I cleared my throat and tried again. "Scott! I'm here!" It came out louder, and my eardrums threatened to rupture.

"Abby?" He sounded close.

"Scott!" My breaths were coming short now. I wanted my husband. I wanted to go home. Leaves rustled nearby. Either I would be animal food, or Scott was here.

"Abby!" I turned my throbbing head toward his voice, and there was my handsome husband, tripping over himself to get to me. A tiny smile found its way to my face.

"Abby, oh my gosh, Abby. Do I need to call an ambulance? Do we need a medivac? I know people at Georgetown Hospital—"

"It's ok, Scott. I'm fine." As I said the words, I had to close my eyes and let my head relax from the sensory onslaught. He knelt and leaned over me. His hand, oh how I loved his hands, reached up and stroked my face. I didn't realize tears had spilled over until his warm fingers wiped them away.

Guilt flooded me over the trouble I'd caused. "I'm sorry, Scott." He didn't respond. His fingers skimmed my neck and shoulders, down my arms, making tiny goosebumps appear. I wasn't sure if he even listened, and suddenly words poured from my mouth.

"The beautiful lady from last night came to the room. And she gave me your favorite sweatshirt. And she said..." I had to pause to catch my breath. I was on the verge of hysterical crying and my brain could not handle the lurching of hiccups. Even with deep breaths and a whispered prayer for help, tears streaked down my face, and my head throbbed. But I had to keep going. "She said you left your shirt... in her room... and I thought..."

Scott brought his hands back up to my face, warming it, drying it again, and looking into my eyes. "You thought I had been with her?" he said, his own eyes full of emotion.

My lips were sealed shut, now devoid of words. I nodded.

"Abby," he said with a voice full of tenderness, and a streak of moisture descended from his face. "Just like in those romance books you read, with all the made-for-each-others and happily-ever-afters—" That made the slightest smile fight its way to the surface of my face, and he kept going. "You are my one and only, made for each other, 'till death do us part'."

He pressed my hand into his face and turned to kiss my open palm. Closing my eyes, I relished the scruffy cheek and warm lips. Warmth spread from my hand through my whole body. Then a stab of pain exploded across my head, making me wince. Scott jolted. "What was that? Did I hurt you?"

"No, you didn't." I glanced at him before looking at the ground. "Since I came to, I've been having stabs of pain in my..." I paused for a second trying to explain the location of the pain without freaking him out. "In my brain."

Scott did a double take and sat back on his heels, surveying the situation. "Your helmet is still on. What happened?" he asked, while reaching for the buckle under my chin and gently unsnapping it.

He yanked his shirt off and put his hand under my neck to help me lift. As soon as I did, my helmet rolled to the side, and Scott tucked his warm shirt under my head like a pillow. "Scott, that's real sweet, but what if you just help me get up, and we can go home? I want to take a hot shower and lie in our bed instead of on the ground in the woods." While I talked, I watched him pick up my helmet. He turned it, and I gasped. A crack stretched from the brim to the back.

"I'm calling the ambulance." Scott grabbed for his phone.

"No, Scott. It's fine. We don't need an ambulance." I fought the urge to squeeze my eyes closed against that wretched sunlight. No need to give him ammunition.

"Abby! You broke your helmet!" He looked at the helmet, then at me. "You could have died! You may have a serious brain injury. We need to call for help."

"Yeah, but the helmet saved me! That's why I wear it. And how would an ambulance even find me? How did you find me? Actually, why are you here? How did you know?"

He mumbled something, but I didn't catch it.

"What did you say?"

"I said, Juan called. Henry came back to the barn without you, and he called me. So I left my client and came straight out."

It was hard to believe my super salesman husband would walk out on a client for me, but here he was. I reached for his hand and gave it a squeeze. "Thank you. Was Henry ok?"

Scott rolled his eyes. "Why are you worried about a horse when you're out here in the middle of the woods with a head injury?"

I leveled him with a glare, and he quickly backpedaled. "Sorry, Abs. I know you care a lot about that horse. But I get so worried about you and what we would ever do without you."

"Ok, Scott. I think I'm good to go. Why don't you help me up, and we can go check on Henry?"

"Hello!" A voice sounded far away. I remembered Juan saying he'd wait for me, and I realized I'd ruined his plans for the day.

Scott stepped to the side before responding. "Hey, we're on the trail by the road."

"We call it a carriage path," I corrected, and Scott repeated what I said. Soon Juan came into view, jogging toward us.

"Abby, you ok?" he asked, ignoring Scott to crouch by my side. I noticed my husband stiffen and a wave of guilt hit me over the moment in the tack room.

"Yeah, Juan. We were about to come take care of Henry, and then Scott is taking me home to rest." The guys stared at each other—a silent man conversation. Whatever they were doing, it was taking too long. I was ready to go. I rolled to my belly and pushed up onto my hands and knees.

"Whoa, Abby!" Scott interjected as Juan said, "I'm not sure you should do that."

My head spun, but I had no desire to be a damsel in distress with these two overcautious heroes. I paused to allow my brain time to find its balance while it competed with my stomach for most likely to fail me.

"Abby," they both scolded. From where I perched on the ground like Baxter on all fours, all I could see were their feet.

"Abby, we should call an ambulance." Scott insisted.

"No. Just give me a minute."

"You hit your head so hard it cracked your helmet. You need an ambulance."

"Her helmet cracked?" Juan exclaimed.

I ignored them, placing my left foot on the ground in preparation for standing. "How about y'all help me up?"

Both men rushed me and grabbed an arm. Soon, I was standing on two feet, anchored on either side by a man, and wondering if I could hold back my vomit.

33

Broken

Juan promised to take care of Henry and jogged off while Scott and I made a slow trek through a thin strip of woods. We stumbled over a stone wall, and I practically had to slap Scott away when he tried to carry me across the road to the car. My husband took a moment to scour the road, but I had no idea what he was looking for, and he apparently didn't find it. Finally, we both sat in the vehicle, and he sped me toward the nearest emergency room.

I reclined my seat like the star of a nineties rap video and closed my eyes in an effort to block out the blinding sun. Everything hurt, but I tried to relax. "I'm getting too old for this," I mumbled.

"Yeah, Abs. Maybe it's time to sell Henry." The words hit like a lash from a bullwhip.

I searched my mind for a rebuttal. *Maybe you should chop off a hand* was a bit excessive. *Maybe you should live in a cardboard box?* I don't know. My brain was functioning 30% at best. All I was sure of was I'd finally figured out that denying myself horses had been a mistake. They made me come alive. They brought me joy. Horses were a part of me. Non-horse people didn't get it.

Self-care for some people meant going to the spa. For others, it was going for a run or taking time to read a book. For me, barn time refueled me—cantering up to a jump, facing all my insecurities, and choosing to press down my heels, keep my eyes up, and trust Henry to give us wings.

"No," I finally responded, with my eyes still closed.

"Abby, we're on the way to the emergency room because of a horse accident," he enunciated each word like I struggled to understand English.

"We keep the horse or you can start preparing for my eventual mental breakdown. Your call." I opened my eyes enough to see his reaction. He shook his head, and I wasn't sure how to interpret it. Was he resigned to keeping the horse or resigned to not arguing anymore?

We sat in silence, and Scott turned the radio up. The voice of an obnoxious poppy female singer came through the speakers, grating on my every nerve. "Change it," I said. A whiny hair metal guy replaced the pop singer, and I considered opening the car door and rolling out. Why do people like this stuff? "Scott," I said, a little louder than necessary.

The station switched to country, which I normally enjoyed, but it was one of those weird talk/rap songs that made me want to take a baseball bat to the radio. "Can you turn it off?"

A button clicked, and we rode to the sound of the motor before Scott asked, "Do you remember what happened?"

It took a moment to gather my thoughts. "Not really. I remember my ride. We had a good gallop and hopped a couple of jumps. I remember Henry was being perfect." Our time in the field replayed in my mind—my horse stood and let me cry into his mane, but that moment would stay between me, Henry, and God. "I turned him back toward the barn, and we were low-key jogging."

I searched my mind for a memory that wasn't there. "That's it. Then I woke up in the woods."

"So, you don't remember how you got to the ground?" he pried.

"No, Scott. If I remembered, I'd tell you." I snapped, then took a deep breath and tried to calm myself. Scott did nothing to deserve my temper. "Sorry." I closed my eyes, guilt filling my chest. "How did you know to come get me? And how did you find me?"

Scott laughed, but it lacked any real humor, and I cracked my eyes to see him. "You won't believe how I found you. First, I was using the phone's shared location all day. That's how I figured out not to call the cops when you disappeared and weren't communicating. I knew no kidnapper would take you to the barn."

He looked at me with a combination of hurt and humor in his expression. "A strange number called. I was with a client, but I had this feeling I needed to answer. It was Juan. I left my appointment and headed straight out."

"What did Juan say? It must've scared you for you to leave a client." I forced my eyes open to appreciate my husband.

"He said he was calling from the barn. You took Henry for a trail, and the horse came back, but you didn't. Something about scraped knees and pulled shoe—"

"Wait!" I interrupted. "Henry had scraped up knees?" The urge to head back to the barn had me gripping the handle on the door. Then I remembered I could trust Juan and Tracy to take care of him. It would be fine. "He must have fallen. Maybe his shoe got stuck on something or he overreached with a back hoof and it made him stumble."

Scott looked at me a little longer than what felt safe, since he was supposed to be focused on the road. "That would make sense, I guess."

"I'll have to text Tracy in a minute and ask about Henry. Anyway, did location sharing bring you right to me?"

"Ok, you may think I'm crazy. Honestly, I'm questioning my own sanity. I was following the GPS, and got pretty close to the location dot, and a huge turtle was blocking the road. That thing looked like he could eat off half my foot."

Words rushed from my mouth. "You didn't hit him, did you?"

"No! But the beast wouldn't get out of my way, so I figured I'd pull over and go look. You were right through the woods from that spot."

For the millionth time that weekend, I fought back tears. *Ok, God, I see you,* I prayed in my head, *and I see you gave me the strangest guardian angel. Thank you.*

"I'm going to drop you off at the door," Scott declared as he turned into the hospital parking lot. His love was a bit smothering.

"The drive-through is for ambulances. Park over there. I can walk."

My husband looked at me with a lifted eyebrow.

"I'm fine, Scott! Just a headache and my body is sore." Well, my back hurt like a mother, but I probably tweaked it in the fall. Scott didn't need every detail.

"Ok, Abs, but you're going to let me help you." I smiled at him, which probably looked more like a grimace. "Hey, you need to talk to Lacy. I sent her a text and told her we were headed to the hospital, but she's worried." There was a pause, and then he confessed, "She may have threatened to remove my manhood, too."

I laughed, which turned into a groan as Scott pulled into a parking spot. "She can take your manhood over my dead body. Unless you really were cheating." I made eye contact. "You've got some explaining to do, Scott." I thought about leaving the conversation there, but more words forced their way out of my mouth. "Now I'm the one who might sound crazy, but when I was on Henry, I think God spoke to me."

Warm fingers grazed the top of my hand. "Yeah?" he asked. "What did God say?"

I analyzed Scott's tone for hints of mockery or fear, but only found curiosity and a hope so deep it bordered on desperation. His fingers trailed from my hand to my arm as I struggled to share this most intimate truth. A prideful piece of me wanted Scott to hurt like I did. After all, even if he wasn't cheating on me with another woman, his job sure did get more of his heart than I did.

"Abby? You ok?" His touch grazed back down my arm until he reached my hand and wove his fingers between mine.

I closed my eyes and took a deep breath. *God help me*, I prayed in my mind before I told Scott the truth. "God told me to trust." I paused to swallow. "And I do. Until I replay the image of that lady... Auri... standing at the door returning your favorite sweatshirt. And then I'm assaulted by these feelings of fear and betrayal all over again." I stared at our hands, my insides hollow. How quickly peace could be chased away.

"Will you look at me, Abs?"

The emotions in my chest were as chaotic as if I'd handed little Tucker a pack of markers and a white piece of paper. I wanted to trust him. I was afraid to trust him. The truth was, I was angry at myself and angry with Scott and Auri for making it so hard to trust. But I finally plucked up the courage to lift my eyes to meet Scott's gaze.

"I changed clothes in her room." His words were kind and explanatory. "She wasn't even there. I think she was getting her hair done. Since I was planning to come home last night and not check into a room, I borrowed Auri's to change. That's it."

My head pounded, and I had to take deep, steadying breaths. Even so, a tear leaked out, and I swept it away. "Then why did she look so smug, Scott? She winked at me when she dropped your shirt off. Winked!"

His warm hand cupped my cheek, and I leaned my head into it, instantly relieved that he bore some of the weight of my heavy head. "If I were to guess, I'd say probably because of your whole Cassidy charade. She was going crazy over that whole thing and kept elbowing me during your speech. She thought you were incredible."

I closed my eyes and replayed the scene from this new perspective and almost believed it. Shame flooded me.

"Or she winked because she figured we had a hot night!" Playfulness had entered his voice, and it brought the tiniest smile to my lips.

"Ok, Scott," I sighed, closing my eyes for a quick rest. "Thank you." I had jumped to so many conclusions.

Scott's thumb grazed my face. "Abby. I love you. And I'll talk about whatever you want to discuss later, but right now, I need you to get checked out."

"Fine." I sounded like a petulant teenager, but I couldn't help it. I wanted to be home in our bed.

"Hey. If something happened to you on my watch, Lacy Lee would dismember me. Then you'd be gone, and we'd all be depressed, and I'd be a eunuch trying to raise three kids by myself."

"Ok, let's go then. But only because it would be humiliating for the kids to have a eunuch as a dad. Word would get around, and that's a tough rumor to have following you through middle school."I smiled and opened my car door. When I leaned forward to step out, it felt like I rode a Tilt-a-Whirl. "I'm going to let you come around and help me. I think standing is going to be the hardest part of this whole ordeal. Also, will you text Lacy from my phone? Please."

"Sounds like you took quite the tumble," the ER doctor declared. "Have you ever considered a gentler hobby? Checkers or chess? Some women are into crafting."

It was amazing how I politely chuckled at his lame joke instead of cutting him down with my glare, but the laugh sent waves of pain through my head. I noticed Scott nodding at the doctor and reached up to press the heels of my hands into my eyes.

"Ok, well, we'll need to get you in for an MRI. If your helmet is cracked and you have memory gaps, we need to make sure there's no significant brain bleed. Does anything else hurt?"

I hesitated, trying to decide if anything else was worth mentioning. It would throw everyone into a tizzy. "I mean, I apparently took a hard fall, and I'm not 15 anymore. My whole body hurts."

The doctor and Scott simultaneously grimaced. It was two against one in here—an unfair fight.

"Is there significant pain anywhere besides your head?" Dr. Smith persisted.

I groaned before responding, "My back started hurting in the car. It's probably just muscles locking up now that the adrenaline has worn off. That's what backs do, right? They hurt?" A memory of my back spasming before church not long ago had me grimacing.

"Back spasms are a thing, but while you're here, let's get images just to be safe."

Team Avoid Risk At All Costs was blocking me from what I really needed—a good Epsom salt bath and a day in bed. Everything would be fine after a long soak, a few ibuprofen, and some sleep. That's how these things worked. It's not like it was my first fall or even my tenth. You fall off countless times when you're learning to do hard things, especially when you're a kid who rides naughty ponies.

"Ok, Abby, I'm putting in the order for x-rays on your back and an MRI. We'll do the x-rays first. I'm going to ask one more time. Does anything else hurt?"

The two men stood over me with their arms crossed. Tweedle Dee and Tweedle Dum. I gritted my teeth, sending shots of pain through my skull, so I immediately stopped. Which made me want to punch someone, but that would require quick movement. Can they give me some ibuprofen already?

"Abby?"

"I already told y'all. My whole body hurts. Let's do the imaging things and get it over with. I'm tired and ready to go home."

Dr. Smith opened his folder and jotted notes as he exited the room. Scott's hand found mine, and I took a deep breath, closing my eyes. The memory of waking up next to him in the hotel room this morning had me pulling on his arm, dragging him closer.

He leaned over, and our breaths mingled. I reached up and touched his scruffy face. "Thank you for coming to find me," I whispered.

"I'll always find you, Abby," he said and pressed his warm lips against mine.

"Knock knock! We're here to deliver Abigail Aberdeen for x-rays."

34

Texts

Scott followed as they wheeled me back into the room. The initial news wasn't great. I tried to remind myself it could be so much worse, but I imagined the amount of hovering that was about to happen in my life and the long days in bed, and groaned.

"What's wrong? Are you ok?" Scott was at my side in an instant.

It was starting already. "I'm fine, Scott. Really." I wanted to tell him how I just needed a couple days in bed, but unfortunately, the imaging said otherwise. "Will you text Lacy Lee for me?"

Scott pulled my phone from his pocket. "What do you want it to say?"

I sighed, deep and disappointed. "I guess just tell her what the doctor said."

Abby:

I have a concussion and a broken back.

Lacy Lee:

> What? Is this Abby? My best friend Abby would never text me this kind of news. Who stole Abby's phone?

Abby:

> Technically this is Scott. Abby isn't supposed to look at the phone bc of her head. But I promise those are the words she sent to you

Lacy Lee:

> WHAT?! WHAAAAAT?!!!! IS SHE PARALYZED? THIS IS ALL YOUR FAULT

> WHAT HOSPITAL? I'M ON MY WAY

Abby:

> Abby wants me to tell you it's not my fault. Not paralyzed. "Just" a compression fracture. Doc is sending us home with orders of lots of resting.

Lacy Lee:

> Is she ok? What happened?

Abby:

> I mean, she's not great, but she's not paralyzed or dead. Abby says—I'M FINE EVERYONE CALM DOWN

But between you and me, she's not fine. It's going to be a long haul. And she needs to sell the horse.

Lacy Lee:

I'm pretty sure Abby would rather you be a eunuch than sell her horse. And it may be a good possibility if you actually have a girlfriend

Abby:

My only girlfriend is my wife. Promise. You can interrogate me later when you visit Abs, who said to tell you she loves you and she's sorry she can't go to mom and me workout class. ??don't you need a kid for that??

Lacy Lee:

Ok…we'll see…me and Abs share the kid

Is she in miserable pain? Surgery? Did they put her in like a full body cast or what?

Abby:

She says and I quote—I mean yeah it hurts, but I didn't think it was broken

Lacy Lee:

She's cray

Abby:

Also we'll see a specialist this week. No idea about surgery, but if we do, it'll probably be "easy." They gave her a posture support brace?? It's weird. And she needs to lay low. Concussion protocol is lots of rest, dark room, no screens for a couple days. The more she rests, the faster her brain heals.

We'll learn more about her back when the specialist looks at the images, but the ER doc said probably just lay low. Don't lift heavy things. Don't do anything strenuous for 8 weeks. Because she's on the young side and healthy it shouldn't be a deal.

Lacy Lee:

Ok so what happened?

Abby:

Doesn't remember. Henry's knees are scratched and he's missing a shoe so he must have fallen. Her helmet was broken.

Lacy Lee:

HELMET BROKEN?!!! SHE COULD HAVE DIED!!!

Abby:

I told you the horse is for sale.

Lacy Lee:

SCOTT

What do y'all need? Kid coverage? Food?

Abby:

Kids with parents. Abby says—I love you, can you come tomorrow? She wants to go to bed. (I'm going to force feed her first and then get her to bed.)

Lacy Lee:

Ok I'll be there in the morning. Tell her I love her.

Abby:

I'll tell her. And not too early

Lacy Lee:

;)

35

Home

"M uuuuuuuuuu!"

"Muuuuuuuuuu!"

The wailing hit my ears, but today, at least, it didn't pound like someone beating a bass drum on the side of my head. For the first time in three days, I didn't want to hide under the covers from the sunlight bleeding through my eyelids. A low-key pressure still weighed on my brain, but I would survive.

"Muuuuuuuu!"

"Hi, Krista!" I turned and tried my best to smile. Krista returned the grin, sitting back on her haunches and holding a stuffed animal in her mouth. Bax trotted in with his favorite duck toy dangling from his jowls and sat beside her.

"Y'all! Really?" I laughed. And then I saw it. "Scott!" I yelled, attempting to extricate myself from the covers and exit the bed quickly but carefully. "Scott!"

"Daaa," Krista yelled around the death trap, posing as a stuffy. I jammed my fingers between her gums and pulled the toy from her mouth, turning her happy yell into a blood-curdling scream that grabbed every nerve ending in my head and twisted them, making me grimace and want to curl into a ball.

"Stop it," I scolded. "Stop screaming."

Krista melted into sobs as Scott rushed through the doorway with a laundry basket under his arm. "What's happening? What's wrong?"

"She could've died, Scott! She could've choked! And where were you, anyway? She just crawled in here. What if she'd gone down the stairs instead? Are you even watching her?"

He narrowed his eyes. "Abs, what are you talking about? Why are you out of bed? I've got the stairs gated. She's just crawling around pretending to be a dog."

"What's wrong is this." I brandished the stuffed sloth with its beady, sleepy little killer eyes. "If these eyes came out while she's playing dog," I threw my arms into the air, "she would choke and die."

"Abs," he rolled his eyes, and I seriously considered punching him. "The chances of that happening are so slim. And if she's copying Baxter, she's seen him chew on the eyeballs and spit them out."

"Scott!" I didn't know how to respond. His flippantness over the situation shocked me. Krista used the leg of my pajamas to pull herself to her feet. She forgot her sadness as she reached her hands up, opening and closing them in hopes I'd pick her up.

"Muuuuu!"

I reached down and squeezed her fingers with my own. The motion of bending over made my back twinge and my brain feel too big for my skull, but as soon as I was upright, it was fine. I leaned against the bed so Scott wouldn't notice.

"Abs, I'm sorry. She must have gotten into the boys' stuffies while I put clothes away. Why don't you get back in bed? Between your back and your head, you're supposed to be resting."

"I'm tired of the bed. And I need to pee." I trudged to the bathroom to relieve myself. When I returned, the covers were straightened, and the TV was on. Scott waited with Krista in his arms.

"I know resting is hard, Abs. But it's the doctor's orders. Two more days and then you can move around a bit. Within reason, at least."

I sulked, climbing carefully back into bed so it didn't hurt.

"Would you like to snuggle with Krista?" he asked like a penance. I gave him a weak smile and patted the spot next to me. He released her, and she crawled over and burrowed into my side. Scott adjusted my pillows, and I flipped through the TV shows, looking for something to take my mind off the never-ending bed rest.

"Knock knock!" Lacy Lee's voice called from downstairs.

"She's up here!" Scott hollered and threw me an apologetic sideways glance.

"It's fine. Loud noises don't bother me as much today." It was true as long as Krista didn't go Tarzan.

Lacy Lee walked into the room, or at least I assumed that's who it was. She was hard to see behind the basket in her arms. If the grunting and squeaking of plastic wrap was any indication, it must be heavy.

"Uh, hi!" I greeted my best friend as she plopped the package onto the bed.

"Hey, Bae! You look so much better! How are you feeling?" She reached in for a gentle hug, and I sighed.

"Better? I haven't seen you since the banquet." Heat rushed my cheeks at the memory of that night.

"I'll leave you two to catch up." Scott grabbed the laundry basket and made his escape.

"Girl, I've been here twice already. You were dead to the world both times. I brought you a Chick-fil-A sandwich yesterday, but I think Scott ate it."

"It's in the fridge!" he yelled from the next room. "But I did eat the fries. They're disgusting reheated."

I rolled my eyes.

"She says thank you!" Lacy Lee called.

Scott popped his head in. "Actually, since Lacy's here, I may go grab some lunch. Cava sound good?"

My stomach rumbled at the mention of my favorite quick Mediterranean restaurant. "Yeah! That would be great! I'll get the usual. Lacy Lee, you want something?"

"I'll have what she's having!"

"Ok, y'all are in charge of Krista," Scott said. "I'll grab the boys from preschool while I'm out."

"K love you!"

Lacy Lee and I stared into the hallway, silently waiting. The front door slammed, and words spilled from Lacy's mouth. "Do I need to take care of Scott?" A big smile threatened to overtake my face. Not the time for smiling, I told myself, but Lacy Lee acted so natural in front of Scott, all while holding this in.

The look she gave me brought up an image of Lacy dragging a body bag through the dark. "So what's going on?" she pried. "Last I heard, his girlfriend came by your hotel room and then this happened." She gestured toward me in the bed. Krista was uncharacteristically tranquil, in a trance from the cartoon playing on the TV.

"Well... it's kind of hard to explain." I chewed my lip while I tried to come up with the words. "We had an incredible night, and I thought surely everything was back on track. Then, that morning, Scott left to grab our coffee, and I took this incredibly long, hot shower. When I got out, someone knocked on the door.

"I figured it was Scott with his hands full of coffee. But when I opened the door, it was the lady who wore the goddess dress the night before. You know, the one who kissed his cheek? She said she was returning Scott's sweatshirt that he had left in her room. I mean, what would you think if some lady brought a shirt to the door saying your husband left it in her room?"

Lacy Lee's mouth hung open until she gathered herself enough to respond. "I think the cops would have to be called, and I'd have a lot of repenting to do." The expression on her face told me she was completely serious.

"Yeah, ok, glad I'm not the only one. I immediately jumped to the conclusion that Scott had lied to me. I threw the sweatshirt on the floor and got out of there as fast as I could. I didn't want to look at Scott. So I panicked and got an Uber home. I escaped to the happiest place I could think of, which was Henry's back. Things always seem clearer there, you know?

"Scott didn't even know what happened, but he tracked me on his phone and knew no one would abduct me and take me to the barn." I chuckled, but there was a sadness to it. "I had an amazing ride, and I know he's a horse, but I felt Henry's happiness, too." Scenes played through my mind, and I yearned to be back there.

"At one point, we stopped in a field, and I was crying and praying, and I saw a bee on a wildflower. It was an incredible moment, like a whispered reminder from God that He takes care of the bees and wildflowers, and He'd take care of me, too. He kept telling me to have faith."

I looked up to see Lacy nod knowingly. "Anyway, this sense of peace filled me, and I realized things aren't always how they look. That I should give Scott a chance to explain, so I started back to the barn. A few minutes later, I woke up in the woods, and Henry was gone."

She sat on the bed next to me. "Is it ok if I sit here? I'm not hurting you, am I?"

"No, it's fine."

Lacy shimmied until our bodies pressed together, and I tilted my head, resting it on her shoulder. With Krista on one side and Lacy Lee on the other, I found myself cocooned in love.

"Have you talked to him about it?"

"Before all the drama went down, I asked him point-blank in the hotel room, and he promised me he'd been faithful." My voice trailed off.

"So, what exactly happened that night?" Lacy Lee cut in. "After I left. Did y'all work things out? Was our scheme a success?"

The memory made my cheeks flush.

"Abby Aberdeen, are you blushing because I mentioned one night? With your husband! It sounds like a very juicy story, and I would like the PG version!" Her smile spread from ear to ear, and I chucked a pillow at her face, which she, of course, deftly dodged. "If you're throwing pillows, this must be good!" she laughed.

I took a deep, centering breath and tried to calm my quickly heating insides at the mere memory of that night. "Well, you left, and I went up to his hotel room. He immediately tried to jump my bones, but I said we needed to talk first. I asked him if he was—" I glanced at Krista, who I'm pretty sure didn't understand more than very basic English, but I still felt the need to not say certain words around her. She was entranced by the TV, not paying us a lick of attention.

"Anyway, he said he never had and never would cheat on me. And in that moment, you know, before the lady showed up with his sweater the next morning, I believed him. We had probably the hottest night of our marriage. Wendy from book club was totally right, and I'm officially advocating for you to meet your husband in a hotel room sometime because, wow."

"Ok, I know what I'm asking for for my birthday." Lacy Lee smiled before getting serious again. "Did you ever ask him about the sweatshirt?"

"Yeah. He said when he found out he needed to fill in for his coworker and attend the banquet, he rented a tux from somewhere downtown and changed in her hotel room. She was getting her hair done and wasn't in the room. They were never alone together."

Lacy Lee raised an eyebrow at that. "Why didn't he change in his own room?" I loved her defensiveness over me.

"He had planned to come home after the banquet, so he didn't want to get a room. But once he saw that I was there, and the kids were at my parents, he got one."

Remembering that night was like riding an old wooden rollercoaster. There were some incredible moments I'd never forget—good and bad. My overall takeaway was a massive headache. Literally.

"You really trust him, Abs? I mean—"

"Yeah, Lacy." I smiled. "I do. And he's been so good to me since we got home, and I've been on bed rest." We paused in companionable silence, letting the truth sink into both our hearts. We can trust Scott. He's a good man.

We sat pressed together for a while. Finally, she broke it. "I never heard what the doctor officially said. Honestly, I expected you to be in a body cast when I got up here."

"My head feels worlds better, and the doctor wasn't too concerned with the back thing. The specialist reviewed the imaging. He said it's a mild compression fracture, and it's stable, so I just need to lay low for several weeks. Once my head feels better, he actually wants me on my feet. The hardest part is I'm not supposed to do anything strenuous, which includes picking up my kids and riding. So..."

"So, Aunty Lacy Lee will be popping by even more often?" She spoke about herself in third person, making me laugh through the pain of looking into the next few months of "laying low."

"If she would." I batted my eyelashes at her. "And Scott said he's talking to his boss about options for working from home some. He may take on more of a sales management role instead of being in the field. He doesn't have a solution yet, but he said if it comes down to it, he'll leave his job if he has to and find something else. He's determined to be around more."

"Wow! That's—" As she spoke, Krista emerged from her snuggle spot, crawled over my thighs, grabbed the crinkle plastic of the gift Lacy Lee brought, and let out a delighted shriek.

As Lacy Lee climbed down from the bed to catch Krista in case she dove over the edge, the baby stuck her wide open mouth onto the side of the basket like a starfish and started sucking.

"Ew! Krista!" I scolded, and she turned to look at me with smiling eyes and drool pooling on her chin.

"So, what's with the basket? Should we open it?"

Lacy scooped the baby into her arms while she answered. "Oh yeah! I came from book club, and the girls put it together for you. Everyone pitched in a favorite item to help you pass the time. It was Cathy's idea, and Gabby did the wrapping."

"Gabby wrapped this?" I asked with a lifted brow. It may not be my style, but it looked like it came from Harry and David or something.

"That girl. She just whipped a whole roll of clear plastic out at the end of our discussion and made this gigantic bow right before our eyes. I mean, it's kinda gaudy but also kinda magical."

"She made that bow? I thought you had to buy bows like that!"

"No joke, Abs. It took like half a roll of ribbon and 3 minutes."

There was a very brief moment of silence as we mulled over the hidden talents of the Bible study and book club ladies.

"Wait. You said this was Commanding Cathy's idea? I mean, she's great and all, but she didn't seem like the gift giver of the group."

"Yeah! She gave everyone an assignment. But I did my own thing and got what I knew you'd want." Lacy smirked.

Krista leaned out of Lacy's arms and squeezed the edge of the plastic, letting loose a throaty giggle when it made a crackling noise. "Help me unwrap it, boo!" Lacy said as she plopped Krista into the center of the bed and handed her the bow to distract her. She pulled off the plastic and tossed it to the floor.

"Oh my gosh, is that a pink Stanley?" I leaned forward to get a closer look.

Lacy Lee grabbed it and pointed out the S|M on the top. "Definitely a dupe, but I've got friends who love their Simply Modern cups."

"Well, at least I'll be well hydrated."

"Girl, this thing holds 40 ounces of water. That means fewer trips downstairs to refill!"

"It means I'll be making way more trips to the bathroom." I laughed, which shot a twinge of pain to both my back and my head, so it was short-lived.

"Based on the color, I'm going to guess Priya contributed this."

We went through the basket. There was a stack of books—a romance, a self-improvement, a mystery, and a fantasy all tied into a bundle. An expensive-looking bottle turned out to be nonalcoholic wine, nested with some fancy crackers, cheeses, and jelly jars. Next to that were canned boiled peanuts, and another laugh escaped me.

"I'm guessing you brought the boiled peanuts?"

"Hey, I know what my girl likes, and it ain't fancy jelly."

"Touché. If Scott doesn't want it, why don't you take this?" I handed her the jar that said rose petal jelly on the side and wrinkled my nose. Gross.

I pulled out a beautiful box, and when I lifted the lid, an envelope fell out. A set of bath bombs with different scents nested inside. One said, "Lavender—rest well," and another label read, "Peppermint + Eucalyptus—sore away." Several more were lined up, but curiosity had me reaching for the note instead.

Hi Abby,

I'm so sorry about your accident. I hope you love your at-home spa!

I also wanted to offer to take the kids off your hands so you can enjoy it! How about Wednesdays after preschool? Gabriella said she'd love to help as well! We can start next week.

Sincerely,

Gabby

"What'd she say?" Lacy Lee had been sniffing bath bombs while I read.

"She offered to take the kids on Wednesday afternoons." My smile was weak, but my heart was oh so full. What did I do to deserve this? Am I the kind of person who would do this for others? Sometimes, it felt like everyone else was more kind and giving than me. I should volunteer at a homeless shelter or something.

"Wow, that's really sweet! You could use that time to ride Henry when you're better."

"Yeah, well. Scott is convinced we're selling him. He's decided horses are too dangerous and has concocted this whole plan of offering him to the teenager who leases him and putting the money into the kid's college funds." Bitterness filled my chest at the mere mention of this plan.

Lacy Lee studied me for a moment before responding with a lifted eyebrow. "And how do you feel about that?"

"I don't know. I mean... for a moment, before the fall, I was riding Henry and felt like I had finally found myself again. Like, I realized that while I love being a mom, and am so grateful that God gave me the opportunity to raise these three beautiful kids, I had abandoned this part of my spirit that loves and needs horses in my life. I was making all these plans to make riding a priority again."

"Yeah, Bae. I've been hoping for a long time that you would see that because I could see it from a mile away."

"Why didn't you say something?" I had to ask.

"You've been so busy being a mom, and you're so good at it. I mean, hello. You have three kids under four and your house is cleaner than mine will ever be, and your kids are happy, and they love you. I know you go nonstop. But I was just waiting, hoping you could get back to the horses when it was time."

I chewed my lip, taking in what she said. Lacy Lee was a beautiful, free spirit. Just because my house was clean didn't make me a better woman. Sometimes keeping a clean house is the only thing I had control over. It was a sign of my obsessive and perfectionist tendencies. "Yeah, well..." I finally said, unsure what else to say.

"Well, why are you letting Scott talk about selling Henry? Are you going to get another horse?"

I wasn't sure if I should laugh or cry over her question. "No, not getting another horse. Henry's been with me for a while. We click. He's like family."

"Exactly," she deadpanned. "So why are you letting Scott talk about selling him?"

I sighed, deep and frustrated. I couldn't decide if I wanted to cry or punch something, but I did neither. "I just... he's right. Horses are dangerous, and what if I got even more hurt or killed? What would my family do?"

"Abby Aberdeen. Driving a car is dangerous. Walking down stairs is dangerous. Life is dangerous. You could live a perfect life in a bubble and still get cancer and die. You can't tell me that you, my friend Abby, who is an excellent and skilled horse-woman with the most level head who knows her limits and her horse's limits, is really going to stop riding because of danger?" She glared at me and lifted an eyebrow.

"Well..."

"You know what's dangerous? Raising kids who think the world revolves completely around them. Raising kids who watch their mom quit the thing she loves most and become a shell of herself for their sake. The worst kind of adult is the one who thinks the entire world revolves around them. It's the whole put-the-oxygen-mask-on-yourself-before-helping-others thing."

I took a breath to talk, but Lacy Lee kept going.

"Have you ever been in the home of a family with an unhappy mom? Everyone in the house is unhappy! But if Mom is happy and fulfilled, she's a better mom, and the kids are better kids. Seriously. When I used to babysit, those Carter kids were rotten.

They had all the toys, fancy furniture, everything they wanted. But their mom was always on the go and never happy, and those kids were the meanest kids I'd ever been around. And then the Fosters had a smaller home, less stuff, and you'd think those kids would be mean or unhappy. But Mrs. Foster was such a joy, and her kids were a joy. Don't give up what you love because it's dangerous. You're not riding races or anything."

"Ok, Lacy! I hear you!" I borderline yelled, but she'd made her point, and I didn't want to hear it anymore.

"So are we done with this crazy talk of selling Henry?"

"We'll see." I was silent for a few seconds before the words spilled out of me. "I also feel really guilty about the money. Horses aren't cheap, and I'm not exactly bringing in anything to help the family. We've got three kids. I could sell Henry and put the money towards their futures, and the money we spend every month on the horse would go to them. I just feel so selfish sometimes."

Lacy Lee reached out and grabbed my hand. "Remember what I said about how a happy mom raises happy, kind, better human beings?"

"It's—" I started, but she talked over me.

"Are y'all struggling financially?" she asked.

"Well, no. Scott—"

She cut me off with her next question. "Is your horse keeping you from being able to put dinner on the table?"

"No. It's just—"

"Abs. If you want to sell Henry, then sell him. But as your friend who's known you since before kids and before Scott Aberdeen, your friend who had to hang out at the barn if I wanted to see you and learned to clean saddles to help you get ready for shows—I don't think you want this to happen. Don't make big decisions based on fleeting emotion or when you're in a compromised state. And I'm pretty sure you're emotional and compromised in your current situation."

My answer came out in a whisper. "You're right. We're all emotional right now."

"Abby," Lacy Lee made sure I was looking her in the eye before she kept going, "I don't think God would give you this deep passion for something and then take it away from you. Promise me you'll talk to Scott more about it, and pray about it. Don't just give up."

"I promise," I said as I clutched the note from Gabby in my hand.

For the first time since the ride to the hospital when Scott brought up selling Henry, I felt a little peace settle in my heart. Lacy was right. We're both still riding the wave of emotions from everything. We needed to talk more and pray about it.

36

Disorganized

"H ey, Babe," Scott's gaze pierced my soul. "Are you sure it's ok for me to leave for a few hours? I can have someone else take care of my client."

It had been six days since the accident. Six days since I had done something myself. I loved and appreciated how helpful and serving Scott was, but I wanted to pour my own cup of coffee. He always put too much creamer in it. My perfect cup of coffee is an art that my husband had not quite mastered.

"Thank you, Scott. But I'm fine. I promise. My head barely hurts. I'm sure I can hold down the fort for a few hours."

"You sure?" One iota of hesitation on my part, and Scott would have me back on bed rest, serving my every need. Who would have thought I wouldn't want such a thing?

"You did the hard part," I assured him. "The kids are fed, and Krista's napping. The boys and I will lay low. They can play with blocks and watch cartoons or something."

He looked me up and down and then paused on my face, apparently attempting to discern if I told the truth. The truth was, I needed some space. "Honest! Go take care of your client.

Lacy Lee may come over. Just bring dinner home. I'm not up for cooking yet."

I couldn't decide if I was using my injury to get out of cooking or if I really wasn't up for it. But I'd rather eat Pho and throw away the takeout containers when we're done than prepare food and clean the after-mess. The extent of our dishes will be forks and spoons because the plastic ones they give you aren't safe for the kids.

"Ok. Then I'm going to go. But call me if you need anything. The teenager next door has been walking Bax once a day." The dog appeared, pushing his wet nose into my hand as if called. "And if he needs to go, just let him out back. I'll clean up the poop later."

"But sweetie," I smiled, "you always tell me not to let him out back to pee because it makes our backyard stink and the kids step in his poop when they play!"

"It's true. But sometimes it's ok. It's been a lot, taking care of you, the kids, and the dog. It's fine to do it on occasion." He smiled, and I bit my lip to keep the bitterness reined in. I walked to the back door and opened it, watching Bax jog out and cock his leg on the corner of the play set. It looked like some of the overspray landed in the kid's sandbox, and I slammed the door closed.

I reminded myself of all the ways Scott had served me since the accident, and it wasn't too difficult to add cheer to my voice. "Have a good appointment, Scott. We'll see you in a few hours. Everything will be fine!" The boys were quiet in their rooms, so I turned on the water and opened the dishwasher. It was time to tackle the things I oddly missed while sitting in bed binging Netflix and romance novels.

"Bye, Babe." Scott leaned in and kissed me on the cheek.

"Bye!" I said with a smile and turned back to the dishes.

He lingered for a moment, and I cocked an eyebrow. "Everything ok?" I asked.

He turned and grabbed his bag, shuffling towards the door. "Yeah." His voice was gruff and hard to understand. He cleared his throat and said it again. "Yeah! Text me what you want for dinner. Love you."

He came back and kissed my cheek, then disappeared out the door.

I surveyed the main level of the house. It was in pretty good shape, considering I'd been in bed for days. Scott kept everything afloat. I had mildly expected dishes to be piled everywhere and food to be dripping from the walls, or at the very least, globbed on the floor underneath the kids' chairs.

What appeared to be one spot of ketchup and three goldfish sat under Krista's chair. Were the kids better for him?

He'd clearly let the boys eat in front of the TV a time or two, based on the handful of dishes scattered around. The sink had dishes in it, but he'd kept up with the work pretty well. It was nice not to have a complete pigsty to clean up, but I was surprised he held down the fort so effortlessly. A dog bark drew my attention to the back door, where Baxter waited to be let back in. Well, there is that.

With Bax back inside, I returned to the sink. I rinsed a cup, rolled out the top rack of the dishwasher, and shook my head at the sight. Rows of tines made it pretty obvious how you should load it, but Scott had plopped dishes wherever they landed. Double the amount of dishes would fit if he loaded the thing half-decently.

Ten minutes later, the sink was cleared, the plates from the living room were put away, the dishwasher was running, and I was attempting to wipe crumbs off the table without leaning over.

"MOM!" Tucker screamed from upstairs. Panic flushed through my body. What if something's wrong? And then it hit me. What if he wakes up the baby?

"MOM!"

"Tucker!" I tried to shout, using an inside voice. How could I get him to hear me enough to shush without my own voice waking up the baby?

"MOOOOOOOM!"

I sprinted for the stairs, and a wave of dizziness assaulted me. "MOM!" Tucker shouted again as I grasped the stair rail for balance.

"Tucker Aberdeen, you stop yelling. Your sister is asleep!" I shouted with my head resting on my arm while my brain caught up with the onslaught of noise and movement.

"But I can't find my Bumbee Transformer!"

Time out for everyone, I determined, as I started up the stairs. "I'm coming! It's in the blue basket, Tucker. All your Transformers go in the blue basket," I scolded as I grabbed the correct container, ready to pull Bumblebee out and show Tucker how much he had overreacted.

"It's not there!" he whined.

"It's the only place it should be if you put your toys away properly." I glanced down into the basket and gasped.

"Dad hepped me cwean." Tucker's voice faded into the background as I took in the hodgepodge of items in the Transformers/action figures basket. Tiny board books, race cars, blocks, and Magnatiles were piled inside. And was that a diaper?

I grabbed the red basket for race cars and pulled it out. This one had transformers, an unopened pack of goldfish, a stuffed bear, and a single race car. The air in the room was getting thin. "You ok, Mumma?" Tate's little voice broke into my spiral. "You west?"

"No baby. I don't need to rest. I need to clean. How did the baskets get so disorganized? We have a simple system. What happened to our system?" I tried to use a kind voice, but it shook.

"Daddy cweaned while we bwushed teef!" Tucker said with pride.

"Oh." I sang the word, trying to keep it light. "But is this daddy's room or Tucker and Tate's room?"

How did three-year-old twin boys clean better than a grown man?

A bloodcurdling scream tore through the house, and I had to rest my head against the wall for a second. After the scream came a giggle and then, "Muuuuuuuu!"

Am I ready for all three? Maybe I should call Scott home. But then I remembered the disarray and decided he should stay gone a while longer.

"Hey, babe!" Scott walked into the door a few hours later, with pizza boxes balanced on one arm. "I brought home dinner! Looks like y'all had a restful day."

Krista stacked cups, beating them with a wooden spoon. I laid on the floor next to her, trying to protect my face every time she knocked over the pile. The boys stretched across the sectional, zoned into the TV.

I wasn't ready to broach the "restful day" topic. Nearly the entire time he was gone, I'd been organizing and cleaning. "I thought we were getting Pho."

"The wait was nearly an hour for that, so I swung by Mod Pizza instead. You like their crust, right?"

I stared at Krista's tower of cups, dreaming of Pho. "Thanks."

"How are you feeling?"

"I may have done a little too much today. I think I need some time in bed to recover." My eyes stayed closed while I talked.

"No worries! I've got the kids. Do you need help getting upstairs?" He walked toward me as he talked and reached over to help me up.

"It's fine. I'll just be in bed." I lumbered to my feet with Scott's help.

"Ok, I'll bring dinner up to you in a bit."

My stomach growled, gnawing at itself and killing every effort I made to sleep. When Scott was out of town and I solo-parented the kids, I daydreamed about naps. So why, when I actually had the opportunity, could I not drift into oblivion? Just let me sleep, I scolded my stomach.

A whoosh of air told me the door had been opened. I rolled over to find Scott with baby Krista on his hip, setting food on the bedside table. "Here's some pizza." He reached into a pocket and pulled out a peach-colored can, setting it next to my plate. "And a can of seltzer. Need anything else?"

"Nope."

"You ok?"

"Yes."

"Ok." He hovered for a second, staring at me like he wasn't sure.

"Dad! Dad!" one of the boys called from downstairs.

"Coming!" he yelled back and stood there for a moment longer.

"You sure you're good?" he asked again.

"Yep. Thanks for dinner."

"Dad!"

Krista smacked him in the face and giggled. "Ow!" he protested. "Ok, better go check on the boys. Call if you need anything." He closed the door gently behind him.

As I chewed on pizza, my mind drifted to the boys' room with its cubbies in complete disarray. How hard was it to put things back where they belonged? Even the three-year-olds did that. A twinge of pain in my back made me gasp and pause eating for a moment. If I hadn't spent all day cleaning, I would be fine. I had barely hurt for the last couple of days until I clearly overdid it today.

I reminded my mouth that calories were necessary for healing, but I couldn't make myself eat anymore. I set the plate back on my nightstand, cracked open the seltzer, and took a couple of sips. Setting it down, I rolled over and tried to sleep again.

Thoughts spiraled through my brain like I'd had three cups of coffee before bed. The joke's on me because I'd only had one, and it had been a long time since that morning brew. Tucker's scream from when he couldn't find his toy replayed in my mind, and I wanted to punch something. It was such an unnecessary stressor that led to waking baby Krista up from her nap early. Not to mention what that entailed. I broke a lot of the doctor's orders finagling her out of the crib.

The messy dishwasher and Baxter peeing on the sandbox came back to me. We probably need to replace all the sand now. Or could you spray it with bleach? That probably wouldn't be good for the kid's skin, but then neither is dog urine. I wondered what other crazy stuff Scott had done when he was "taking care of things."

I wanted to see Henry. With Scott taking care of the kids, it was a good opportunity to visit the barn. I could probably drive just fine. But then I realized Henry was turned out for the evening, and if I wanted to see him, I'd have to traipse across a half mile of pasture in the dark.

What was I even doing with a horse? I didn't have time to compete or show. It was selfish. What little time I spent with him was time away from the kids. Henry deserved more, too. He could be a top show horse, and I didn't have the time or money to get him there.

I had a foot in a canoe and one on the shore, and it wasn't helping anyone. Not to mention the money.

A tear made its way from the corner of my eye to my pillow. I'm a mom of three kids. Having a horse was completely selfish and irresponsible. I grabbed my phone from the nightstand and pulled up a text to Tracy.

Abby:

Hey Tracy, how's Henry doing?

Tracy:

He's good. The vet checked him over and said he looks good. Teenager took him on a long walk today and all seems fine.

How are you?

Abby:

Fine. Slow recovery. Tired of laying low.

Tracy:

Lol. Every time I get injured and have to lay low, I get depressed. It's awful.

Abby:

Yeah.

The bedroom door opened, and Scott tiptoed in. I stashed my phone in the drawer of my bedside table, not wanting him to see I'd been looking at my phone screen in case he lectured me.

"Hey," he said in a low tone. "Kids are asleep. Want some tea or something?"

Pressure built in my chest. No one even came in to give me a goodnight hug. I had dreamed of Scott being home to help with bedtime more, but I never imagined I would be pushed out of the process. They didn't need me anymore.

"No." I finally responded.

"Is something wrong?"

I rolled my eyes at that question. "No, Scott. Everything's fine." My molars ground together.

"Are you sure? You seem a little upset. Did I do something?" He took a step toward me.

"I just wanted bedtime hugs is all." I heard how silly I sounded, but the words were out. He laughed. It was short and quiet, but I heard it.

"Abs, I'm sorry. I thought you might be asleep, so I told them to be super quiet and leave you alone. They were champs and got ready for bed quick. We read a book and turned out the lights."

This was a punch in the gut. How many times had bedtime gone on for over an hour for me? Sometimes, it felt like two hours, though I'd never timed it. The process left me spent and exhausted. "You know what? Maybe I should go to work, and you can stay home since you're so much better at it than I am."

"I don't... what?" He stumbled incoherently. "What are you talking about?"

"Since you're so good at keeping the kids. They're happier for you, and quiet, and they go to bed. You should stay home, and I'll go out and wine and dine clients."

"Ok, first of all, you're welcome to get a job. No one told you that you had to stay home. I'm happy for you to be home if that's what you want." His voice, normally so calm and relaxed, was developing a harsh edge. "And second, we're all just trying to live up to this impossible standard you've set, Abby. So I don't know where you get off thinking that the kids are happier and better with me. We all know you do everything better."

His words were a slap in the face. "What are you even talking about?" I nearly yelled.

"It took about 5 minutes to see how you, who were supposed to be resting and taking it easy, came behind me today and redid everything that I've been doing for a week. I don't even know how you can get that much done in a few hours, especially with a broken back and concussion." He emphasized my injuries, like I was putting myself in danger by rearranging some toys. "You make it impossible to even help you."

"I'm sorry. I didn't think it was that hard to put cars in the car bin. Even the three-year-olds do it." My words were biting. I knew I shouldn't have said it, at least not like that.

"And you wonder why I work all the time? At least at work, I can make people happy. I can bring them joy and make some kind of difference."

"Yeah? And who else are you making happy?" I jabbed.

"Well, obviously not you, even though I have served you in every way I know how for the past week. And if you're implying again that I'm cheating with that question—no, Abby. I wasn't cheating on you, and I'm not cheating on you, and I'm not gonna."

I studied his expression, searching for some tell for a lie, and when I couldn't find one, I studied myself. Why was I so worried that my husband wasn't faithful?

When I didn't say anything, Scott kept going. "I don't know what it is that has you convinced that you're not enough for me."

Those words snapped me out of my mental fog, and words leaped from my mouth before I could stop them. "Well, apparently, the real problem is that I'm too much, and no one can live up to my standards."

Scott shook his head, making a clear effort to remove any emotion from his tone. "I'm getting ready for bed. Do you need anything?"

"No. I can handle it."

"That's the thing, Abs. You don't have to. I want to help you."

"Yeah, but—" He walked into the bathroom, not listening to anything else I had to say. Which was just as well because I had run out of words. This was ridiculous. Clearly, I did everything wrong, starting with being selfish enough to own a horse.

I grabbed my phone and wrote a text to Tracy.

Abby:

Do you think the teenager would be interested in buying Henry?

Clicking send killed a piece of me, but the fear of more bedtimes missed because of future accidents left my insides hollow. I felt like a shell of myself lying in bed, which randomly made me think of that turtle who seemed to crop up everywhere.

"God, can you please fix this?" I prayed. "You can even use your weird angel. He's actually starting to grow on me." A tiny bit of warmth filled me at that thought, and I finally drifted off into darkness.

37

Brownies

"We goin' to pick abbles!" Tate yelled into the bedroom. I cracked my eyelids open.

"Abble butta, abble pie, abble ice cweam, abble—"

"Hey, Babe," Scott leaned against the door frame with Krista on his hip, and for a moment, I thought I was dreaming. His muscles looked unusually...

"Have you been working out more?" I mumbled, half asleep.

Scott smirked. "Yeah. What did you think I do in the garage during naptimes?"

I wanted to cover my face. Here was more proof that Scott was better at life than me. How did he have time to work out during naptime? My body melded to the bed, and I wondered what it would be like to be so firm that nothing spilled to the side. Apparently, I could have been working out during naptime. My heart rate picked up at the idea of skipping all the things that needed to be done and exercising instead.

"Anyway," Scott's voice rumbled, "I thought I'd take the boys apple picking."

"Abbles!" Tucker ran into the room and started dancing. He wiggled his tush around and moved his arms so they looked almost like a sprinkler.

"You want me to take Krista? I, uh—" his eyes shifted to the side. "I don't want you to feel left out, but I don't want you to overdo it either."

I took a slow, deep inhale and closed my eyes. A tear threatened to squeeze out. If I hadn't had that stupid ride and that stupid accident, I would be able to go with my family. This was the kind of stuff I had always dreamed of doing together, and now I wouldn't be there.

"Do you think you can handle all three?" A part of me was resigned, knowing Scott could handle it. But a niggling fear still existed. What if he neglected something, like with Krista and the stuffed sloth? Things with kids could go south so quickly, and he wasn't used to having them.

"Yeah, Abs. I've got it. You can take a long, hot shower or clean up behind me." He smiled, and I saw a hint of apology in it. "Just don't overdo it, ok?"

"Actually," a little excitement welled in my chest as I remembered, "I ordered new canisters for organizing the pantry. Did they come in?"

"Oh yeah. I stuck them in the dining room."

"Ok! I'll just work on that!" I felt better already. I threw the covers off and crawled out of bed.

"Promise me you won't overdo it?"

"I promise."

"Abbles!" Tucker said and clapped. "Abbles! Abbles! Abbles!"

Soon, all the kids were chanting along, Krista squealing and pounding her fists on Scott's shoulder.

"I'll take them down and get some food in them while you get dressed." Scott and the kids sounded like a stampede going down the stairs.

I took a second to check my phone. Tracy had responded.

Tracy:

Are you sure? I can talk to her parents. I know they love him.

I stared at the text, contemplating a response. No, I wasn't sure. I felt more *me* on a horse than anywhere else, and I missed me. But I was also missing out on a day of apple picking with my family because of my selfishness and determination to be a "horse girl."

Abby:

Just feel them out. I'm looking at options.

Tracy:

Ok.

Abby:

Btw, how's your horse's back?

Tracy:

Ugh. Chiropractor said it's the saddle. Had a saddle fitter out. She said it's probably bc he's gained so much muscle since he went into training. And his back will keep changing. Why can't they make a pad to help with this? I've tried every one at the barn.

Abby:

That stinks. Horses are tough.

As I pulled on my favorite leggings, my brain spun with ideas about this saddle pad issue. Like, how different was cushioning a horse's back from a saddle than cushioning a person's residual limb from their prosthetic? Could the same technology apply?

When I made it down a few minutes later, all the new containers sat stacked on the island. My heart did a little flutter when I saw how clean and clear they were, with perfect little latches on the tops. I glanced to the table where Tucker and Tate were devouring jelly toast, shirtless. "Um, Scott?"

"Hey! It's a lot easier to clean them this way." He shrugged.

I shrugged my shoulders. It drove me a little crazy to see their delicate, white skin on display at the table, but I loved knowing their shirts weren't being ruined.

"Want me to fix you some coffee?" my husband offered.

"I've got it. Thanks, though." I grabbed a mug and poured myself a cup. The aroma wafted up, and I soaked up the perfection of the moment. We were all together, and no one—

"Oops," Tate's solemn voice said. "Sorry, Mumma."

His half-eaten toast lay jelly side down on the tile floor.

"No worries, bud." Scott grabbed the toast and tossed it in Baxter's bowl while I got the sponge from the sink. "I've got it," Scott said and grabbed the sponge from me. "No need to bend over. You're supposed to be taking it easy, remember?"

"Yeah," I sighed and chose to shift my focus rather than dwell on my limitations. "Tate, did you have enough to eat? Want another piece of toast?"

"Yes, peas," he said, and my heart melted.

"Me too, me too!" Tucker hollered before shoving his last bite into his mouth.

"Babababa!" Krista said before grabbing a handful of cheerios and stuffing them in her mouth.

I put two more pieces of bread into the toaster and grabbed the sugar for my coffee. The container we kept by the coffeemaker was low, so I made a mental note to refill it once everyone left. For now, I scraped a teaspoon and a half out and put it in my mug, followed by a splash of half-and-half. The toast popped as I took my first sip of coffee. So good.

Scott grabbed the boys' food, slathered it with jelly, and handed it to them. "Eat up! We need to get to the orchard before everyone else picks all the apples!"

Tucker gasped before screaming, "Abbles! Hurry!" He took one bite of his toast and declared, "I'm full."

Tate started whining, "I'm not done!"

"It's ok, boys." I tried to console them. "Your dad was joking. You have plenty of time. There will still be apples if you take the time to finish your breakfast."

I glared at Scott. Rookie mistake. Tucker didn't buy it. He yelled at his brother to hurry, and big tears rolled down Tate's face. "I'm trying." Krista squawked like a pterodactyl. Or at least how I imagined one would sound. It was ear-piercing, and I considered leaving the room.

Eventually, everyone shuffled out the door. Scott got them buckled in and drove away, and I sat in the kitchen and drank my coffee in silence.

My phone buzzed, and I checked it. Apparently, I had missed a few texts, but the most recent one was from Scott. He must have messaged me as he pulled out of the driveway.

Scott:

> Love you, Abs. Have fun organizing.

His text filled all the cold spaces in the room with warmth. I realized this alone time was a gift. Another text waited

Lacy Lee:

> Hey bae! How are you?

Abby:

> Good. Fam left to go apple picking. I'm going to organize the pantry!

Lacy Lee:

> Oh fun! LOL! You can do mine next!

I stashed my phone and ate Tucker's toast as I pulled out all the baking goods from the pantry. Paper sacks and cardboard boxes were scattered across the floor with flour, sugar, and other things. It made my head itch to see the mess, but I reminded myself it would be cleaned up soon. I was halfway through dumping the sugar into a canister when it hit me—these containers need to be washed.

Should I throw the sugar out? Leave it and trust the factory isn't that dirty? Pour it back into the bag and wash the container? I texted Lacy Lee, and she said to clean a different canister and dump the sugar into that one. Surely five minutes of contamination from a brand-new, unwashed bin wouldn't kill anybody.

Soon, my baking shelf looked like a professional organizer's Pinterest board. I snapped a picture with my phone and sent it to Lacy Lee.

Baxter nosed my leg and sat, waiting on his walk. How he knew I planned to take him out was beyond me, but I grabbed his leash. We headed out into the sunshine together, and I took a minute to thank God that Baxter never pulled on the leash. My body was healing, and I wouldn't be able to walk him if he was a puller.

He picked up a stick from our sidewalk, and I assumed he'd found it on another walk. He carried sticks like the kids carried stuffed animals. I waved at neighbors, and he peed on a fire hydrant, all with a stick between his teeth. When he sniffed at a bike laying in a yard, I pulled him away, not wanting him to pee on some kid's toy. This reminded me of the sandbox, and my moment of peace abruptly ended.

Scott was trying, and I appreciated it, but really? Why was the sandbox even uncovered? I shook my head, trying to shake off the frustration as we headed back into the house. There were brownies to bake and only a little time left before they came home from apple picking.

Pulling up a recipe I'd pinned months ago, I preheated the oven and started gathering ingredients and setting them on the counter. The ease of finding and scooping everything I needed felt indulgent. These containers were life-changing. It was incredible that I had spent most of my life digging for what I needed and scraping measuring cups against the side of crinkled paper bags.

For the first time ever, I beat the recipe prep time by an entire minute. It reminded me of when Henry and I beat the time for a jumper round, and I did a little victory shoulder wiggle. The text I'd sent Tracy popped into my head, stealing the joy of the moment. The oven beeped, and I put the first batch of brownies in, letting the door slam closed.

It's what's best for my family, I reminded myself.

My phone vibrated in my pocket.

Scott:

We're on our way home with lots of ap-ples!

Crap. The kitchen was a mess, and stacks of containers still waited to be filled and put away. I set the timer on the brownies and got lost in the business of putting things away and rear-ranging the pantry.

"Mumma!" Tate said as he walked in the door.

"Abbles!" Tucker hollered and ran to me, an apple in each hand, and one of them half eaten.

The joy on their faces ripped my heart in half. I loved that they had a wonderful time apple picking, but I imagined all the times I'd tried to do something fun with the kids. They never had this look on their faces. With me, the twins argued and Krista was forever hungry or tired. This was apparently another thing Scott was better at.

Tucker took a huge bite of his apple. "Did you clean that?" I looked to Scott who seemed a little frazzled.

"We wiped it off. It's fine," he said.

"Eat, Mommy!" Tucker thrust an apple at me.

I smiled. "I will in a minute. Did y'all have fun?"

Scott held Krista, who cradled an apple with tiny bite marks on the surface. *It's fine,* I told myself. I took the first aid safety course. I can save her if she's choking.

"We certainly missed Momma, didn't we, kids?" Scott said as he leaned in for a quick kiss. My face heated, but I stood my ground and let him kiss me. His lips were warm and soft and once I had a taste, I wanted to lean in for more. I didn't with the kids around.

"Smells yummy!" Tate said as the oven beeped.

"Oh yeah, I made y'all something!" Grabbing the oven mitt, I pulled a platter of brownies out of the oven, setting them on the stove. I went ahead and stuck the book club batch on the rack to bake.

"Oooooh I want!" Tate insisted, and I smiled. It was my turn to bring the kids joy.

"Ok, bud! We just have to wait a few minutes for them to cool. How about everyone wash their hands? And where are all the apples y'all picked?"

The boys rushed to the bathroom, and Scott and Krista led me out to the van to show me their spoils. "What are we going to do with all those apples?"

My husband blushed. "I don't know. Eat them? Can we make applesauce or something?" His face brightened like he had a fantastic idea. "Henry likes apples, doesn't he? You can give them to Henry!"

I stared at him, trying to decipher what he was saying, but not grasping. "Scott, I thought you said—"

"I know what I said, Abs," he interrupted. "But I was upset. I've been thinking about it, and if Henry makes you happy, you should keep him. He's practically family."

My blood was boiling, and my face was hot. I probably resembled one of those apples. "I thought it was selfish of me to keep the horse. That it was too dangerous, and you wanted me to give it up." Krista's head was pinging back and forth as we talked.

"I'm sorry. I've been thinking, and I was wrong."

"MUMMA!" Tate hollered from the door. "Bwownies!"

I glanced up at Scott, shooting daggers with my eyes, before heading back inside. "Coming, bud!"

I grabbed a butter knife and started cutting. "Who wants a corner piece?"

"Ew!" Tucker yelled.

"Me!" Tate said, and I smiled.

"One corner piece, coming up!" I stuck a fork under it and lifted it out, setting the brownie onto a napkin and giving it to Tate. "Here you go!"

"Tank oo!" he said, and for a moment, I was his hero.

I scooped the next piece out of the pan and handed it to Tucker, just as Tate tapped my leg and said, "Mumma!" Once Tucker had his brownie, I turned to Tate. Tears spilled from his eyes, and my heart dropped to my feet.

"What's wrong, Tate?"

Vomit noises started coming from the other twin— loud, dramatic coughs and dry heaves. "Tucker! What is going on?" I said with a bite to my voice.

"It yucky," Tate said between sobs.

Tucker yelled, "Blugh! Ew! Blugh!"

"Guys, you love brownies!"

The sound of the trash can opening and Scott spitting into it had me turning my attention to him. "Abby, I think you mixed up the salt and sugar. That is..." he paused to spit into the garbage can again, "disgusting."

And there it was. Proof that I, Abby Aberdeen, was a failure as a mom. I couldn't even make a basic batch of brownies.

38

Intervention

"Get up, sleepyhead! This is an intervention!" Lacy's voice pulled me from my half coma.

She stood at my bedroom door with a huge smile and two coffees.

"Praise the Lord for good friends and coffee!" I mumbled with a contented smile. "What's this intervention? Are we going out?"

The idea of some time away from the house with Lacy Lee was making me actually want to get out of bed. I imagined us at the nail salon, sitting in adjacent chairs and chatting away while someone rubbed the tension from my feet and legs. "Nope! I'm here to watch Krista so you and Scott can go on a date."

My balloon of excitement deflated, replaced with a smidge of guilt for not being more excited about going out with the man I vowed to love 'til death do us part. "Don't get too excited!" Lacy Lee broke my inner spiral with her sarcastic remark.

I attempted a grateful smile, but I was pretty sure it came out as a grimace. "Thanks, Lacy!"

"Really, though. You and Scott need some time alone, without kids. I'm your best friend, and I can tell when you need to work on stuff." She scooped Krista into her arms and started tickling her. Krista squealed and contorted her body, melting into laughter. "First step is a shower, though!" Lacy nearly shouted to be heard over the baby's giggles. "Take as long as you need! I'm entertaining Krista."

Those words were something I might expect to hear on my birthday or the day after Christmas. Not a random Wednesday. "Are you sure? What time does Scott want to leave?"

"Scott said he's doing admin work this morning at the office and to text him when you're nearly ready. And the boys have lunch bunch today, right? If y'all get carried away..." She took a moment to lift her eyebrows suggestively, "just shoot me a text, and Krista and I can take your van and pick the boys up."

"But Lacy, don't you need to work sometime?"

"I mean, sometime, yeah! But I already did the billing for Luke's personal training clients, and I just have some calls left to do, which can be done after your hot date. And I have a couple of Mary Kay orders to deliver, but again, that can happen later. Now is your time. Shoo! Get in the shower! I think I can smell you!" She held her nose, and Krista copied her, attempting to pinch her tiny little upturned nose between her thumb and forefinger.

"Ok, ok!" I ducked into the bathroom. "Thank you!"

An hour and a half later, I ran my fingers through soft, clean hair. I spritzed myself with perfume, and Lacy helped with makeup while Krista played on the floor. For the first time since we crashed the banquet, I felt pretty. It had been two and a half weeks by the calendar, but years in every other way.

Scott walked into the kitchen, where I stood pointing out food options for the kids. I smiled and kept talking to Lacy, who played with the baby and only half listened. "Hey, Abs!" Scott greeted me with a trace of hesitancy. "You ready?"

"Yeah, let me—"

"I've got it, Abby," Lacy cut me off with a wink. "You go on and have a nice date."

Something warm touched my hand, and I jerked before realizing it was my husband. I turned to make eye contact, and he looked toward the door, avoiding my gaze. "Bye, Lacy."

"Thanks a ton, Lacy Lee," Scott said, opening the door and waiting for me to exit first.

"You kids have fun!" Lacy joked, and Krista yelled, "Baaaaaaaaaa!"

Scott opened the car door for me, and I climbed into the passenger seat. Time to be with my husband. Alone.

Scott adjusted the radio. His fingers pushed buttons and turned dials, like an adult fidget spinner. He went through at least six stations before landing on a decent song. It played for twelve seconds before he reached forward and twisted the knob to the left, creating a deafening silence.

He smiled at me, and I attempted to return it. "Any place in particular you'd like to go?" he asked.

"Oh. I hadn't thought about it. It seemed like you and Lacy had this all planned out."

The hum of the car was the only sound, so I drummed my fingers on my knee. I appreciated my husband more than ever, yet I was so frustrated with him that it was hard to talk. It was a block in my chest, unyielding and making it painful to be in his space. Not to mention the Henry thing. First, Scott said to sell him. Then I convinced myself my husband was right. Now, Scott says to keep him. Which is great and all, but maybe I shouldn't have a horse. Wasn't it like the number one rule in the mom handbook that you have to make sacrifices for your kids?

Scott got on the interstate and headed west. He laid his hand on the console, and I wondered if he was hoping I'd reach over and weave my fingers between his. He was always such a toucher. "I know you like to make decisions." There was a hint of humor in his voice. "I have some ideas, but if there's something you really want to do, I'm happy to do it!"

"What, like apple picking?" I crossed my arms.

He changed lanes before responding, "Yeah, Abs. We can go apple picking if you want. We've got plenty of apples at home, but I'm pretty sure you'd make much better company than the kids."

Anger tore through my chest. "Better company?" I spat out, "Everyone looked so happy when y'all got home. Like a big, happy family." I flinched as I realized my words may have revealed a wound I'd planned to keep covered.

"If it looked like they were happy, it's because they were happy to see you." He glanced at me as he said it.

"Good cover, Scott. Lamest response ever."

He laughed humorlessly and then shook his head. "Abs, I'm not joking. The boys spent the entire time asking why Mumma wasn't there and telling me how you do everything—from getting them out of the car to putting Krista in a stroller, which was a bad choice in an apple orchard, by the way. I should've figured out the baby carrier or just held her the whole time."

"But if you'd been carrying Krista, who would have carried the apples?"

"My thoughts exactly. Although, we did eventually get to a super bumpy area, and I decided to just carry Krista and put apples in the stroller. Tucker kept trying to push the stroller into other people. Every time I corrected him, he'd yell, 'I want Mom!'"

A laugh escaped when I imagined that scenario, and a little guilt accompanied the satisfaction that filled me.

"At one point, Tucker threw an apple at Tate's head. Thankfully, he missed, but it was close. That kid's got an arm for a nearly four-year-old."

"Yeah, I've looked into signing him up for t-ball, but he's too young. Next year, I think."

Scott took the Middleburg and Plains exit before he grabbed my hand. "See, Abs, you were missed. And once you're one hundred percent, I'd love an apple-picking do-over with the entire family. I'm not sure I'll ever take three kids by myself again." He lifted his eyebrows at that.

"We can go pumpkin picking, instead? What's in season next?"

"I'm not sure," he said as we cruised down a country road with beautiful farms on either side. "I've just been driving towards Middleburg, but did you think of something you'd like to do?"

"Um... I'm more of a planner, and this is a surprise. Let's do your ideas. I'm just glad to be out of the house." As I said it, I realized how true it was. "Oh, and can we get coffee? I would love to sit at a coffee shop."

There was a pause, as if Scott was thinking, before he said, "I have a confession to make."

His words cut through me, sending an instant wave of dizziness to my already compromised brain. My mind spun for confessions he might make. All I came up with was something about selling Henry or him with another woman. Again. Why can't I escape this? Was I wrong about him? Was he with Auri? I can't handle this. *God*, I prayed in my head, *help me with this rollercoaster.*

"Ok," I said, hoping it would get him talking. He needed to rip off the Band-Aid. If he's been with someone else, I'll leave. I'm done. In fact, I'll tell him I'm going to the bathroom when we get wherever we're going and never come back. I'll call Lacy Lee and then call a lawyer, and we'll be done. But how on earth will I support my family? I can't even make brownies right.

"I've been reading that book you told me about. You know, the one your Bible study is reading?" His tone was so sweet and sheepish, and I was still trying to find the oxygen in the car. My chest rose and fell like I'd sprinted a fifty-yard dash.

Wait.

"Is that the confession?" I asked in disbelief, with enough bite to take off a hand.

"Were you expecting something else?" he asked, still in his trademark, easygoing tone.

"Well, yeah, Scott. It hasn't even been three weeks since a lady returned your sweatshirt, saying you left it in her hotel room. And later that day, you decided we should sell the one thing that makes me happy. And once I finally decided you were right, you said never mind, and I can't keep up. So I guess I was expecting something a little more earth-shattering when you say you have a confession." Pressure built behind my eyes. *Wow, God, I'm a mess.*

Scott's hand reached for mine, and I jerked from his touch. "I'm sorry, Abby, I." He slammed his hand against the steering wheel. "I freakin' screw everything up. I thought we were clear, Abs. I chose you a long time ago, and I'm still choosing you every day until I die."

I was crying now, surely ruining the beautiful makeup Lacy Lee had helped me apply. The days of slow-building fear and resentment poured out of me.

Scott steered the car onto the wide shoulder of the country road and threw it into park. He turned to me, and I looked away, wishing I could hide. Maybe I should run. I didn't want him to see me like this. "Abby. You're stuck with me." His words were gentle yet full of resolve.

I pressed my face against the cool window, trying to control the waterworks, and in turn, only making them worse. I felt so unlovable. And did I love Scott with the same commitment? Moments ago, I was planning my escape. What kind of wife am I? "Thank you, Scott," I said through hiccups. "I just... I can't. I'm such a mess lately. And at this point, I'm not even sure why you'd want to be stuck with me." The cold glass grounded me, keeping me from floating away.

I heard a seatbelt click, and his door opened and slammed closed. I pressed my face into my hands, racked with guilt, overwhelmed by his commitment, and overtaken by sobs. My car door opened, sending a wave of slightly cool Virginia air across my skin. Scott's strong hands grabbed my wrists, pulling them from my face. Then he tilted my chin, so we looked into each other's eyes.

"Abby Aberdeen, would you do me the honor of stepping out of the vehicle?" He bowed low and grabbed my hand like a gentleman from a Regency-era movie— Mr. Darcy helping Elizabeth Bennet down from a carriage. I huffed out a wet laugh.

"Excuse me for a moment, m'lady," Scott said, still clinging to one hand and using the other to tap on his phone. Soon, Jack Johnson crooned about being better together. "May I have this dance?"

I smiled, and one more tear squeezed out. A final rally of all the emotions I'd been holding in for days. "Let me relieve my nose of its burden first, good sir!"

"Ah, but of course! I but thinkest I may offer a butt wipe for the lady!" We both laughed, and Scott grabbed the pack of wipes that had become essential to life since having kids. I cleared out my nose and dabbed at my face. I didn't want to wipe off any makeup that might be left. When I was no longer a blubbery mess, I stashed everything back in the car and returned to my very own Mr. Darcy.

Words were on the tip of my tongue, but before they escaped, Scott's firm hand met my waist, gently guiding me to him. His other hand found mine, holding it out to the side. He tilted his head down so our foreheads touched, and we swayed side to side.

"I love you." His voice was barely above a whisper. "And I know you. And I know that you're struggling to like yourself right now." I set my eyes on his shirt, embarrassed to look up. "But you need to understand that whether you feel good enough or pretty enough or deserving enough or whatever, doesn't matter. What matters is the truth, and the truth is you are beautiful, and incredible, and loved." His words caressed my cheek, and I closed my eyes, allowing them to absorb into me.

"But—" I started to talk.

"No buts, Abby. You can make salt brownies for the rest of your life, and we'll still love you and be blessed to have you."

We moved back and forth, and I took deep, steady breaths, inhaling this truth and trying for all I was worth to exhale all the unworthy, ugly, not-enough feelings that had slowly taken over my brain.

"I love you, too, Scott." I closed my eyes, trying to keep the guilt from eroding the hold I had on my emotions. "And I'm sorry I'm so mean sometimes. I'm sorry I get so frustrated. I see you trying hard. I see you working and providing for us."

The song started over, and we ignored it. Scott's hand left my waist and found a home on my cheek. I tilted my face up toward his. "Hey. It's ok. I piled basically everything in the boys' room into the race car bin." He laughed and winked. "I think we're even."

"That is not even—"

His warm lips touched mine, interrupting whatever I was going to say. The slight taste left me wanting, needing, more. Scott's eyes looked into mine, asking permission, and I answered by meeting his mouth with my own.

The kiss was a warm blanket by the fire on a cold day, stepping into your house after a long and tiring trip, a gallop across a field on a horse you trust and love with the wind whipping your hair and making tears stream from your eyes. Which made me wonder for a brief moment how I could consider giving up the horse.

One hand cradled the back of my head, and the other found the skin at the bottom of my shirt. His touch was so gentle, goosebumps erupted across my torso. "Scott," I moaned his name into his kiss, wanting more.

He stepped into me, moving us toward our SUV, while the hand under my shirt held me close. My back pressed against the vehicle, his body flush against mine, and the years slipped away. Before the baby weight, the responsibilities, the frustrations that come with sharing a home and a life. It was college us, but so much better.

His kiss migrated toward my ear and then down to my neck. I gasped as awareness shot through my body. A car whooshed by, blaring its horn and breaking the trance.

Scott pulled back, grinning. His face was flushed with color. "Wow, Abs!" he said, and I exploded into a fit of giggles.

"Were we really about to? Here?" I squeaked out, and my small chuckles morphed into convulsive laughter that sent tiny waves of pain into my head. I didn't care, though, because each touch, smile, and laugh shook the cobwebs off our marriage. Scott grabbed my hand, and we held on tight to each other, bracing against all the forces trying to tear us apart.

A loud pickup truck with tires almost as tall as me approached. They slowed and rolled down a window. "Y'all ok?" a loud voice yelled over the engine.

"We're good! Thank you," Scott shouted back, waving him off.

I stood up, the fingers of my left hand still intertwined with Scott's and a giddy smile stretching across my face that refused to be wiped away.

The guy in the truck lifted his eyebrow. "What's so funny, then?"

Scott pulled on my hand, tugging me into his arms. "Man, we're just glad to be alive and to have each other."

"Touché," the guy tipped his hat. "Y'all have a great day now!" Popping noises came out of his pipes as he sped off.

"I love you, Abs, but we better get on with our date. I may not be able to stop myself if we stay here, and I'd hate for a cop to come knocking while the car is rocking!" A blush rose to my cheeks.

"Scott!" I smacked him on the arm.

"Hey, don't blame me! I'm pretty sure you were every bit as into it as I was." He stepped into my space again, and my body flushed with anticipation. "I love you, Abby Aberdeen."

He darted in for a quick kiss and then stepped away, leaving me cold and wishing for more.

He opened my door and waved his hand to the seat like a fancy driver. "Ladies first!"

Once I was in, he made his way to the driver's side, and we were back on the road, on our way to wherever he was taking me for our date. Scott wove his fingers between mine again. I was so used to pulling away, but in this moment, I couldn't remember why I ever did. Why would I pull away from his touch that was everything to me?

Scott cleared his throat, "So as I was saying before all that," his voice was raspy, and I swear his cheeks were turning red, "I read your book on Love Languages, and I think it's really good. I think it could help us, Abs."

39

Love Languages

"Y ou read the whole thing, and I didn't even notice?"

"Well, you've been in bed a lot, recovering. And I got it on audio too and listened while I was doing chores and stuff." His smile was sheepish.

"Oh really? Did you use one of my credits?" I poked at his arm with my free hand.

"Hey, you can listen too! I thought you'd appreciate it!" Scott squeezed my hand, and the sensation warmed me, momentarily stealing words from my mind. "Let's play a game," he said. "Let's guess each other's Love Languages. You first."

"Hey, no fair! I haven't finished the book yet!"

"Ok, fine," he grinned. "Your choices are words of affirmation, gifts, acts of service, touch, and quality time."

I stared out the window at an old stone fence. Three weeks ago, I thought I knew this, but now my brain was muddled. Scott's hand squeezed again, sending an idea to my head. "Touch! One of your Love Languages is touch!" The victory drained from my voice as images of me shunning my husband's touch pervaded my mind.

"Yes, I think so," Scott said, his voice still full of cheer, yet quieter. Like he imagined the same things I did.

I raised our joined hands into the air and ran my fingers down his arm, staring at Scott. His chest lifted with an inhale. Enjoying the effect I had on him, I grazed my fingers up his arm and under the sleeve of his polo shirt. His body was completely still until he grabbed my hand. I looked up to see the heat in his gaze.

"Abby." His voice was rough. Scott Aberdeen could have had me right here if we weren't at a stop sign about to pull onto a highway. Pink tinged his cheeks, and I smiled with mischief. Scott Aberdeen loved my touch.

He cleared his throat, and I pulled away so he could focus on driving and talking, but I left my hand tangled with his. "Ok, I'm going to guess that your primary Love Language is quality time." I glanced over to find his eyes boring into me. His look had the same hollowness I felt. The years of Scott's long work hours and my loneliness hovered over us like a ghost.

A few seconds of silence stretched between us. Scott's hand gripped mine a little harder, and he returned his gaze to the road. I finally rasped out, "Yeah. You're probably right."

"I'm sorry."

I barely heard him. It seemed the guilt over all the hours he spent at work, away from me, weighed as heavy as the pain I felt over his absence.

"Me too."

I reached over and rested my free hand on top of our clasped ones. "We're on a date, spending quality time together, holding hands. If this isn't the first step to fixing things, I don't know what is."

"I may sound like a broken record, but I haven't said it enough lately. I love you, Abby."

"I love you, too, Scott."

The speed limit dropped to twenty-five, and my heart leaped in my chest. We were coming into the town of Middleburg, and

I had to remind myself that we were still in Virginia. This town reminded me of a little English village. The main street was lined with shops, restaurants, and a couple of churches. Some of the buildings dated back to the 1700s and were made from stone.

My favorite part was the horses. Middleburg was known as the Nation's Hunt and Horse Capital. Horses and foxes were everywhere—from the store signs to statues. A trailer drove past us going the other direction, and I couldn't stop myself from trying to see what kind of horses rode inside.

Some of my favorite little stores came into view. "What should we do first? Books, Fun Shop, or coffee?"

"I'm still buzzing from my morning cup." His fingers tightened around mine for a second before releasing his grip to focus on parking. He seamlessly maneuvered into a parallel spot in front of the bank. Little things like this made me fall more in love with this man. He could parallel park with ease no matter how many people pretended not to watch.

"Let's meander around town, then! I really want to stop by the Play Store and see if they have anything for Krista's birthday coming up."

"We can buy books at the bookstore and then sit outside Common Grounds and read and drink coffee!" Scott lifted his eyebrows in question, as if he thought I might not like this idea. For a moment, I was lightheaded. Did he just describe the literal perfect date? This would go viral if I posted it on social media. If Scott were in a book, that line alone would make him everyone's preferred book boyfriend. I smiled to myself, knowing I had scored the perfect book husband.

We were close to the Fun Shop, so we popped in there first. Room after room was filled with the most random stuff. There were wind chimes and yard flags, Breyer toy horse barns, kitchen gadgets, soaps, greeting cards, books, and so much more. We purchased local artisan bubble bath for the boys and headed to the Play Store.

The owner greeted us with a huge smile. One time, I'd brought the kids in and let the boys loose. They spent nearly an hour tinkering with blocks and making masterpieces while I read to Krista with a puppet on my hand.

The store was full of beautiful toys that made me want to get down on the floor and play with my kids. There was even a wall of science toys for older kids.

I got Krista the most beautiful ballerina doll that looked handmade. I imagined her falling in love with it and dragging it everywhere—even to her dorm room when she moved to college one day.

"Bye! Thanks for coming in!" The owner waved as we stepped back out into the cool air and warm sunshine. Scott took the bags from me and pressed a gentle kiss onto my mouth. I wanted to cry and laugh and dance down the street. Instead, I did the next best thing and grabbed his hand, walking close enough that, occasionally, my shoulder brushed against his.

We paused at the real estate office that always had properties posted for sale. "Look, Scott!" There was a 100-acre farm with a temperature-controlled indoor riding arena, a state-of-the-art barn with chandeliers, an eight-bedroom brick mansion, and two caretaker cottages. I had to wipe the drool from my chin when I saw the barn, but when I remembered the eight-bedroom house, I blurted, "Can you imagine cleaning that thing?"

Scott laughed, "Abby, I'm pretty sure if you can afford that place, you pay someone to clean it."

"Still. Can you imagine having to furnish that many rooms?"

"How much is it?"

"I didn't see yet. Let's take guesses!" I said.

"Four million."

"No way! I'm going with seven point six mill. Did you see that barn?" I scoured the board looking for the price, and when I finally found it, I couldn't hold back my shout. "Nine million! I wonder if it includes a Grand Prix horse that's already Olympic-qualified."

"Ha. You'd be living your dream for sure." Scott moved on to look at the next property, apparently not noticing my silence or the way my hand had gone clammy in his.

"Dreams are for kids and those whimsical, irresponsible adults," I voiced the thing I had recently decided, and Scott paused.

"You think so?" he asked.

"I think once you have kids and responsibilities, you've got to put those things behind you. Then it's all about the kids' dreams."

Scott was quiet for a second, and then he said, "Why would God give you a passion that stirs your soul and brings you joy if He didn't want you to have it?"

It was my turn to be silent. *God, he's right. Why did you give me this passion if I'm supposed to give it up for my kids?*

"Ready to go to the bookstore?" Scott asked, turning that way.

"Sure!" I forced cheer into my voice.

We turned off Main Street and meandered over uneven sidewalks, past beautiful old storefronts. The sign for the bookstore came into view, dangling from the roof. As we neared the door, I saw the window display of "spooky season" books. It was a reminder that Halloween was approaching and we needed to get the kids' costumes and cold weather clothes. You never know if it will be seventy degrees or snowing in October in Virginia.

Scott opened the door, and a bell tinkled, announcing our entrance. I stepped over the threshold to smiling faces and a "Hello! Welcome to the bookstore!"

"Hi! Thanks!" Scott's hand touched my back, and in a strange turn of emotions I was still getting used to, I hoped it never left.

"Anything specific we can help you find today?"

"We're just browsing," I said with a smile. I almost asked for help to find the horse books, but then I remembered my decision. If I wanted to survive selling Henry, I needed to distance myself from that world—find something different to be interested in. "Actually, where's your romance section? Uh, the clean ones, please." Scott smirked at me as the sales lady led me to a section and started pointing out her favorites.

Scott and I met at the register, each with a book in hand. None of the romance books looked interesting, and I ended up with one about a horse. Other patrons had trickled in, ringing the bell each time the door opened. I smiled and nodded as a group of three, all in dirty riding boots, burst in. They headed for the horse section, and for a minute, I wished I was wearing something that identified me as a horse girl as well. They'd know I was one of them. But then I remembered I wasn't anymore. I had made my choice.

As the lady handed Scott the receipt and bag of books, a loud noise erupted across the store. Silence followed. We all attempted to act normal while deciphering if it was the bodily function it sounded like. I glanced around, looking for furniture that had been moved, but I only found the group of horse girls snickering and elbowing each other. A lady with spectacles perched on her nose and a wide grin sat in a reading chair. When our eyes connected, she winked, and I smiled back before whipping my head back to the sales associate.

I grabbed Scott's hand and ran for the door. As soon as it closed behind us, a laugh exploded from me. "Did you hear that?"

"It sounded like a Mexican barking spider was in the bookstore somewhere," he shrugged.

"Oh my gosh, Scott, was that you? That lady with the spectacles winked, and I was sure it was her! She reminded me of my grandma, letting one fly in public."

He grinned, and I moaned. "Scooooooott! Did you just... just.... pass gas out loud in the bookstore?"

"Pass gas? You sound like my mom."

"Scott Aberdeen, I can't take you anywhere."

"Hey!" He pulled on my hand and smiled, trying to act sexy. Impossible after that display. "It wasn't me. I'm telling you, it was a Mexican barking spider," he insisted.

"I can't." I shook my head, trying to hide my laughter from him.

"Hey, Abs."

"Yeah?"

"It's proof that God has a sense of humor. No matter how young or old you are, farts are hilarious!"

"Scott!" I tried to scold, but I was openly laughing now, like I had the intelligence of my three-year-old boys. But Scott was right. Farts would always be funny. Gross, but funny.

40

Coffee Date

"Cuppa Giddyup or Common Grounds?" Scott asked as we made it back to Main Street.

"Well, if we were getting it to go, I'd say Cuppa Giddyup. But since we're sitting for a while, let's go to Common Grounds and sit outside." His skin was warm against mine, and I wondered why I had so often shunned his touch. Maybe touch was one of my main Love Languages, too, and I had been so worried about Scott noticing my fat rolls that I rarely let either of us experience it.

We sat at a table out front by the Common Grounds sign. An iron fence separated us from the sidewalk, but there was plenty of room for the dogs being walked to stick their heads through for an ear scratch. *This is Heaven*, I thought as I took a sip of my coffee, thinking about the adorable Corgi who'd just come by.

A horse trailer cruised past us down Main Street. Through the barred windows, I caught sight of soft muzzles and curious ears. It reminded me of Henry and all the adventures we used to go on, adventures I had been hoping to start going on again until... yeah. Not anymore.

The cold brew had a hint of dark chocolate that blended perfectly with the heavy dose of half-and-half. I wanted to drown myself in it while also relishing every sip so it would last all day. I finally pulled my new book out. It was called *Dragon*, about a crazy Thoroughbred racehorse turned showhorse.

I had to swallow a knot in my throat, realizing this could have been about Henry, except he hadn't reminded me of a dragon since his first days off the track. No matter how much I told myself my horse girl days were over, this was the only book in the store that caught my interest.

"Do you hear that?" Scott asked, pulling me from my thoughts.

"Hear what?" I asked, and we both got quiet while I strained my ears. What should I be listening for? A helicopter? A bird? A screaming kid? The unmistakable sound of hooves thundering across asphalt answered my question. It was faint at first, but quickly grew louder.

Shouts came from a few blocks away. "Loose horse!"

I looked in the direction of the noise and finally saw him. A large bay horse was about four blocks down main street, galloping in our direction. He wore a saddle and bridle, but his gear was missing one important element—a rider. The stirrups flopped around, banging into his sides with each stride, while the reins still rested over his neck.

The whites of his eyes showed from three blocks away. People emerged from businesses and stores to yell, "Loose horse!" and rush at him. This only spurred him forward.

I glanced at Scott. "He needs help!" I declared.

"Be careful," he said, and for a fraction of a second, I was in awe that my husband didn't hold me back, even with my healing injuries. Empowered by his belief, I looked around for anything that could distract this horse. A shiny red apple sat in my sandwich basket. It was worth a shot. I stood in my chair and gripped the fence as I gently and efficiently climbed over and lowered myself onto the sidewalk while Scott helped steady me. The horse was two blocks away, and I had seconds to make this happen, so I strode to the center of Main Street.

The door to the post office banged open, and people rushed out. A man in a suit took a deep breath to yell, and I leveled him with my best mom glare—perfected by keeping toddler twin boys in line. "Quiet!" I growled. "Come stand next to me. Quick!"

Five people, one in a postman uniform, filed out into the middle of the road and formed a line on either side of me, like we were playing red rover with a horse. Their eyes got big, but the street quieted. "Stand there, but move if he gets close and isn't stopping."

The vibrations of hooves on asphalt rattled my nerves, but I took a step forward from the line and stood in the center of Main Street. I whistled, grabbing the attention of the runaway horse, and stretched my arm out, extending the apple. He was fifteen strides away when he zoned in on me. My heart pounded in my ears.

The whites of his eyes softened, and he took a deep breath. The muscles in his neck relaxed, but he kept coming. "Whoa, boy," I crooned, as his pace slowed. "Whoa. Easy, bud." My voice was firm but gentle. This was it. He was three strides away. His pace dropped to a perky jog as he lengthened his neck toward me, stretching for the apple. For a brief second, he paused. "What a handsome boy! And so smart!" I grabbed his reins as he went for a bite of the apple. Got him!

The door to the coffee shop slammed, bursting our peaceful and safe bubble. "Who's letting their horse loose in Middleburg? Some people are so dumb they shouldn't even be allowed to own animals!"

Some people shouldn't be allowed in public, I thought as the quieting horse startled, exploding into motion. I tightened my grip on the reins, not wanting him to get loose again or for anyone to get run over. The row of people from the post office scattered back to the sidewalk, and the horse danced in a circle around me. I stood my ground, talking to him in a low, calm voice until he relaxed.

His nose found the apple, and I held onto it. He nibbled at the top until he managed to get a bite without getting his teeth near my fingers—a gentleman. "Hey, Abby!" Scott called, and when I looked up to see what he wanted, I realized we were still standing in the center of the street. Cars were now lined up, waiting for us to move.

I clucked the horse forward. His sides heaved, and sweat poured from under his saddle pad. He kept his head by my elbow, and together, we walked to the sidewalk next to Common Grounds. Scott sat in his seat, staring at us. His eyes were round saucers like a cartoon character.

"Look at what I caught!" I said as if I had been fishing. The people of Middleburg went back to business as if a runaway horse was a normal thing in this town. Another truck and horse trailer ambled up the street.

"Abs, that was incredible. I thought you were going to get run over. It was the most terrifying thing, and then you were like a horse whisperer."

Now that we were out of the road, I let the horse work on the apple some more. "I'm not a horse whisperer, Scott." I rolled my eyes at the idea and wondered if that was even actually a thing. "I just... I don't know. The horse was scared and he needed help. When I saw it happening, I knew he needed to be caught. He was looking for a safe person."

"But what if he ran over you? You're still healing from your last accident." Awe filled his voice, but also a hint of anger over the position I'd put myself in.

"Well, I was pretty sure he wouldn't. Horses don't want to hurt us. Running over me is dangerous for him, too, because he could get tripped up and hurt himself in the process. I was going to get out of the way if I needed to."

Scott looked skeptical, and I kept going, "Plus, he's outfitted in foxhunting gear. Most hunt horses are brave and level-headed. Sometimes, horses panic over dumb stuff and kind of lose their minds. They just need something to bring them back to their senses."

At that moment, I was transported back in time to the hotel room, when the lady returned Scott's shirt. Maybe I wasn't so different from this horse. I'd certainly lost my mind for a bit, and Henry helped me return to reality. Truthfully, even the accident helped.

"Yeah. I guess you're right," Scott said. I smiled at him, grateful we were finally working together on our relationship.

The horse finished the apple, leaving my hand damp and sticky. I wiped the juice onto his mane. "Shouldn't you wash your hands?" Scott asked, obviously grossed out, and I laughed.

"Do you want to hold the horse while I run to the bathroom and wash up?" I offered him the reins.

"Oh yeah. No thanks," he said. "So, how do we find its owner?"

I'd been so lost in the moment that I hadn't thought about it. "I figured someone in riding clothes would have appeared by now, but maybe his rider didn't see where he went. I have an idea. Can you hand me my phone?"

I pulled up the local Facebook group, took a selfie with my new horse friend, and posted it with the words, "Is somebody missing something? I found a new friend running amuck down Main Street. He's currently enjoying afternoon coffee at Common Grounds with my husband and me. Come quick before I fall in love and take him home :)"

I couldn't help myself. This horse was clearly a solid citizen who just had a bad moment. I wondered what would startle a horse like this so badly that he'd end up running through town.

The bay horse and I stood on one side of the fence blocking the sidewalk, forcing pedestrians to find a workaround, while Scott sat at our table. The books lay next to my food basket, and I mused over how I'd thought a bookstore and coffee was the perfect date. That was way off. The new addition to our day, who kept trying to rub his itchy, sweaty head on me, made it the actual best date ever.

The noontime sun burned away any coolness in the air. Scott and I talked while I munched on my sandwich, pulling the vegetables out and offering them to our new friend. He loved the yellow bell peppers but mouthed the lettuce before dropping it onto the sidewalk. One of the birds lurking around the patio darted under our feet and grabbed it.

People stared as they walked by, but I kept my shoulder to them, pretending this was normal and soaking up the moment.

"That was incredible!" someone shouted as the coffee shop door banged closed behind him. The horse startled, but went back to nudging at my sandwich. The barista strode toward us, juggling two coffees and a bowl. "This round is on the house! I'm so sorry about that crazy customer. Some people can't be reasoned with. You should hear the complaints I get every day about his coffee, but he keeps coming back."

We shared an eye roll and a laugh as he set down two cold brews and a bowl holding apple slices on the table.

"Thank you!" we said in unison. The horse stuck his nose in the air, lifting his top lip and wriggling it around, drawing attention from everyone around us.

"Can I give him one?" the barista asked, nodding to the bowl.

"I mean, I just met the horse, but he seems pretty friendly. He's probably fine. Hold your hand flat so he doesn't accidentally nibble a finger."

The guy grabbed a slice of apple and stretched his tattoo-covered arm across the fence. The horse nuzzled his hand, gently lipping the treat off it. When the barista pulled his hand back, a grin stretched so wide across his face that the tattoo on his forehead lifted. "That was epic!"

"Pretty great, right? I love the feeling of their lips against my hand. They have these huge teeth and powerful bodies, yet most of them are so gentle when they take a treat."

"Can I give him one more?"

"Yeah! But then we probably need to stop. He already had a whole apple and a lot of stress. I don't want to give some stranger's horse a bellyache." The horse nudged my elbow as if to say *Hey! I'm fine! Give me all the treats!*

The barista gave him one more slice before heading back inside.

I slurped down my first coffee until it made bubble noises in the straw and discarded the cup. Scott looked up at me. "I really want to kiss you right now," he said. I blinked slowly, feeling drunk and heady in this perfect moment.

"Same," was all I was able to croak out. I wanted to tell him how happy I was, how perfect this day was. I wanted to leap into his lap and teleport into another hotel room and have a night like two weeks ago. And I also wanted peace in my heart over this horse thing. Selling Henry was best for my family, but shouldn't the decision make my heart lighter? Instead, it was like an anvil had been tied to it.

"So this is fun and all," Scott said, "but what do we do with the horse? What if its owner doesn't come? Do we keep it? Don't they call it a husband horse or something?" He grinned, and I laughed nervously. Why was he making this so hard?

"Well, to be a husband horse, the husband has to know the front end of the animal from the back," I said, and chuckled. Our new friend stuck his head in the air and wriggled his top lip again.

Scott's cheeks turned bright red as he realized not only was I laughing at him, but so was the horse. "Ha ha," he deadpanned.

I smiled, giving the horse an apple slice as a reward for helping with the joke. "I swear, as horses get older, they understand English."

Scott lifted an eyebrow at me.

"Yoohoo!" someone called, breaking our moment. I turned around to see a truck and trailer stopped behind us on the road. In the passenger seat sat an older lady dressed in traditional fox hunting attire, grass clinging to parts of her hair. She flung herself out of the truck onto the sidewalk, and I hoped I had even half that energy at her age. "Rixy, boy! Did you get so tired from hunting you had to get a cup of tea?"

"Uh, hi! I'm guessing this is your horse?" I held the reins toward her.

"Yes, that's my little troublemaker, Rixy! And I'm Bunty!" She smiled and stuck out her hand for a shake that about crushed my bones.

"I'm Abby!"

Scott's eyes bulged when she shook his hand, and I had to smile over this tough little horse lady. "I'm Scott! Pleased to meet you, Ms. Bunty," he managed to get out.

Her British accent made me feel like I was in a movie. "Oh, you absolute darlings, thank you ever so, for catching that rascal! It's been quite a morning, I must say!" With an air of effortless composure, she plucked a stray leaf from the sleeve of her jacket.

I reached up and patted Rixy's neck as I talked, "What on earth happened? Rixy doesn't seem like the type to take off down Main Street." What I didn't say was that I imagine Ms. Bunty may have aged out of riding the type of horse who startles easily. But what do I know? She seemed tougher than me, even if she was double my age.

"We were having a delightful gallop back in from the hunt—Rixy here never puts a hoof wrong, you know. Absolutely fabulous hunter. I trust him so implicitly I'd put my grandchildren on him without a second thought. But heavens above, we popped a little coop, landed beautifully, and what did we find? A monstrous tortoise! Enormous thing, the sort you'd expect to see in the Galapagos rather than the countryside. I do believe they call them alligator snapping turtles? Beastly creatures."

Her eyes widened as if reliving the moment. "Well, dear old Rixy, who, as I said, is normally as solid as they come, took one look at the thing, and, before I could say 'hold hard,' he was six feet to the side. And I, regrettably, was not."

She paused for effect, giving us time to absorb the image of this grand lady being unceremoniously unseated. "I daresay, the tortoise, combined with the frightful racket of me hitting the ground, gave Rixy such a start that off he went. Never in my wildest dreams did I imagine he'd gallop all the way into town! You ridiculous boy, Rixy! If you do that again, I'llbe forced to get you a GPS tracker."

Rixy, now fully engrossed in his owner's presence, nuzzled each pocket of her jacket, clearly expecting a reward of some sort. I'd guess a sugar cube.

Scott and I exchanged incredulous glances. "I'm sorry, did you say a turtle spooked your horse?" I asked, hardly believing that my turtle was the cause of so much havoc.

"Yes, yes, I know it sounds absurd, but I assure you this creature was positively prehistoric in stature! When I found my-self rather ungraciously sprawled on the ground, for a fleeting moment, I did wonder if it intended to take a bite of my derriere! Can you imagine? But thankfully, it merely lumbered off into the undergrowth, and we've all had a jolly good laugh about it back at the hunt."

Scott and I shared another look, barely suppressing our laughter. I couldn't wait to tell Lacy Lee about my guardian angel causing trouble again.

"How did you know to find him here?" Scott asked.

"Well, naturally, we assumed he'd turn up at one of the nearby farms, so we started making calls. Then one of the young girls in the hunt—far savvier with these mobile phones than I am—saw a post about him on Facebook. I must say, this could have gone in all sorts of frightful directions, but what a delightful outcome! And you, my dear, must be a horsewoman yourself. Do you hunt?"

I felt a faint blush creeping up my cheeks. "I used to ride hunter/jumpers, even rode professionally for a few years. But since having kids, my horse has been leased out."

"Oh, I do remember those days! Such a juggling act when they're little, isn't it? How old are your kids?"

"We've got three-year-old twin boys and an eleven-month-old girl," I said, pride warming my voice.

Bunty's eyes softened with nostalgia. "Enjoy every moment, my dear. My children are your age now, and I'd give anything to relive those days. But listen to me—don't give up the horses. I know how impossibly difficult it feels, carving out time for yourself. And the guilt—oh, the ghastly guilt! But my love, horses are in your blood. You need them as much as they need you."

My throat tightened, and I couldn't do much more than nod. *God, did you send Rixy and Bunty here for me?*

Bunty turned to Scott with the same commanding presence that I imagined had animals and humans alike hopping to attention. "Now, Scott, darling. Don't you dare let her give it up, do you hear me? You strike me as one of the good ones, and if I could impart just one bit of marital wisdom after forty years, it would be this—make sure she gets her time in the saddle."

"Yes, ma'am." Scott nodded solemnly.

"Good man. You see, she'll either get her madness out on horseback, or she'll let it loose on you and the children, and I rather think you'd prefer the former." She shot me a knowing wink, and I laughed, nodding.

As she turned to leave, I found my voice. "Mrs. Bunty—have you ever had a bad fall? I mean, I want to keep riding. It's part of me. But a couple of weeks ago, I took a spill and ended up in the hospital. The guilt, the what-ifs... it's all been weighing on me."

Bunty's expression shifted. For a moment, we stood in silence, and I knew she was reliving her own tough moments.

Scott's words were soft as he said, "We couldn't live without her."

"Oh, Scott, my dear boy." Bunty reached for his hand, then mine, with Rixy's reins looped through her arm and him standing sentinel over our conversation. "Most people are so consumed with avoiding danger, with tiptoeing through life unscathed, that they forget to actually live. But when God grants you a passion, it's in the pursuit of that passion that you are most alive—and that is when you shine His light the brightest."

Rixy nudged me, and I absently handed him a bite of apple I'd been holding, too transfixed by her words to do anything else.

"Thank you," I whispered.

Bunty smiled. "Accidents happen, my love. We do our best, and then we trust."

A sharp honk rang out, and we looked up to see Bunty's friend waving impatiently from the driver's seat of their pickup.

"Oh, I must dash! Such a pleasure meeting you both. Thank you again for minding my boy!" She enveloped me in a fierce hug, then swatted at Rixy when he grabbed at the pocket of her jacket, searching for a treat.

"Thank you so much!" I said again, and Scott repeated the sentiment.

Bunty and Rixy checked for traffic and walked across the street to where her friend waited with the horse trailer. They loaded the lovely hunt horse up and closed the door behind him. We smiled and waved, and the trailer slowly made its way to the road. I turned towards the coffee shop, heart light and full of hope. The anvil that had weighed me down since I had decided to sell Henry, lifted.

"Abby! Excuse me, Abby!"

I turned around at the sound of my name to find Bunty hanging out the passenger window, waving a piece of paper. "Coming!" I walked quickly to the truck.

"Do reach out, darling! And remember—never, ever give up." She pressed a note into my hand.

"Thank you so much, Bunty. I won't!" I promised, tucking the paper into my pocket to read later when I had a quiet moment. As we turned back to our table at Common Grounds, I sent Tracy a text.

Abby:

He's not for sale. :)

The response was nearly immediate.

Tracy:

> Finally! I knew you would come around.
> Never talked to the teenager's parents ;)
> When can you visit your boy?

A raindrop hit the top of my head and then my arm. "Are you feeling that?" I asked my Scott.

He looked up at the sky, and I followed suit. "Looks like a storm is rolling in fast!" He turned back to me, searching my face. "Should we wrap this up?"

I knew he was thinking the same as me. No. This has been perfect. I never want it to end.

41

Rain

I thought about Lacy Lee and the kids. The boys would be home from preschool now. This amazing day with Scott made me long for time with the kids, too. Scott's fingers wove between mine, and peace settled over me. For the first time in a very long time, Scott Aberdeen felt like home.

"Let's go," I told him, looking up into his face. A raindrop landed on my eyelashes, and I blinked it away. "Together," I added.

"Together," Scott repeated.

"I want to get Lacy a thank-you gift real quick. I saw something in the Play Store."

"Ok, but we better hurry. The storm is rolling in!"

I rushed to grab our bookstore purchases and tuck them into the plastic bag while Scott cleared our table. Then we made a mad dash up the block as the sprinkle became more insistent. The sky darkened above us, a loud crack exploding from the clouds. We ducked into the Play Store, and the heavens opened. Rain drummed the roof of the building, making it hard to hear anything else.

Next to the cash register, dangling from a wire rack, was the item I'd wanted for Lacy Lee. I pulled it from the hook and handed it to the lady to ring me up. "It's quite the storm out there! You're welcome to linger in here until it lightens up!"

"Thank you," I smiled, handing her my credit card.

Scott stepped up next to me, and I relished the warmth of his body. "Do you have a couple of extra plastic bags? We can pay for them if we need to."

"Of course! That won't be a problem. Big or small?"

"Big enough for this stuff and whatever she's buying." Scott held up the bags containing our purchases from the day, and I smiled to cover my confusion.

The lady dug around behind the cash register for a moment before popping up with two large empty store bags in her hand and a tiny brown bag with tissue paper containing Lacy's gift. "Here ya go!"

"Thank you!" we said in unison.

I meandered around the store with one eye on Scott. He put Lacy's gift in with the books, then he nested everything in a plastic bag, wrapping it like he was wrapping a gift before sliding it all into the third bag. "You ready to head out?" he asked.

The steady drumbeat of rain on the roof made it hard to hear him, so I was sure I heard wrong. I glanced outside and then back to my husband with a lifted eyebrow.

"Let's go!" he said and grabbed my hand.

"What are you—" But before I finished my statement, Scott pulled me out the door into the rain. "Scott!" I screamed. Thunder echoed across the sky, and water ran down my face and hair in rivulets, and above all that noise and rain, I could hear Scott laughing.

My husband stepped into my space, and I saw a light in his eyes that had been missing for years. He dipped his head, so his lips brushed my ear as he spoke. "May I have this dance?"

I stared at him, momentarily dumbfounded, until he lifted our joined hands into the air and put his other around my back. "Where's the music?" I yelled over the storm. My body automatically followed his, swaying back and forth.

"This is the music!" he yelled back. "The rain! The storm!" A deep peal of thunder filled our ears for a moment, as if God was proving the point for Scott. "Us, Abby. We're the music." He stepped back and tugged on my hand so that I spun into him. Then he wrapped both arms around me, holding me tight, and swayed back and forth.

I pressed my head against his chest and closed my eyes. Puddles formed between our bodies until they rolled down to the sidewalk in tiny streams. I thought about our song, with its highs and lows. How the hardest parts of life were often the best. I realized if that lady had never come to our hotel room, if I hadn't had that accident on Henry, we probably wouldn't be right here, right now. And it was so worth it.

Scott pulled away a bit, and I started to panic. I didn't want it to end. But then his fingertips touched my chin, tilting my head up, and his hand moved to cradle my face. He trailed a thumb across my cheek, his eyes roving from my eyes to my lips.

I lifted onto my toes, needing to be closer, needing him. With the fervor of the storm, his mouth crashed onto mine. It tasted like coffee and rain and hope, and I let myself get lost in it. I pressed my body back into his, wrapping my arms around him and deepening the kiss.

We stood in the rain, making out like young lovers until a loud wolf whistle pierced the air, breaking our trance. Rays of sunshine warmed my soaking wet skin. We had kissed the storm away. Scott smiled, and I felt it against my mouth. I wondered why we always made kissing such a serious thing. This was incredible and joyous. The townspeople emerged from their hiding places, sporadic applause and whistles cheering us on.

Scott pressed one more kiss onto my mouth. "I love you, Abby Aberdeen. Now, let's go home."

"Let's!" My body buzzed as we headed to the car. Inside, Scott cranked the heat, but my teeth still chattered as we drove.

I pressed as much of my skin against him as I could get over the console without sitting in his lap.

"Hey, Abs." His fingers grazed my arm when he spoke, making my goosebumps even more pronounced.

"Hey, Scott." I smiled, closing my hand over his. I loved his touch, but right now, I needed his warmth.

"I'm sorry I've been gone so much and about all that 'sell Henry' talk."

"You've already apologized for that, and I forgive you. And I'm sorry for being so—" I searched for the right word but came up with several and paused between each one. "Unpleasant. Mean. Biting."

"Hey, you can bite me whenever you want!" He turned and winked at me, and I just shook my head and smiled. "But really, Abs, I want to do better. To be better. I was so lost in my work that I hadn't realized how far we'd drifted. If you and Lacy Lee hadn't hatched that completely insane plan, I don't know..." He rubbed his thumb along the side of my hand. "I just know we wouldn't be here. I always wondered how couples who were so in love and so perfect for each other ended up hating each other. I guess I see it now."

I wanted to say, "I could never hate you." But hadn't I come so close? My anger and frustration at life turned me into someone I never expected to be. Pressing my head against his arm, I said, "I want to be better, too, Scott. I want to learn about your Love Languages and show you love in a way that fills your cup."

"Same. Starting with, I promise to do regular date nights and family outings," he declared, and I wanted to cry. It was all my heart wanted.

"Have you thought more about the work-from-home thing?" I asked.

"Yeah. And I've been talking to my boss. He says a sales manager role is available, but he's not sure if the pay will be able to match what I make in a sales position."

"This is going to sound crazy, but I have an idea. I wonder if MedDev—"

"Could make saddle pads?" Scott finished my question.

"You're freaking me out, Scott. How did you know I was going to say that?"

His thumb rubbed my hand as he answered. "I started thinking about it at dinner that night, when you said it's something that cushions the horse's back from the saddle. Even a custom saddle ends up not fitting, as muscles change."

I remembered talking about it at dinner when Tracy texted about borrowing Henry's half pad. "So, do you think the MedDev technology that helps prosthetics fit would also help a saddle fit better?"

"It's worth a shot," he shrugged, and for the first time in recent memory, I felt like Scott and I were playing on the same team again, and it was an incredible feeling.

"Mumma!" Tate screamed as we came in the door.

"Daaaaaa!" chorused Krista.

"You caught us just in time! We were about to go out for a walk!" Lacy Lee did a double-take as she took in our appearance. "Wow, did you get caught in the rainstorm or something?" she asked over the ruckus of the kids.

Scott and I shared a look, and my entire body flushed with warmth even as I shivered from being wet. "Yeah, you could say that! We had a great time. Thank you so much!" Tucker clung to my leg. "Buddy, you're gonna get soaked!"

"Hey, Lacy." Scott set his keys on the counter. "Could you stay with the kids for a few more minutes? We could both use a warm shower and dry clothes before we catch a cold."

Lacy Lee shifted Krista to her other hip. "Sure! Want me to wait on y'all to go on our walk?"

"Wait, please!" I wouldn't let Lacy take all three kids on a walk solo. Plus, there were so many things to fill her in on. "We'll be quick!"

"Hey, save water and shower together!" She grinned at us as we fled up the stairs.

Thirty minutes later, Scott and I descended the stairs, warm, dry, and blissful.

I shared a look with my friend. "Thank you again, Lacy. I can't tell you what a lovely time we had."

"Don't thank me, thank your husband! It was all his doing."

Scott scooped Tate in his arms while he talked. "Yeah, but we couldn't have done it if you hadn't watched the kids."

"Oh, I got you something!" I exclaimed. "I need to grab it from the car."

"Actually, how about I put Krista down for her afternoon nap, and y'all can take the boys on a walk?" Scott offered, setting Tate down in exchange for Krista, who was rubbing her eyes and babbling, "Dadadada."

"Paygound!" Tucker shouted, running for the door. We all laughed, Tate grabbed my hand, and we headed outside. I grabbed Lacy's gift from the car, tucking it into the little gift bag while she wasn't looking.

"Oh my gosh, Abs, you shouldn't have."

"Don't start with me, Lacy Lee. I got this for you because I wanted to. I'm sorry the packaging got squished, but the gift should be fine. Now open it!"

She jerked the tissue paper out and reached her hand in. When the bag dropped away, a key chain with a turtle on it dangled from her fingers.

"Wow, Abby! Uh... thank you?"

I snorted out a laugh before explaining. "Remember the whole guardian angel thing?"

"Oh yeah! Aw!"

"Well, my scary turtle angel has been working overtime the last couple of weeks, even making an appearance today. Things with me and Scott are finally back on track."

"Yeah?" Her eyes searched mine.

"Yeah, Lacy. It's really good. We both have some stuff to work on, but now we know it and can work together." Nodding toward the keychain, I kept going. "I think it's your turn. I'm not sure how God does this whole angel thing, but I'm passing her on to you. You're so full of love. You're the best friend I've ever had and the best backup mom to my kids. And maybe, with some help, well..." I paused, trying not to cry. "God will bless you with mini Lacy Lees and Lukes."

Lacy's cheeks were wet, but her face was bright with hope.

"Mum! Is Aunty Lacy ok?"

"Yeah, bud. We're good."

"Thank you, Abby." Lacy wrapped me in a hug, and we stood there together, crying and silently begging God to make her story beautiful, too.

42

Book Club

"Hey, Abby! Welcome back!"

"How are you feeling?"

"We missed you!"

"Give the lady some space, will ya?" Lacy Lee interjected over all the book club ladies while simultaneously winking at me from across the table. Gabby's daughter had carted Krista off, and I was finally back at book club, coffee in hand.

"I'm doing much better. Thank you so much for your gifts and prayers and everything else." I smiled back at the ladies.

"But how's your head? Does it still hurt? And your back?" Gabby asked.

"My head seems good. My back hurts a bit, but honestly, if I hadn't had the accident, I wouldn't think much of it. I'm not supposed to lift heavy things, which is hard with the baby and not always possible. And I have to be careful because the biggest danger now is in getting a second concussion before the first one's fully healed."

Everyone's eyes bulged as I shared about my injuries, but I kept going. "So, I'm praying for protection from circumstances

I can't control, like car accidents, and I'm trying to make smart decisions everywhere else. Riding is out of the question for a few more weeks, but I'm still visiting Henry and grooming him."

Priya, Wendy, and Gabby all started talking, but Gabby plowed forward with her question. "Ride? I didn't think you were riding anymore. And especially not after the accident. I'd never get near a horse if something like that happened to me."

Wendy exploded into a story that she had apparently been holding in for a while. "One time on vacation, Ray and I decided to go riding on the beach. There were so many bugs; it was disgusting. But anyway, they took us on a path through these little trees, and I swear the horse tried to sweep me off. It was awful. He kept taking me right through low-hanging branches. And then when we got to the ocean, the guides rode out into the water."

"You got to ride in the ocean? That's amazing!" Lacy Lee piped in.

"For everyone else. I got the rotten horse. He started pawing in the water. I thought he was playing, and it was real cute, right? Until he laid down and rolled in the water! I could have drowned!" The pitch of her voice had risen with each sentence. "Thank God, I didn't. But when I stood back up, everyone laughed at me. The guides totally knew what would happen. I told Ray we should sue them. What if I didn't know how to swim?"

"Did they ask you if you could swim?" Priya asked, a knowing look in her eye.

"Not that I recall."

Sara spoke up, "Did they ask if everyone was ok going into the ocean?"

"Well, yeah, but I didn't think my horse would…" A loud clap interrupted her.

"It's time for us to get started," Cathy commanded. I had never been more grateful for her. We all sat up straighter and turned our focus to our fearless leader, who started us with a question. "Does anyone have any insights into the Love Languages? Would anyone like to share how it's helping in their relationship?"

I looked around the table, trying to decide if anyone else was going to speak up. Surprisingly, Sara spoke first. "I figured my husband's Love Language is words of affirmation, so I've been leaving him little notes by the coffee maker every morning."

"Ooooh! Such a good idea!" Lacy Lee said.

"I wish someone would leave me notes at the coffee maker," said Gabby.

Priya had her pencil out, ready to take notes. "Are you using stationary or Post-It notes or what?" she asked.

"Priya, it doesn't matter what they're written on," Cathy piped up.

"It does! If she uses the same sized paper, they can be saved and turned into a book. Or use post-it notes and collect them on a board."

"Great idea! A scrapbook of love notes!" Gabby interjected.

"I've been writing them on 3-by-5 notecards," Sara said. "But that's a good idea. I'll tape them in a notebook for him to flip through sometime."

"Or you could reuse them and set an old one out when you're in a hurry," Lacy Lee said with a laugh. I shook my head. She totally would.

"That's wonderful, Sara!" Cathy wrangled the conversation back on track. "Anyone else?"

My heart pounded against my breastbone, trying to escape as I spoke up. "I'd like to share."

"Great!" Cathy said, and nodded for me to go on.

"Ok, well, Scott and I have honestly been having a rough patch until recently. He was working a lot. Like, I was convinced he was avoiding being home because he worked so much. I even wondered if he was cheating."

I swallowed. Knowing nods around the table helped me realize I wasn't the only person here with marital struggles. It gave me the courage to keep going.

"But then when he was home, I was just so mad at him. And I didn't even know why. Nearly every time I talked to Scott, my words or my tone were cutting at him. I was so mean. No wonder he didn't want to be home. Except when he's not there, I'm alone with three kids and barely able to hold it together.

"This book got me thinking. A lot has happened in the last couple weeks aside from the accident, but basically we're working on loving each other in our own Love Languages now."

Lacy Lee smiled like a proud mom or, in this case, best friend. The other ladies nodded enthusiastically.

Our fearless leader was the first to speak. "That's wonderful, Abby. Is it working?"

I closed my eyes for a brief second. Was it working? "Honestly, I've never felt more loved by my husband. I mean, I know that marriage won't always feel like Hollywood love. My mom told me when we got married that sometimes it will be hard to even look at the man, much less lie in bed next to him. But she said to stick out the rough patches. Love is a choice, not a feeling. She said to choose to love him in the bad, and then when the good comes, it's easy.

"And we made it to the other side of our roughest patch so far." I smiled at everyone, holding back my emotions that threatened to spill over. "And I've never been more grateful for Scott Aberdeen."

43

Six Months Later

"Rider 183 is now on course."

Henry's ears perked forward, searching for the first jump. I steered him in a circle, getting a good forward canter while my heart pounded fiercely in rhythm with his hooves. I lined him up to our first obstacle and as it grew closer, I thought my heart might beat out of my chest. For a second, I considered bailing. No one would fault a mom of three kids gracefully exiting the arena. But before I could make a decision, the jump was right in front of us. Henry's weight shifted back, he sprung into the air, and we flew.

His front feet hit the dirt on the other side, and a laugh bubbled out of me. *We did it!* I nearly squealed out loud. Henry's head lifted as he searched for the next jump, and I realized I still had eight jumps to go.

"We can do this," I whispered, more for my own sake than his. Henry clearly knew his job, and I just needed to tell which jump was next. We made a sweeping left turn, and I kept him in a rhythmic pace. A metronome tapped away in my mind, and I kept his hooves in sync. We aimed for the next jump. Hay bales covered in flowers filled the space between the poles and the ground, but Henry wasn't phased by the colorful distraction that might have scared a less experienced horse.

He cleared it in stride, and I followed the motion of his head with my hands, giving him the freedom to move. We landed, and I remembered Tracy saying we needed to fit seven strides between this obstacle and the next. One, two, three... I counted and pulled the reins a half inch to make sure we could make it happen. "Seven," I whispered, as Henry launched into the air again.

The bustling atmosphere of the horse show faded away. Warmup rings with trainers yelling at riders, horses being led by grooms, the constant bathing outside the temporary barns, were a silent blur. My world was Henry—the way we tapped along in rhythm, even the hum of his breathing had joined our song. And every few beats, just as the music hit a crescendo, his feet left the ground and it all paused. The sound faded away and we soared.

As we landed our final jump, the cheers of the people who loved us broke the bubble I'd just floated through. I glanced up at the sky, knowing that every bit of this moment was a gift from above. We cantered a final circle, and I leaned back, allowing Henry's pace to dwindle when he was ready.

Reaching forward to rub his neck, I whispered, "We did it, Henry! Thank you!" His left ear swiveled back to me, and I knew he was listening. "You're the best boy."

"Abby! Abby! Abby!" the tiny crowd chanted, and I pumped my fist to the rhythm, laughing along. Scott and the kids, my parents, Lacy Lee, Tracy, and Juan all cheered us on from the rail by the in-gate. Even Gabby and her daughter came since they watched the kids on Wednesdays while I rode.

I can't remember ever crying in the show ring in my life, and I'd had some terrible rides that were definitely worth tears. There had been great ones, too, but since having kids, my emotions stayed on high alert.

Today, back in the show ring with Henry, and all the people on the sidelines who helped me get here, had me swallowing back tears like crazy. I promised myself that later, when we were alone in his stall, I would let Henry's mane catch them all.

Scott and Tracy met me at the gate as we exited. "That was brilliant," he said, and I leaned over for a fly-by kiss.

"Thank you, Scott!" I squeezed the hand he had rested on my thigh. "Thank you so much."

"You two were amazing out there!" Tracy patted Henry's neck and walked us out of the arena so the next rider could get in.

"It's probably that new saddle pad." Scott interjected with a cheesy grin. He wasn't wrong. Scott and I had worked together to create a half pad using the same technology MedDev used to cushion prosthetics. Tracy's horse, Oz, was finally moving pain-free, and his back issues were behind us for now.

Scott had transitioned to a mostly management position and worked from home. We were working together to build MedDev's equine branch. He still worked in person with local clients, but he was done with the crazy amounts of travel.

"Hey, if you get to the house and I'm not there, I'll be on the trail. Your parents offered to watch the kids, so I'm taking my bike out for a couple of hours."

I smiled. Scott had found a thing that made him come alive in the form of a matte black Canyon endurance bike. I had a feeling it wasn't the bike itself as much as time alone in nature to recharge, combined with the thrill of speed and staying in shape. Ok, it was the bike.

"How'd he feel?" Tracy piped up.

"Amazing!"

"And how did you feel?" Tracy gave me an eyebrow quirk.

"Aside from the insane nerves at the beginning where I thought I might retch over Henry's shoulder and considered quitting before we got to the first jump, it was like I never left the show ring."

"Ha! That's what it looked like, Abby. You rode great, and Henry is such a good boy. You do realize you're responsible for that, right? You got him from the track and trained him."

Heat crept up my cheeks at the praise. I reached forward and scratched under his mane. Tracy was partially right. I had trained Henry. But he's also a good horse with a big heart and drive to work.

"I haven't seen too many rounds as good as y'all's. You might win the class, Abby!"

"Really?" I squealed.

The sound of hoofbeats drew our eyes to the ring. A teenager cruised around the course on a gigantic Warmblood that looked to have cost more than Scott's income for a year. "Ok, maybe not," Tracy laughed. "If she puts in a clean round, this judge tends to pick the heavy Warmbloods."

I kicked my feet out of the stirrups as Tracy slipped Henry a treat. "I love to win as much as the next person, but to be honest, regardless of a ribbon, I already won."

"You know, if you switch to jumpers, no judge can give you a lower ribbon because your horse isn't fancy enough," Tracy said with a laugh. She was always trying to get me to switch from the show hunters, where a judge decides which horse jumped the best to show jumpers, where the fastest horse with a clear round wins no matter how good it looks.

"Don't listen to her, Henry! You're the handsomest boy in the barn!" He swiveled his ears back to listen to me while I slipped down to the ground. Juan grabbed his reins, leading him toward the stalls. "I'll be there in a minute to put him away, Juan. Just—"

"MUMMA MUMMA!"

"I need a—"

"MAAAAAAAAA!"

"No worries, Abby." Juan winked and sauntered off with my horse as two little boys tackled me in the grass.

"Be careful with Mom!" Scott scooped up Tucker as he playfully scolded. "Her head and back!"

"And my fancy new show outfit! No grass stains on the new pants!" I said it with humor, but was completely serious. These show pants were too expensive to ruin on the first wear. I mentally calculated which stain remover would be best as Krista toddled over and joined the pile.

"Kids!" I heard the stress in my husband's voice.

"I'm fine, Scott!" I called and tickled Tate and Krista, which caused raucous laughter.

"But we really do need to quiet down. We don't want to spook any horses," Tracy called before following Juan back to the barn.

Lacy Lee grabbed Krista and plopped in the grass next to me. Scott joined us on my other side, his body close enough to brush mine every time we moved. The boys scampered off to see what their grandparents were doing. Grooms, trainers, and riders went about their business, but I noticed the knowing, wistful smiles from people older than me. Smiles, I assumed, told a similar story to Bunty's.

"Juan was real sweet to take Henry, but I want to go help take care of him. That horse deserves a hug and an entire bag of carrots! And y'all deserve whatever the human equivalent of a bag of carrots is. Everybody does. I couldn't have done this without y'all."

Scott's arm gripped my waist. "Of course, Abs."

"That's what friends are for." Lacy Lee's arm wrapped around my shoulder, and they cocooned me in love.

"Yeah, well. I just am so blessed. I pray that every other mom out there can find her village. Because things like this," I smiled, soaking up the moment, "are impossible without one. And it's so beautiful with one."

A voice boomed over the loudspeaker. "Alright, we have the placings for the adult amateur three-foot hunters. In sixth place, we have..."

The three of us froze. I wasn't here for the ribbons, but dang if I couldn't help the way my heart raced over the idea of winning. Placing after placing, other names and numbers were called. As we got closer to the top, hope drained away.

"In third place, we have competitor number 208, Sally Castle on A La Mode."

There was no way I could place in the top two. I hadn't watched the other horses go, but this was my first show in years. "Ok, I'm going to help Juan with Henry." I stood, brushing grass and dirt off my new show pants.

"In second place, congratulations goes to..." The announcer paused and Scott grabbed my hand, holding me in place. "Number 183, Abby Aberdeen on My Ebenezer."

"Whoop!" Lacy Lee screamed and, in a move that defied gravity, leaped from her seat on the ground into the air, all while holding a giggling Krista, causing a nearby horse to jump backwards a few steps.

"Sorry!" I called to the rider, and then let loose a squeal. "Oh my gosh! We got second!" I high-fived everyone within ten feet, including a few strangers who congratulated me and laughed.

"You're incredible, Abs! And I thought his show name was Stride For Me Henry?" Scott asked.

"I found out that with a mere $60, it can be changed." I looked toward the barn where Henry was waiting. "And Henry is my Ebenezer. My stone of help to remind me that when I humble myself, God comes to my rescue."

Scott stepped into my space, and our breaths mingled. I peered up to see his eyes squinting at the sides in happiness as his arms pressed against my back, pulling me to him. "Is *humble* the right word for yours and Lacy Lee's shenanigans?"

I almost snorted into his face at that comment but held it in. Snorting into Scott's mouth is the opposite of sexy.

"Hey, it worked, didn't it?" Lacy Lee piped in from somewhere behind me.

Thinking of our turtle, I said, "That and the help of Raphael."

Scott's brows furrowed. "Who's Raphael?"

"That's what we named our guardian angel turtle!" I grinned.

"Like the Ninja Turtle?"

"Like the Archangel in the Bible!" Lacy Lee exclaimed. "Duh, Scott. Don't you know anything from the Bible?"

I grinned at Scott. "And like the Ninja Turtle." I stretched up for my kiss, tired of waiting.

"Ew, gross!" Tate's voice chimed in the background, along with the sound of Tucker's gagging noises, which only spurred me to deepen the kiss. For their sake, of course.

"Get a room!" a voice called, and I broke away to see Tracy smirking at me. "And go show Henry his ribbon. He's still waiting for you!"

I blushed. How could I forget? I grabbed Scott's hand, and my entourage followed me to the show office, where I walked out brandishing a shiny red satin ribbon. They oohed and aahed, and I felt incredibly silly for the big deal we were making over this piece of fabric. This would definitely be hanging by the front door for a while.

We practically jogged to Henry's stall at the showgrounds. "Henry!" I hollered as we made it to his aisle. His head poked out, hay hanging from his mouth and ears pointed forward. "Henry, look!" I rushed to him so he could see.

I slid his leather halter over his ears. An engraved nameplate on the side read, "My Ebenezer." The metal hook on the back of the ribbon slid into the halter against his cheek. Everyone pulled out their phones and snapped pictures of us. Each kid had a turn posing with Henry and his ribbon, and then the grandparents took photos, and we even did one with Juan, Tracy, and me.

I elbowed Scott in the side. "Send a pic to my favorite Med-Dev rep, Cassidy! She had a barrel race this weekend!"

"Hey now! I thought I was your favorite rep!" Scott mock pouted.

"Well, you're now in management and the head of the equine department, and therefore, Cassidy, who laughed her head off over my acceptance speech for her award, is now my favorite Texan and MedDev rep."

I still couldn't believe that I, Abby Aberdeen, had done that. But my crazy leap of faith had been so worth it.

A bag of carrots later—many of them eaten by tiny humans—my friends and parents returned to their lives, taking my kids with them. I stayed behind to clean tack and pick Henry's stall. "I love you, Abby Aberdeen," Scott said, leaning in for a parting kiss.

"I love you, too, Scott. Thank you." He wrapped his arms around me, and I leaned into his embrace, breathing in the scent of his cologne. We swayed back and forth, dancing to the music of Henry munching hay and the faraway sounds of a horse show.

A few minutes later, I stood alone in Henry's stall, scooping the morning's manure and thanking God for my life. I fished into my pocket and pulled out a wrinkled piece of paper. Bunty's name and phone number were scribbled across the top, and on the bottom she'd left a note.

Sometimes your cup is overflowing with so many blessings, all you can see is the mess. Cherish those blessings, dear, and don't give up the horses.

Thank you for saving my Rixy. Come hunt with us sometime.
Love, Bunty
P.S. Help that cute hubby of yours find something that brings him joy. He's a catch!

I imagined her winking at me every time I read it.

Yes, ma'am, I thought as Henry nudged me for another carrot.

I have a few things to say...

When I was creating a best friend for Abby, I mentally scrolled through all the women I've known. I had a college friend who always had a smile on her face, brought the fun wherever she went, and made everyone in her space feel loved. In the words of my college-aged self, "She rocked my face off."

I transferred to another school junior year and am not sure I ever saw her again, but we stayed connected through Facebook. When I was having babies, she was battling cancer. Lacy Lee passed away several years ago, but her light still shines — so much so that I modeled a character around her. May we all have a Lacy Lee in our lives and *be* a Lacy Lee for our friends.

The real Lacy Lee was not the only source of inspiration for Abby's bestie — I have incredible friends, and some of the quotes in this book are direct rip-offs from our conversations. Sorry, ladies! Nothing is completely sacred when you're friends with a writer.

I have a bone to pick with my beloved Bunty. She shared some inspirational advice with Scott and Abby. You might remember this line: "...when God grants you a passion, it's in the pursuit of that passion that you are most alive—and that is when you shine His light the brightest."

She forgot to give a warning, so I'm going to drop my own. God has given me a few passions, and I'm the kind of girl who goes for it. All in. Both feet. If God called me to it, I'm running. This book is proof of that, and I hope you loved it! Here's the warning: Don't let that passion grow bigger than your love for Him.

This was a hard-earned lesson for me. True story — when I was in college, I loaded up my horse and dog and moved to Louisville, Kentucky, to chase a dream of riding racehorses. Horses and that dream became an idol — the reason I woke up in the morning and the thing that made my heart sing. I held the gifts from the Creator in higher esteem than the Creator himself.

There's a reason The Ten commandments warn about "having no other God's before me." So be passionate, shine God's light, but let's remember who made us this way, and keep Him first.

The story about going to Kentucky to chase that dream was pretty insane, and was what started my career as a writer. If you want to read about it, check out my award-winning memoir, Finding Gideon.

A final note on marriage. The little kid phase can be brutal on a relationship. The dishes pile in the sink, the baby spits up on your favorite sweater, the toddler throws a fit because her cup is the wrong color, and you have to figure out what's for dinner...*again*. All your patience is poured into the kids, which often leaves angry words that cut like a knife for your spouse. Life can so easily become a blame game.

This story is my rally cry for couples who feel trapped in the cycle. Maybe it can't be fixed in one magical day in Middleburg, but wounds can heal and marriages can survive. The best things in life were never meant to be easy. The strongest relationships are those refined in the fire.

But that doesn't mean every relationship needs to continue. A couple of years ago, my good friend kept coming to me for marriage advice. How did I handle my husband's moods? How did we handle our finances — separate or together? What were my tips for getting his support for our girls' weekend/business conference?

I knew she was struggling, but I didn't know the extent of it until he nearly threw her out the window of their eighth story apartment and left her so beaten she hid in the truck for the night. She is strong, beautiful, and independent, yet he convinced her she couldn't go to the cops. She was embarrassed to go to friends.

Not every relationship issue should be worked through. You shouldn't need to lock yourself in the bedroom to feel safe. There's a difference between being worried about a conversation because your spouse gets grouchy and being afraid you won't survive it. If you need to, please get out.

Now I'd like to end on a happy note, so I'll remind you of the thing that has been making me laugh for months. Maybe your guardian angel can shape-shift and the next time you have to stop for a goose waddling across the road, check to see if she winks at you. You never know what her little diversion has protected you from.

Acknowledgements

I'd like to make this quick...but I can't. Here goes my best effort.

Thank you to my Creator – the OG Storyteller. I never thought I'd be able to write fiction, but when I asked for an idea, You delivered. All glory and honor to God.

To Joey – when I started reading books on marriage, you got nervous, thinking something was wrong. The truth is, things are so right with you that I have to research to find out what to write about. Thank you for loving me. I'm messy, horse obsessed, and have half my brain in a book at all times, and you're still here. As I said in the dedication, you're my favorite human. Sometimes I secretly cry myself to sleep because I feel so dang grateful to be married to you.

To JJ and Essie – thank you for looking forward to this book even though you're not old enough to read it (yet). I *love* being your mom. Essie, maybe we'll sell enough copies to get you a horse!

Joey and I were blessed to grow up with parents who were committed to each other. Through thick and thin, the good and the bad, fun times, mundane times, and hard times, the D word wasn't an option. In a culture that's quick to jump ship when things get hard, we were shown the importance of leaning in. I don't think I'd be able to write a story like this without your example. Thank you to the Hickner's and my parents.

Ok, here's where I'm worried about missing people because I've had so many friends help me with this book!

When I stuttered out my idea of a romance series about married people, Mallorie said it was genius without a lick of hesitation. It gave me the confidence to start typing. I sat on Katie's couch in Mississippi where the idea of Abby's mom bag and a banquet crash were born. I've had brainstorming sessions on horseback with Caitlin and Amanda. Hope has listened to endless droning via voice text about everything I wrote and rewrote and would drop everything to read a chapter.

My friend Katherine convinced me to make Scott a salesman, and my cousin Rachel lost her leg just so I could come up with an idea for a fictional company for my book. Ha! Just kidding. But she did inspire me and answer any questions without hesitation. For the first couple of years after her accident, when I asked how she was doing, the repeat answer was – I'm good except the stump hurts in my prosthetic (this is my paraphrased version of what she said, and she said it much more gracefully). That's how my fictional company MedDev was born. I wanted to help people like Rachel.

Sara was my first reader and together we nerd out over romance books and plotting so many stories we'll never have enough years to write them. Katrina, everyone needs a cheerleader like you in their corner, and y'all should read her book, Dragon: The Story of a Fiery Thoroughbred and the Girl Who Loved Him.

Susan – for someone who doesn't read romance, you gave me incredibly helpful feedback.

Thank you Rachel Keith for an amazing proofread.

For all my advanced readers – THANK YOU!!! Your feedback was so helpful and encouraging. I can't tell you how much even a one line email telling me you loved it meant. It took me from nervous about book launch to chomping at the bit, ready to get this book out to the world! Please, let's do this again next time.

About the Author

Sarah Hickner is a dreamer and a doer. She's been obsessed with horses her entire life, which has led to some epic highs and really hard falls. Those experiences have been chronicled into short stories, magazine articles, and a memoir titled Finding Gideon.

Now she's blending the lessons she's learned about life and her love of romantic comedy novels for the sweet romance market.

When Sarah isn't at the barn, you can find her at home with her husband, two kids, and coonhound mix.

Your free short story

Before I started writing fiction, I lived a fairy tale! Enjoy this true story about the lead up to the wedding of my dreams. This will also sign you up for my newsletter, where I will soon be delivering the first two chapters of Lacy Lee's story,
All the Things We Can't Have.

Go to www.liveridelearn.com/freeshortstory

Also by Sarah Hickner

Finding Gideon: A Broken Dream, a Missing Horse, and the Faith of a Mustard Seed

Sarah is a horse-obsessed dreamer from small-town Mississippi, who hopes to earn a job riding on the track. When she loads up her horse and dog and moves to Louisville, Kentucky, her newfound dreams are quickly shattered by tragedy and the disappearance of her beloved horse Gideon.
Follow Sarah as she discovers a deeper understanding of the power of faith, the importance of resilience, and the true meaning of courage.
If you were captivated by the classic racing novel Seabiscuit by Laura Hillenbrand or the movie Wild Hearts Can't Be Broken, then you'll love Finding Gideon.

Stories from the Barn Aisle:
Real Life Tales of Humor and Grace from a Horse Obsessed Girl

Enjoy five short stories from Sarah's adventures before Kentucky!

My Stories from the Barn Aisle:
A prompt journal and guide to writing epic short stories

A great gift for horse lovers!
Includes fun activities as well.

Storyteller:
A creative writing journal and guide to unlock your inner wordsmith

shop at
www.LiveRideLearn.com/books

shop at Amazon:
https://amzn.to/44q8W9F

Thoroughbred horses doing different sports

A Thoroughbred Life Horse Coloring Book
Thoroughbred horses are known for their speed and prowess on the racetrack, but there is so much more to these majestic creatures! This coloring book takes artists from the first days of life to the racetrack and beyond. Pictures are based on real Thoroughbreds and the people who love and work with them. Drawings are done by Sarah Hickner.

Now all glory to God, who is able, through his mighty power
at work within us, to accomplish infinitely more than we might
ask or think. Glory to him in the church and in Christ Jesus
through all generations forever and ever! Amen.
Ephesians 3:20-21

www.ingramcontent.com/pod-product-compliance
Lightning Source LLC
Chambersburg PA
CBHW021027310726
48969CB00006B/1569